Praise for the Baby Boomer Mysteries

"Santangelo has come up with an intriguing premise, drawing on the much-publicized fact that the baby boomer generation will soon be facing retirement, and she develops it cleverly....We'll look forward to more Boomer mysteries in the years to come.... Pure fun—and don't be surprised if retired sleuths become the next big trend."
—*Booklist.com*

"*Retirement Can Be Murder* is a fun chick lit investigative tale starring Carol Andrews super sleuth supported by an eccentric bunch of BBs (baby boomers), the cop and the daughter. Carol tells the tale in an amusing frantic way that adds to the enjoyment of a fine lighthearted whodunit that affirms that 'every wife has a story.'"
—Harriet Klausner, national book critic

"*Moving Can Be Murder* is jam-packed with Carol's cast of best buds and signature Santangelo fun! The author has penned a magnificent cozy that will leave you panting from the excitement, laughing at the characters, and—no surprise here—begging for more."
—Terri Ann Armstrong, Author of *How To Plant A Body*

"With her Baby Boomer mystery series, Susan Santangelo documents her undeniable storytelling talents. *Class Reunions Can Be Murder* is an especially well crafted and entertaining mystery which plays fair with the reader every step of the way....An outstanding series."
—*Midwest Book Review*

"*Funerals Can Be Murder*, Susan Santangelo's latest *Baby Boomer Mystery*, will keep you chuckling, as well as wondering whodunit, until the very end."
—Lois Winston, Award-winning author of the critically acclaimed *Anastasia Pollack Crafting Mystery* series

"I love this series! With *Funerals Can Be Murder*, author Susan Santangelo has done it again—successfully mixed the challenges of

aging boomers into a stew with hilarious events, winning characters and nimble storytelling. I've read every book in the series and can't wait for more."
—Barbara Ross, Author of the *Maine Clambake Mysteries*

"With the fifth in the *Carol and Jim Andrews Baby Boomer Mystery* series, *Funerals Can Be Murder*, Santangelo doesn't let up the pace or the humor on this one."
—Kaye George, Author of *Death in the Time of Ice*

"Can it be possible that Carol Andrews somehow attracts murders— or at least their discovery and subsequent solution—into her life? As this fun romp opens, Carol is simply attending the untimely funeral of her very hunky handyman. *Funerals Can Be Murder* is the fifth installment in Santangelo's *Carol and Jim Andrews Baby Boomer Mystery* series, and it doesn't disappoint. Another 'must-read'!"
—Anne L. Holmes ("Boomer in Chief"), National Association of Baby Boomer Women

"Susan Santangelo continues her delightful *Baby Boomer Mystery* series with *Funerals Can Be Murder*, in which savvy sleuth Carol Andrews, despite her husband and detective son-in-law's skepticism, digs up the dirt on a lustful landscaper and the ladies who loved him."
—Carole Goldberg, National Book Critics Circle member

"In the mood for a light mystery? Susan Santangelo's *Funerals Can Be Murder* is a fun, relaxing, read, with a great voice. Protagonist (and busybody) Carol Andrews could be your new best friend. She's funny, bright, ironic, a great listener . . . her only problem is finding too many bodies. "
—Lea Wait, Author of *Shadows on a Maine Christmas*

To Joyce
Love Paulette

Funerals
Can Be Murder

Every Wife Has a Story

A Carol and Jim Andrews Baby Boomer
Mystery

Fifth in the Series

Susan Santangelo

SUSPENSE PUBLISHING

Susan Santangelo

FUNERALS CAN BE MURDER
by
Susan Santangelo

PAPERBACK EDITION
* * * * *
PUBLISHED BY:
Suspense Publishing

Susan Santangelo
COPYRIGHT
2014 Susan Santangelo

PUBLISHING HISTORY:
Suspense Publishing, Paperback and Digital Copy, October 2014

Cover and Book Design: Shannon Raab
Cover Artist: Elizabeth Moisan

ISBN-13: 978-0692244722 (Custom)
ISBN-10: 0692244727

This book is dedicated to Donna Schaefer, for all the years of friendship and support.

Acknowledgments

Thank you to my wonderful family—Dave, Mark, Sandy, Rebecca, Jacob. And especially to Joe, who inspires me every day.

To Beverly Russell, who won character naming rights at a fundraiser to benefit the West Dennis MA library, and chose to honor Isaac Weichert. And to Helen Konisburg, who won character naming rights at a Cape Cod Hospital, Barnstable Branch, wine tasting. I hope you both like how your characters turned out!

To Pompea Sanderson, who keeps me looking my best when I'm down south.

A big thank you to Sandy P., Cathie, and Jersey Shirley. I think you know why.

Special thanks to Marie Sherman, who allowed me to "ride the mower" in Brewster MA, as research for *Funerals Can Be Murder*. And my apologies to Husqvarna, the manufacturer of the mower mentioned in this book. I'm sure Carol Andrews must have done something wrong to make it behave that way!

Thanks to Elizabeth Moisan for her imaginative plot ideas, and the terrific cover art.

A bouquet of shamrocks to my high school classmate and pal Pat Sinon Branciforte, my official Irish wake consultant.

Thank you so much to Paulette DiAngi for the creative and delicious Irish wake recipes, found in the back of this book.

To everyone at the Breast Cancer Survival Center, and cancer survivors everywhere, God bless! And to those who are continuing to fight the fight, never give up!

A big thank you to everyone from the Cape Cod Hospital

Auxiliary, Barnstable Branch, and the Cape Cod Hospital Thrift Shop, for allowing me to play with them. Which I do as often as I can.

For Carole Goldberg from *The Hartford Courant*, and Melanie Lauwers from the *Cape Cod Times*, I appreciate your help more than you will ever know.

To my own First Readers Club, I couldn't do this without your input. A special shout-out to Marti Baker, who always keeps me on my toes no matter what.

To all my friends and cyber friends from Sisters in Crime, especially the New England chapter, thanks for sharing your expertise with me. I always learn something new, and the support is fantastic.

To Shannon and John Raab, and everyone at Suspense Publishing, who help me in so many ways.

And to everyone who's enjoyed this series—the readers I've met at countless book events and those who have e-mailed me—thanks so much! Hope you enjoy this one, too. And keep those chapter headings coming!

Funerals *Can Be* Murder

Every Wife Has a Story

Susan Santangelo

Mallory and Mallory Funeral Home, Fairport, Connecticut
Another Finnegan's Wake

"I hate wakes," I said, turning my car into the parking lot of Mallory and Mallory Funeral Home on Fairport Turnpike and cruising for an empty spot.

This pronouncement was greeted by a heavy sigh from my passenger. "Mom," said my usually patient daughter, Jenny, "first of all, nobody likes wakes. Or funerals. Especially the guest of honor. And Dad was right. We didn't have to come at all. You weren't that close to the deceased."

I matched Jenny's sigh with one of my own. "I know," I said. "But when I saw his obituary in yesterday's paper, I was so shocked. It was only last week that Will Finnegan was raking our leaves and getting our yard in shape. He seemed fine. And now, he's gone. Just like that."

I sighed again.

"Life is too short for so many people we know," I continued, easing the car into the perfect parking spot for someone my age— the kind I can drive straight out of without having to back up. My neck isn't as flexible as it was when I was younger. Nor are several other body parts, to tell the truth.

"It just seemed appropriate that I come to pay my respects to his family." I reached over and squeezed Jenny's hand. "I appreciate your coming with me, sweetie."

"I didn't want you to go alone," Jenny said. "And Mark's working. I hate it when he works nights. I always worry more about him than

I do when he's on the day shift. I guess I should be used to being married to a police detective by now, but I'm not. Maybe, after we pay a quick visit to the funeral parlor, we can go out and grab a quick dinner at Maria's Trattoria. My treat."

"I'm never one to turn down the chance of a dinner I didn't have to cook myself," I said. "And your father has plenty of leftovers to graze on, plus there's a UConn game on television tonight. I bet he won't even notice how long I've been gone."

I frowned. "Maybe I should get a pair of pom poms and pretend to be a college cheerleader. What do you think?"

"Please, tell me you're kidding, Mom," Jenny said as we arrived at the front door of what some locals have dubbed M & M, the funeral parlor of choice for many Fairport, Connecticut residents.

I smoothed my hair down and tried to make myself look presentable. The late fall winds had been especially punishing on our brisk walk from the parking lot. I could hear organ music— probably pre-recorded—coming from Slumber Room A. There was a sign near the door marking it as the parlor for the William Finnegan wake, as well as a guest book to sign.

I couldn't help but notice, as I wrote "Mrs. James Andrews," that I was the first person on the page. I handed the pen to Jenny.

"I didn't think we'd be the first ones here, Mom," she whispered, adding her signature below mine. "Where's the family? Didn't he have one?"

"According to the obituary, he did," I whispered back. "Maybe they didn't feel they needed to sign the guest book."

Jenny nodded and pushed me in front of her toward the sound of the organ music. "You first, Mom. At least you have a tenuous relationship to the deceased. I never even laid eyes on the man."

Slumber Room A was dimly lit, but it took me only half a second to realize that Jenny and I were the only people here. Except for the recently deceased Will Finnegan, whom I presumed was residing in the open casket at the other end of the room.

The organ music reached a crescendo, then the room became eerily silent.

"What'll we do, Mom?" Jenny asked. "There's no one to pay our respects to."

"We sit down and wait a few minutes," I whispered back. "The family is probably in another room, composing themselves for a long and emotional night." I looked at my watch. "I don't think I got the time wrong. I'm sure the obituary said the viewing started at seven o'clock. It's ten past seven now."

The organ music started up again. Not exactly a toe-tapper, but at least it made me feel like we were in the right place.

Or were we?

"Jenny," I whispered, "I think I'll just go up and say a prayer at the casket. And be sure I haven't made a mistake." I smiled weakly. "If I have, dinner's on me."

I threaded my way through the rows of empty chairs and found myself gazing at the waxen face of our late landscaper, sleeping in his casket.

Yup, Will was dead all right.

But just to be extra sure, one mourner, who'd gotten to the casket ahead of me, had plunged a scissors into Will's chest.

Chapter 1

If at last you find a sale, buy, buy again!

Jim and I were having a "domestic." A disagreement. A squabble. An argument.

Oh, all right. We were having a fight.

Not the WWE kind of fight. And for once, it wasn't about the credit card bill. I do consider it patriotic to shop as much as possible—anything to boost the economy of the USA.

No, this fight was a stupid one about—of all things—how we divide the household tasks. Not that it started out that way.

To tell the truth, this argument was a typical One-Thing-Leads-To-Another, Then-To-Another squabble that's so common between long-time spousal units. The kind that goes on until neither of the participants can remember what the fight was supposed to be about in the first place.

Except for me. I *always* remember.

Of course, this argument, like so many others we've had, began as a direct result of Jim's retirement.

To be completely fair and objective (to myself), when My Beloved Husband of thirty-five-plus years decided to leave his stress-packed, demanding job at Gibson Gillespie Public Relations in New York City—an easy commute via Metro North from Fairport, the bucolic Connecticut suburb we've called home for most of our married life—I was incredibly supportive.

Forget about visions of sugar plums dancing in my head. I had visions of luxurious cruises to exotic ports, annual trips to Europe, and, well, you get the idea.

Unfortunately, Jim didn't. Get the idea, I mean.

Instead, he was perfectly content to stay home (admittedly, it's a beautiful antique home and I love it dearly) and, with a few (minor) hiccups that disturbed the tranquility of his retirement, reorganize my kitchen, take over the laundry, make the morning coffee, and in every other way become a household diva.

Oy vey. What a career path.

And I resented what I interpreted as an unwanted, unnecessary, inexcusable intrusion onto what had Always Been My Turf. Some of you may say I overreacted. But I dare any of you to invite Jim to *your* home so he can put his newly discovered domestic talents to work on *your* turf and see how you like it.

Any takers? I didn't think so.

Oh, and by the way, My Beloved's foray into micromanaging and controlling household tasks doesn't extend to chores which I absolutely hate, like cleaning the bathrooms, vacuuming, and cleaning up after meals. And he never tells me when we're running low on groceries—like our favorite cereal, for instance. Instead, he leaves that for me to discover, usually on a morning when there are no other breakfast choices but Lucy and Ethel's kibble.

Our two English cocker spaniels don't like to share.

If I'm being completely honest, I have to admit that Jim is a whiz with the outdoor home maintenance—trimming bushes, touching up exterior paint here and there, mowing the grass, raking leaves, and shoveling snow. The weather in our bucolic corner of New England is rife with its share of ongoing challenges.

Of course, one of the reasons why Jim is so fixated on outdoor maintenance is that he gets to play with some of his toys. The riding mower our daughter Jenny and her husband, Mark, gave him for his birthday, for instance. Or the fancy snow blower he bought at Fairport Hardware during last year's end-of-season clearance sale.

Since Jim had a mild heart issue a while back, and he refuses to hire anyone else to take over any of these chores on a regular basis, I encouraged these purchases. Anything I can do to extend My Beloved's life span is okay with me.

Truth to tell, I was dying to try out one of Jim's toys myself. Tooling around our large, fenced-in back yard atop the riding mower held a lot more appeal than swishing the bathroom toilets with bleach.

Which brings me back to the subject of our "domestic." Finally.

"It's only a sniffle, Jim," I said, taking the thermometer out of his mouth and squinting to read it without my glasses. "You're not running a fever. Just take it easy today and drink lots of fluids. I bet you'll feel much better by tomorrow morning."

I gave him the stare I'd perfected after years of motherhood— the one that used to strike fear into Jenny and Mike when they were kids. "And by fluids, I mean juice, water, and maybe some weak tea, so don't get any crazy ideas. And I'm not going to spend the day waiting on you."

I immediately regretted my harsh tone. I was lucky I wasn't a widow like one of my best friends, Mary Alice. Or have a cheating husband like my very best friend, Nancy. Or married to a crashing bore, like my dear friend Claire.

Lucy, who was snoozing in a corner of the master bedroom with her pal Ethel, raised her head and gave me a stare of her own. Which telegraphed loud and clear that I was being extra crabby and should give my poor husband a break. It wasn't Jim's fault if he thought he was at death's door every time he caught a cold.

After all, he was a man.

I wanted to take my words back, but Jim didn't give me a chance.

"Fine, Carol. I won't ask you for a thing. If I need anything, I'll drag myself out of bed and get it for myself. I hope that's all right with you."

He sniffed and coughed for extra emphasis, just in case I didn't get his point.

"I'm sorry for what I said, Jim. I really didn't mean…"

"I think it's perfectly clear what you meant," Jim snapped.

"You're overreacting," I said, "which is something you often accuse me of doing."

Jim sneezed again and I handed him a tissue, then moved the waste basket closer to the bed so he wouldn't litter our bedroom floor with used ones.

I tried again to apologize. "You know how often I speak before I think," I said.

Silence.

"I said I was sorry."

Then I had a brilliant idea. To change the subject.

"What did you have planned today, honey? Anything I can help you with?"

Jim gave a bark of laughter which ended in still another coughing fit. "Not likely, Carol. The lawn is looking pretty high. I was going to give it one more mow before the end of October, and then re-seed any bare spots I found. I can hardly see you doing that."

I stiffened. "Why not, Jim? You do some of the indoor chores"— *which I never asked you to*—"so it seems logical that I take over one of your outdoor chores while you're sick. I only want to be helpful, the way you are to me."

Not.

"There is no way I'm letting you lay one hand on my ride-around mower," Jim said. "It's very powerful, and you'll probably end up crashing it into the picket fence."

Boy, did that make me mad!

"Are you implying that I'm not a good driver, dear?" I asked as sweetly as I could manage under the circumstances. "As I recall, I'm not the Andrews family member who has enough traffic tickets to wallpaper the entire guest bathroom."

Jim closed his eyes. "End of discussion, Carol. I'm going to take a nap."

He opened one eye as I was about to leave him in some semblance of peace. "But I meant what I said. Don't you dare touch my lawnmower!"

Chapter 2

I don't know what's wrong, but I'm positive it's your fault.

I don't know about any of you, but one sure way to get me to do something is to order me *not* to do it. I can't help myself. I guess it goes back to being raised as an only child by a widowed mother, who constantly peppered her vocabulary with verbs ending in "n't" where I was concerned. You know the ones I mean, right? Don't. Can't. Shouldn't. Couldn't. Won't. Wouldn't. And on and on.

By the time I married Jim, I'd broken out of my "n't" phase and was deep into my rebellious phase. Which I'm still in, if I'm being honest.

So I marched myself into the kitchen, muttering under my breath, and poured myself a cup of leftover breakfast coffee. Which was stale, and I ended up tossing it in the sink.

Lucy and Ethel followed me into the kitchen and were now sitting, looking hopeful, by their respective food bowls.

"Not now, kids," I told them. "You just had breakfast a little while ago."

Ethel sighed deeply and padded across the kitchen to catch a snooze in her crate. She always listens to me.

"Who does he think he is?" I demanded of Lucy, who continued to sit by her empty bowl. She does not give up easily where food is concerned. "Forbidding me to touch his precious lawnmower like I'm an infant."

Lucy gave me a hard stare. *Maybe that's because you're acting like one.* Swear to God, that's what she told me.

"Everybody's a critic," I said. "I bet you'd be on my side if I gave you a few Milk Bones."

"I'll be on your side even without the Milk Bones," came a familiar voice from the open kitchen window.

Lucy ran to the door, stubby tail wagging, to greet another of her favorite humans, my BFF Nancy Green.

"How long have you been eavesdropping outside my house?" I demanded, giving her a perfunctory hug. Even though Nancy and I have been best friends since our pre-puberty days, she has no idea how often I talk to Lucy and Ethel. And I planned to keep it that way.

"Not long," said Nancy. "I just stopped in between real estate open houses to check on you. We haven't talked in one whole day, which is a record for us."

She settled herself in a kitchen chair and raised one perfectly sculpted eyebrow. "So, what's up? Why are you carrying on about a lawnmower, for heaven's sake. I thought those chores were one of the main reasons why you're still married to Jim."

"That's a terrible thing to say," I said, pulling out a kitchen chair for myself. "Just because you and Bob are separated doesn't mean you can pick on my husband."

See how I can change sides in an argument in the blink of an eye? It's a gift. It's fine for me to criticize Jim but nobody else—even the woman who was the maid of honor in our long-ago wedding—was allowed to do the same thing.

Nancy looked embarrassed. "If anyone else but you said that to me, I'd probably smack her. But you're right. I do have a jaundiced view of marriage these days. Even though Bob and I are currently dating. Which, I have to say, is working out very well."

Her face flushed, and since we're both way past the hot-flash phase, I figured she was referring to an intimate part of her life that I really didn't want to know about.

I needn't have worried about Nancy sharing intimate bedroom secrets, however. Before I had a chance to tell her about the forbidden lawnmower, she had her perfectly made-up face in my refrigerator, rummaging around to see what she could snack on.

"Is this all you've got to eat?" Nancy asked, waving an apple that had seen better days in my direction.

"Honestly, Nancy," I said, grabbing the apple and steering her back toward the table. "You are becoming a snack-a-holic. I don't know how you stay so slim."

I scouted around in the back of the freezer and came up with a half gallon of mocha chip ice cream. Which probably had freezer burn, but what the heck. I spooned a single teaspoon into a cereal bowl and offered it to Nancy. "Here. This is the best I can do on such short notice. Since I didn't know you were coming. And that you'd be hungry and demanding a snack."

Nancy pushed the bowl toward me. "Just looking at the ice cream did the trick. I'm not hungry any more. You eat it."

"Boy, are you weird," I said, grabbing the bowl and heading toward the sink. "I don't want it. It's only nine o'clock in the morning. Even I can't eat ice cream this early."

Then, I paused. "Maybe Jim has a sore throat. This might help him feel a little better." I looked at the dish of ice cream again and realized it was way past its prime. Kind of like me. So I dumped it.

"Is Jim sick?" Nancy asked. "Is that what you were talking to Lucy and Ethel about? And what's that got to do with mowing the lawn?"

"I suppose I'm overreacting," I said.

"To Jim being sick? I'm not following you."

"Jim has a cold," I explained. "Although, to listen to him, you'd think he had a terminal disease.

"Not that I want him to have a terminal disease," I hastened to explain. "It's just that, when he's sick, he's a real baby. And I wasn't sympathetic. In fact, I snapped at him."

Nancy patted my hand. "I wouldn't worry about it if I were you, sweetie," she said. "Jim is no different than most other men. If they were the ones to bear the children, human procreation would grind to a complete halt."

I laughed. "Perish the thought. But I was mean, and then I felt terrible about it. So I volunteered to mow the lawn today, to make him feel better. And he jumped down my throat. He actually forbade me to touch his precious riding mower. Can you imagine? And this from a man who's spent most of his post-retirement life micromanaging all the jobs I've been doing around the house for years."

I was fuming, remembering the conversation. "He treated me like I was a child instead of his wife. And I was only trying to help. The big jerk."

"It's a riding mower?" Nancy asked. "One of those super big

jobs?"

"Well, it's not a farm tractor," I said. "But it is big."

"Maybe Jim is right," Nancy said. "Your driving skills aren't always the greatest. After all, you did have to take the road test three times when we were seniors in high school before you passed it."

Now, this really frosted me. Nancy has never met a speed limit that she didn't feel was merely a "suggestion" and genuflects at stop signs instead of stopping. Plus, her parallel parking skills are nonexistent.

However, magnanimous person that I am, I chose to ignore her. Instead, I made a show of looking at my watch, then said, "Do you have any more open houses to go to, Nancy?"

"Oops," she squealed, "I must fly. Promise me you won't get into any trouble today!"

"Bye, Nancy," I said, propelling her toward the door. "Happy Open Houses." And I resisted slamming the door after her.

I can act like a mature adult when I put my mind to it.

Chapter 3

Home is where the dogs are.

"Don't get into any trouble! Is that an appropriate way for my very best friend in the whole world to talk to me? Nancy's as bad as Jim," I fumed to Lucy.

My canine housemate gave me a soulful look, making it clear once again—in case I had forgotten—that she and Ethel were my Very Best Friends.

I leaned down and gave her a quick scratch under her chin. "Sorry, Lucy. I didn't mean to hurt your feelings. I meant that Nancy is my very best human friend."

I always stay on Lucy and Ethel's good side. The dogs are in the car with me a lot, and have witnessed a few of my driving "adventures." I didn't need any criticism from them, too.

"I *am* a good driver," I insisted aloud. "And I'm positive I can handle the riding mower, no matter what Jim and Nancy say. But first, I have to figure out how to turn the darn thing on. I wonder if it came with an instruction book."

We have a drawer in our kitchen for instruction manuals belonging to every appliance we've bought since we've been married. I've tried to throw out the manuals that are for stuff we've gotten rid of—old dishwashers, stoves, microwaves—but Jim insists on keeping them all. "You never know when we might need that, Carol," he'll say, grabbing the instruction book and stuffing it back into the drawer.

Beats me why he's so insistent, but I try to pick my marital battles. This is one I'm willing to let him think he's won.

Of course, there was no helpful how-to guide for the riding mower in the kitchen drawer. And I didn't even know what brand it was.

Rats. It might be time for me to make the trek to Jim's garage— one of his sacred spaces—and check out the mower for myself.

But first, I snuck a peek in the bedroom to check on My Beloved. He was snoring like a chain saw.

Excellent.

As I turned to tiptoe out of the bedroom, I tripped over some manila folders, piled haphazardly near the bed. That's Jim filing system. So to speak. And when the pile is high enough, he stuffs them into a drawer in the office. He's fanatical about saving receipts and bank statements. I think he has one for the very first car we ever bought, back in the 1970s.

Hmm.

In a flash of brilliance that impressed even me, I realized that Jim must have saved the receipt for his precious riding mower. And it could be buried somewhere in what I laughingly call the family filing cabinet.

Tripping over that folder was a sign from above. I was sure of it. I would find the receipt, which must have the brand of the mower on it. Once I had the manufacturer's name, I was betting I could find an online crash course on how to operate the machine.

As things turned out, that was a prophetic choice of words.

Humming one of my all-time favorite songs, "Anything You Can Do, I Can Do Better" from *Annie Get Your Gun*—a Broadway musical from the 1950s in case you didn't know that—I logged onto the cyber superhighway and Googled Husqvarna riding mower. Honest to goodness, I'd never seen a "q" that wasn't followed by a "u." Those lawnmower manufacturers knew nothing about proper spelling.

In a flash, I had the user manual on the screen. Which, as far as I was concerned, resembled reading the *Odyssey* in the original Greek. Not that I ever did that, understand. I'm making a point here, so don't take me literally.

Here are a few of the highlights, along with some additional comments from me:

MOWER OPERATING INSTRUCTIONS

* Read, understand, and follow all instructions on the machine and in the manual before starting. **Okay, I'll give it my best shot.**

* Do not put hands or feet near rotating parts or under the machine. Keep clear of the discharge opening at all times. **Unfortunately, I have no idea where the discharge opening is, but this sounds like a good idea.**

* Only allow responsible adults, who are familiar with the instructions, to operate the machine. **This could be a problem. I've never been accused of being a responsible adult.**

* Be sure the area is clear of bystanders before operating. Stop machine if anyone enters the area. **So I guess mowing for an audience of adoring fans is out of the question. Too bad. I love applause.**

* Never carry passengers. **This means you, Lucy and Ethel! So no trying to jump on my lap.**

* Do not mow in reverse unless absolutely necessary. **Trust me, this will never become absolutely necessary.**

* Always look down and behind you before and while backing up. **See previous comment.**

* Material may ricochet back toward the operator. *Oh no!*

* Stop the blades when crossing gravel surfaces. **How does a person stop the blades? More information would be very helpful here! Perhaps I should e-mail the manufacturer and suggest that.**

SAFETY RULES

Safe Operation Practices for Ride-On Mowers

DANGER: THIS CUTTING MACHINE IS CAPABLE OF AMPUTATING HANDS AND FEET AND THROWING OBJECTS. FAILURE TO OBSERVE THE FOLLOWING SAFETY INSTRUCTIONS COULD RESULT IN SERIOUS INJURY OR DEATH. **Good gracious. Am I sure I want to do this???**

WARNING: In order to prevent accidental starting when setting up, transporting, adjusting or making repairs, always disconnect spark plug wire and place wire where it cannot contact spark plug. **I have no idea where this is. Or what it is.**

WARNING: Do not coast down a hill in neutral; you may lose control of the mower. **This is a joke, right? I'm now terrified I'll lose control of the mower on level ground.**

WARNING: Engine exhaust, some of its constituents, and certain vehicle components contain or emit chemicals known to the State of California to cause cancer and birth defects or other reproductive harm. **Fortunately, I am way past childbearing years and I live in Connecticut, so this one doesn't freak me out like some of the other warnings do. Or maybe the State of California is smarter than the State of Connecticut. Hmm. I wonder what other things California knows that Connecticut doesn't.**

* Slow down before turning. **This is assuming I have the courage to turn the mower on in the first place.**

* Never leave a running machine unattended. Always turn off blades, set parking brake, stop engine, and remove keys before dismounting. **See previous comment.**

* Operate machine only in daylight or good artificial light. **This makes sense to me. I don't see that well in the dark, anyway.**

* Do not operate the machine while under the influence of alcohol or drugs. **Too bad. I was thinking of having a small glass of chardonnay before I started this little adventure. I guess that's out.**

* Watch for traffic when operating near or crossing roadways. **I have no intention of driving the mower in traffic, so I'm going to ignore this one.**

* Data indicates that operators, age sixty years and above, are involved in a large percentage of riding mower-related injuries. These operators should evaluate their ability to operate the riding mower safely enough to protect themselves and others from serious injury. **I wonder if AARP has an online course in this. Could this be age discrimination?**

   * Do not try to stabilize the machine by putting your foot on the ground. **I never even considered this!**

Well, I'm not going to lie to you. After reading through the riding mower operating manual, I was ready to chicken out.

This was a lot harder than separating the whites from the colored laundry, a steep learning curve for Jim that he has yet to ace to my complete satisfaction. And more dangerous, too.

No way was I going to take my life in my hands to prove a point. I did want to live long enough to see and hold my grandchildren— which I was planning on having someday in the (near) future. Not that I ever put pressure on my recently married daughter Jenny and her husband Mark, or my possibly married son Mike. And I did want to have two arms/hands to cuddle said grandchildren, and two legs/feet to walk the floor with them whenever they were fussy.

Hmm. Maybe I could print out the instructions and tape them onto the lawnmower, so that, in case I had a problem, I could refer to them.

I immediately discarded that idea. First of all, I doubted there was a place to tape the directions, and second, I needed to concentrate on operating the mower properly, not distract myself with how-to's. Or how-not-to's.

"Maybe I shouldn't try this," I said to the dogs. "What do you think?"

This shows how unsure I was, right? I mean, normally I don't come right out and ask the dogs for advice. Not that this ever stops them from offering it.

Lucy gave a deep sigh and walked over to the bookcase, which is packed with a mixture of books and family photos.

Note to self: This needs to be dusted. Sometime in the far, far distant future.

Lucy turned around and looked back at me, to be sure I was paying attention, then parked herself in front of the bookcase, stared at it, then looked back at me again.

I tried to figure out what was so fascinating. I hoped it wasn't the dust.

"Okay, Lucy. I give up. This time I really don't get it. What is it about this bookcase that's so fascinating?"

My eyes traveled to a row of family photographs. "Oh, look, there's a picture of Jim and me when we brought Jenny home from the hospital." My eyes filled up and I reached for the photo. "That was such a happy day. Although the first few days home, and the nights, were pretty challenging. I had no idea what I was doing. Who knew becoming a mother was so difficult? I worried constantly that she wasn't eating enough. Or that I wasn't holding her properly. And I was terrified to give her that first bath."

I smiled, holding the photo, lost in memories.

And then, I snapped to it. Because it finally dawned on me what Lucy was telling me. When I was a new mother, I was completely unsure of myself. But I persevered, slowly, and finally I got the hang of caring for a newborn. So that, by the time Mike was born, I was a pro.

And in a little while, I'd be a pro with Jim's stupid riding mower, too. I just hoped the labor pains weren't too bad.

Chapter 4

I don't let anyone embarrass me. I do a better job all by myself.

Before I made my official riding mower debut, I gave the dogs a good romp around the back yard. Then I shut them in the kitchen. Firmly. And bribed them with two dog biscuits each.

"No barking," I lectured them. "You'll wake Jim. And I need to do this all by myself, so you're staying in the house. I can't take the chance that either of you will accidentally get hurt by the mower."

Lucy gave me a skeptical look.

"Listen, Lucy, you're the one who convinced me that I am perfectly capable of using the darned mower. So don't give me the evil eye."

I pulled a kitchen chair closer to the window. "Here. You can hop on this and have a clear view of my mowing prowess. I hope that satisfies you."

One more biscuit for each canine, and I was out the door. Approaching the garage. Scared to death. Lying to myself that I could do this. And not believing me for a single minute.

And if I can't convince myself, well, feel free to fill in the blanks.

Even though we're very good friends, I'm not going to give you all the gory details of what happened next. Suffice it to say that this was not my finest moment, and made my first driver's test—which I failed when I backed over a curb and nailed three safety cones and a fire hydrant—look like I was ready for a spot in the Grand Prix.

But I gave it my best shot, and hope you'll give me an A for effort.

Oh, all right. Here's what happened.

I figured that I might have to add some gas to what I now thought of as the Orange Monster. And that, for safety reasons, should be done outside the garage. So I turned the mower operating switch to "on," said a brief prayer, and started to walk the machine outside.

Big mistake.

The darn thing took off like a rocket, with me running after it.

Who knew the mower had so much power? And speed? Good gracious. I'd never run so fast in my whole life. Trying not to scream. Mustn't wake Jim. Praying that the sucker wouldn't hit the fence. Or, worse, the house.

Our gas grill was in its path. Wham! Totaled. No more cookouts this year. Or maybe ever. At least, not on that baby.

Note to self: Purchase new gas grill asap. Preferably before Jim notices what happened to the old one.

Then, the mower headed toward the birdbath and nailed that, too, as well as two shepherd's hooks that were next to my birdfeeders. I was cringing, especially when the machine reversed itself and actually *backed* into our picket fence. All by itself. It was like the machine had taken on a life of its own. Stephen King's *Christine* could take carnage lessons from the Orange Monster.

I finally managed to stop the mower when it got stuck in one of the bushes on the side of the house.

Truthfully, the mower stopped itself. I guess it was tired from all that exertion.

Me, too.

I collapsed beside the wretched machine, gasping for breath. I hadn't had that much exercise since…well, never mind. Let's just say it'd been a while. And the other circumstances are none of your business.

I sat down on the grass and forced myself to survey the wreckage of what had been, until a few minutes ago, my beautiful yard.

You've really done it this time, Carol. Wait till Jim finds out what happened. He's going to kill you.

I closed my eyes and took deep breaths to calm myself. I willed myself to focus on something beautiful. But the only beautiful place my subconscious was willing to take me to was my yard. Before I wrecked it.

I didn't cry, though. For those of you who know me well, I bet that surprises you.

I decided to save my tears and hysterics for my conversation with Jim. I'd need them big-time then.

"Do you need some help, ma'am?"

My baby blues snapped open at the sound of a male voice. And found myself staring at a pair of well-worn work boots. The owner of the boots (he was also wearing jeans and a forest green windbreaker, in case you're interested) squatted down beside me and offered his hand to pull me up from the ground.

I was embarrassed. And also a little scared. After all, he was a complete stranger who had probably witnessed my humiliation and now was in my yard.

I snatched my hand away and laughed. Nervously.

"Thank you so much. I'm fine. Really."

I rolled over and managed to stand up on my own. Not gracefully, but at least I was upright.

The stranger surveyed me skeptically. "Mrs. Stevens didn't think you were fine. That's why she sent me over here to help."

He stretched out his hand again. "I'm Will Finnegan. I do lawn work for your neighbors across the street."

Oh, great. That busybody Phyllis Stevens probably took pictures of my humiliation that she'll spread all over the neighborhood.

Now I was even more embarrassed.

Will Finnegan looked around the yard. "Are you sure you don't want some help cleaning this up? I'd be glad to fix what I can." He gave me a big grin. "Before your husband sees it, that is."

"What makes you assume I'd hide this from my husband?" I asked. "That's pretty presumptuous, considering you don't even know me.

"And how did you know I'm married, for that matter? Or did Phyllis tell you all about me?" The blabbermouth.

"Why, for sure any woman as attractive as you are must be married," Will said, offering me another grin. "That's easy. And as far as keeping this from your husband, well, let's just say that I've had lots of customers over the years who've called me in a panic to come and help them. I don't want to brag, but I'm a very handy guy. And I'm discreet, too."

He made a zipping motion across his lips.

I'll just bet you are.

"I never saw a mower take off on its own like that," he said. "There's supposed to be a safety switch to prevent accidents. You must have done something wrong."

"I didn't do anything," I insisted. "I barely touched the mower and, the next thing I knew, the darn thing took off. Maybe it's defective."

"I suppose that's possible," Will said. Although he didn't sound as if he believed it.

"I can't make the yard look perfect, but at least I can pick up some of the debris and fix the picket fence. I'll even haul away some of the branches. What do you say?"

I hesitated. Then he said two magic words.

"No charge."

I was softening. And although I hated to admit it, I was desperate.

I knew that Phyllis and her husband Bill were the official cheapskates in our neighborhood, so if this guy worked for them, he must be good at his job. Otherwise, he wouldn't have lasted more than ten minutes.

"Call me Will," he said, offering me his hand one more time. "That's what my friends call me. And I have a feeling we're going to be really good friends."

Our hands met and—wow—electric shock. Sizzle City. One of those unexplainable but undeniable immediate attractions that made me jerk my hand right away.

"Is that what Phyllis calls you?" I asked.

"Yes," Will said. "And you know the old saying, where there's a will, there's a way." Then he winked at me.

Well, my goodness. This guy was coming onto me. And my treacherous body had responded.

I could tell from the way Will looked at me that he realized it, too.

I glanced away, sure that my cheeks were flaming. And was confronted once again by the damage that darn mower had done to my previously beautiful yard.

"Can you really fix this?" I challenged Will. "My husband's going to have a fit when he sees what happened out here."

"Sure I can," Will said. "In fact, I can probably make it look better than it did before the mower went berserk." He frowned. "But the whole job will take some time. I might have to get more of my crew over here. And if you hire us, this job won't be cheap. I won't charge you for my own time, because you're a neighbor of Phyllis and Bill's. But I have a payroll to meet. I have to pay my crew. And I may need to rent equipment."

"How much money are we talking about?" I asked. "We never hire anyone without a written estimate."

Especially my super-thrifty, coupon-obsessed husband. I didn't really say that last part, of course.

Will didn't look happy about having to put together an estimate. I'm sure he figured his charm would get him the job, no problem.

Super salesperson that he was, though, he eyeballed the picket fence, part of which was face down in the dirt. "I'll see what I can put together in the next few days and get something in writing over to you, Okay? I can fix that fence right away, though, if you want me to. Looks like you have dogs here. You'll want to keep them safe. This is a pretty busy street."

Lucy and Ethel! Oh, my gosh. What if they got loose and ran onto Old Fairport Turnpike. And got hit by a car. And died. And it would be all my fault.

How could I live with myself if that happened? Oh, God, how I'd miss them. In fact, I was missing them already, even though the rational side of my mind—the part I rarely use—told me that they were both safe in the house.

I'm an expert at fabricating worst possible scenarios. Maybe in my next life, I'll become a fiction writer. Although I'm told that writing fiction is a lot harder than it seems. And doesn't pay very well, either.

"You're hired, Will," I said, hoping he hadn't noticed that my eyes had filled with tears. "I don't know what I'm going to tell Jim, but I'll think of something. Just, please, fix the fence so Lucy and Ethel will be safe."

"Don't worry," Will said. "I'll take care of it. I just have to get a few tools from my truck." He gestured across the street. "That's my rig. Finnegan's Rakes."

"I've seen that truck before," I said. "All over town."

"Well, I don't want to brag," Will said, "but we do a pretty good business. And we have lots of customers in your neighborhood."

He reached out for my hand again and gave it a squeeze. "I'll take good care of you. I promise."

Cue treacherous body again. Which snapped to attention when

it heard a familiar voice.

"What the hell is going on out here?"

Chapter 5

We're staying together for the sake of the dogs.

I jumped a foot. Only a slight exaggeration. I'd had no time to concoct my brilliant fictional account of the Great Yard Debacle.

My Beloved was out of bed and headed in our direction, sneezing and coughing. And wrapped in that horrible, pilly grey sweater that I've been trying to throw out for years.

Focus, Carol. Forget the sweater. How are you going to get yourself out of this mess? I wonder if you're too old to be grounded.

But Jim wasn't wearing his glasses. Eureka! Maybe I could come up with an inaccurate version of the truth after all. (Notice, I didn't use the word "lie.")

I've learned over the years that the best defense is a strong offense. So I went on the offensive.

"Jim, honey, you shouldn't be out of bed," I said, grabbing his arm and steering him back in the direction of the house. "I don't want you to get sicker. What are you doing outside? It's freezing, and you only have a sweater on. Let me help you back inside."

Jim shook my arm off in a gesture of annoyance I know all too well.

"Forget it, Carol. I know something happened out here." He turned and squinted at the fence. "How did this fall down? I didn't hear any wind. Was there a storm? If there was, I must have slept through it."

Every fiber of my being wanted to say, "Yes, Jim. That's it. There was a wind storm. You must have been sound asleep and didn't hear it. And it did a lot of other damage in the yard, too. It totaled the birdbath, and the gas grill."

But I didn't. And the fact that Will Finnegan was within earshot and could call me out had absolutely nothing to do with it.

"I have to tell you the truth, Jim." Most of it, anyway.

"I started the riding mower, it got away from me, and knocked down part of the fence." If he hadn't noticed the rest of the carnage yet, well, why worry the guy when he was feeling sick?

So I skipped over some of the details, cutting right to the chase, as the saying goes. "And this nice young man came to my rescue. His name is Will Finnegan, and his landscaping company is called Finnegan's Rakes. He's kindly offered to fix the fence for free. Today. So we won't have to worry about the possibility of Lucy and Ethel getting onto Old Fairport Turnpike and being hit by a car."

I knew that would work. Jim is a real softie when it comes to the girls.

Jim aimed his squint at Will. "Don't I know you? Aren't you the guy who donated the money to build the new children's playground down by the beach? It's a pleasure to meet you."

Will looked embarrassed. "I don't want to take all the credit for that project. Lots of people pitched in and helped."

"Don't be so modest. You're the one who got the ball rolling," Jim said. "If it weren't for you, nothing would have happened but idle talk. And I understand you donate a portion of your company's profits to the local boys' and girls' club in town. I wish more people in Fairport were as community-minded as you obviously are."

Jim turned to me. "You know, Carol, I was lying in bed thinking about what you said earlier. About how I can't do some of the things around the house as much as I used to. And your offer to help."

He scowled. "Not that I'm letting you off the hook. I knew you couldn't handle that riding mower. But noooo, you didn't listen."

I started to defend myself, but didn't get the chance. Jim sneezed, reminding me that I really needed to hurry him back into the house.

"Anyway," Jim continued, "I've come to the conclusion that it's time to turn over more of these jobs, like lawn care and show removal, to someone else. They're getting to be too much for me to deal with on a regular basis."

He fixed me with a look. "And I don't mean you, Carol.

"So, I guess it was a lucky break that you happened by today,

Mr. Finnegan. Maybe you and I can do some business."

I tried not to look surprised. It was a real effort, let me tell you. This behavior was totally out of character for Jim.

But I wasn't about to give him a chance to change his mind. Something My Beloved frequently does once he figures out that something he's agreed to with great enthusiasm is going to cost him money.

I inserted myself into the now testosterone-dominated conversation with an added piece of information I hoped would really seal the deal. "He didn't just happen by, Jim," I said. "Will does the landscaping and lawn work for Phyllis and Bill Stevens. He was working at their place when the mower and I had our miscommunication problem."

And you know how cheap Bill is. He makes you look like a rank amateur.

I didn't really say that last part, of course.

"If you work for Bill Stevens, that's all the reference I need," Jim said. "I'd shake your hand, but I don't want to give you my cold. How soon can you start?"

Was it my imagination, or did I hear the faint strains of the "Hallelujah Chorus" coming from the sky?

Nah. That must have been me.

I got a reluctant but still sneezing Jim back into bed and made him promise to stay there and take a much-needed nap. Which he only agreed to do after extracting a promise from me to stay out of trouble while he was dozing.

Normally that would have ticked me off, but under the current circumstances, the guy did have a point.

I crossed my heart and said, "Scout's honor, Jim. Now, get some rest." I blew him a kiss from the bedroom door and headed for the kitchen.

I realized my heart was racing enough after my adventure, so instead of fixing myself a cup of black high-test coffee, I decided a cup of chamomile tea was exactly what I needed to calm myself. I'm not a tea lover. Something about the acid in the brew always upsets my stomach, so I needed something to snack on, too.

Which led to my rummaging in the refrigerator and finding a

small piece of cherry pie that was left over from last night's supper. I congratulated myself that Nancy had missed it when she foraged in my fridge earlier today.

Since cherry is a fruit, and Weight Watchers encourages folks to eat five portions of fruit and vegetables every day to stay healthy, I figured this counted.

I'm always impressed with how I can justify anything I want to do.

Lucy padded into the kitchen from the direction of the family room, followed by Ethel. Both canines gave me a reproachful stare.

I tossed them half a dog biscuit each. "Don't look at me like that. If I'm counting calories for myself, I'm going to count them for you, too."

I ignored the dirty look Lucy aimed at me, and continued, "I suppose both of you had your little black noses pressed against the window and saw what happened outside in the yard." Not much escapes their notice.

Lucy gave me another look, telegraphing loud and clear that she thought what happened in the yard was still another ridiculous example of human behavior. As opposed to the far more superior canine behavior mantra—eat, play, sleep.

"You're supposed to be on my side, Lucy," I said. "We girls have to stick together." At least, I hoped that she and Ethel wouldn't blab about my latest misadventure to some of their canine buddies at the local dog park.

Which was more than I could say about Phyllis Stevens.

I don't mean that Phyllis cavorts around the dog park, mind you. She and her husband Bill are members of the "Old Guard" of the area, and one of the few couples in our neighborhood who are older than Jim and me. The self-appointed head of the Old Fairport Turnpike Homeowners Association, her family has owned the house directly across the street from us for three generations.

Which Phyllis interprets as a mandate to comment/judge anything and everything that's going on in the neighborhood, from the exterior color of a house (we live in an historic district in town and all the houses, plus the shutters and fences, must conform to a pre-selected color palate), to the shingles on the roof, to the care and maintenance of anything else she felt like commenting on/criticizing.

Although she and Bill did come to my rescue, however

unwillingly, the night I discovered a dead body in my living room. Maybe some of you remember that. It certainly is a night I'll never forget.

Phyllis is known to have the loosest lips in the neighborhood. Which meant that I had some damage control to do asap, before she had a chance to call or e-mail the neighbors with an overdramatized description of my lawnmower fiasco. And while I was at it, I'd see if I could get some more information about Will Finnegan and his landscaping company. The guy seemed on the up and up, but before we parted with any of our cash, I wanted to be absolutely sure hiring him was a good idea.

I dumped the dregs of my tea in the sink (I finished the cherry pie, but I bet you already figured that out for yourself) and announced to the dogs that I was going to nip across the street for a quick chat with Phyllis.

Lucy gave me another of her looks. Then she butted her head against my legs, forcing me to look down at what I was wearing. My pants were stained with dirt and grass stains. Big oops. I certainly couldn't pay a social call on Phyllis looking like that.

"Okay, Lucy. I'll take a quick shower and change. I appreciate the paws' up, but I hate it when you're right." I gave her a quick thank-you scratch behind her long silky ears.

I pushed aside the thought that the canines in the house were rapidly becoming smarter than the humans. Or maybe they always were, and I'm only noticing now.

My dog, the fashionista!

Chapter 6

Please distract me. I'm trying to think.

I'll be honest with you. I wasn't exactly thrilled about heading across Old Fairport Turnpike in the direction of the Stevens house. So, even though I knew that time was of the essence if I was going to head off Phyllis and her loose lips, I took some extra time in the shower. Hey, washing out a few twigs that had found their way into my hair wasn't easy.

And I took particular care with what to wear, too. I chose a pair of ironed chino pants with knife pleats that would impress any dry cleaner—and which I had done all by myself once I wiped the dust off my iron—topped by a pale blue cashmere sweater that matched my eyes. A little blush, a swipe of lipstick, and I was good to go.

I did tape a note to Jim on the bathroom mirror, since I couldn't count on Lucy and Ethel to give him a message and I didn't want to wake the poor guy.

Mindful of the ever increasing traffic on Old Fairport Turnpike, which runs parallel to Fairport Turnpike—our town's main artery, in case you didn't know that—I made sure to look both ways several times before I sprinted across the street.

Two cyclists swerved to avoid me. Where the heck did they come from? I didn't even see them.

I took my time going up the walkway toward the front door. I wanted to check out the landscaping and see if Will Finnegan did a good job.

What I saw was a neatly trimmed lawn, a well designed pattern of shrubbery interspersed with brightly colored mums, and a stone walkway leading to the main entrance. I was impressed that there was no grass growing between the stone pavers. We always have a problem with that, despite Jim's frequent attempts at weeding.

From the street (or from my living room windows), the house looked like one of the smaller ones on our block. But, although the house had a narrow front, generations of Phyllis's family had bumped out the structure in the back. The latest addition was a large first-floor master bedroom suite.

The main reason I know this is that, five years ago when the addition was completed, Phyllis made sure her house was included in the Historical Society's annual Christmas Stroll, a fundraiser which benefits local charities in our town.

In fact, although our two families have been across-the-street neighbors for almost thirty years, I realized I'd never been invited into the home as a guest. Any party invitations had come from Jim and me, and the parties were held at our house. It's not that the Phyllis and Bill were unfriendly. But they'd never had any children, and had very little in common with most of the other neighbors. Like us.

I pushed away the memory of the only other time I'd landed on their doorstep, squared my shoulders and rang the doorbell. The door immediately swung open to reveal Phyllis, with Bill standing right behind her.

I bet they've been watching me all the time from their picture window.

Phyllis pasted a smile on her face and gestured me inside.

"I was wondering if you'd stop in," she said. *After making a complete jackass of yourself.*

She didn't really say that last part, of course. She didn't need to. The expression of disapproval on her round face said it for her.

"I wanted to thank you so much for sending Will Finnegan over to help me," I said, ignoring Phyllis and speaking directly to Bill.

"Are you all right, Carol?" Bill asked.

"That was quite a spectacle," Phyllis added.

I laughed nervously. "Just my feeble attempt to entertain the neighborhood," I said.

"We certainly can count on you for that," Phyllis replied.

So far, the three of us were still standing at the front door. I wondered how to suggest they invite me inside without appearing too pushy. My mother did raise me to be polite. Under most circumstances.

"As long as you're all right," Bill said. "When I saw what happened, I sent Will over right away."

"It was *my* idea," Phyllis corrected, not wanting to give her husband any credit. "Will's been so helpful to us."

"It was lucky this was the day he did a fall cleanup here," Bill said.

I saw an opening and jumped right in. "Actually, that's the other thing I wanted to talk to you about. Jim and I are thinking of hiring Will to do some work for us. Do you have a minute to tell me more about what he does for you?"

"Come on in, Carol," Bill said, shooting a quick glance at Phyllis. Probably asking for permission.

"Let's sit down in the family room." He turned and headed toward the back of the house, with me and a reluctant Phyllis trailing behind him.

"This is such a beautiful house," I gushed. *The last time I was here, I never noticed.*

I didn't say the last part. But some of you may know that.

I'd hit on the exact right thing to warm Phyllis up. "This is a beautiful house," she agreed, sitting in a comfortable wing chair that I suspected was a recliner in disguise. Bill took his place in its twin, and I settled myself on the sofa facing them. "It's been in my family for three generations," Phyllis said. "We consider it a privilege to live here, a sacred trust. I'm not sure anyone can understand what this house means to us, Carol."

"And, unfortunately, we have no family to leave it to," Bill said. "I'm not sure what will happen to the house when we're both gone."

For a brief second, a flicker of sadness passed over Phyllis's face. Followed immediately by an expression of annoyance.

"You know that's our private business, Bill," she snapped. "Carol doesn't need to know everything about our personal lives."

Bill looked absolutely mortified at being reprimanded like a ten-year-old in front of me. Poor guy.

"There's no need for you to worry, Phyllis," I said as sincerely as I could. "I won't mention what you told me to Jim."

I took a deep breath, then said, "And I hope I can count on you to do the same for me about my lawnmower adventure, Phyllis."

Now, it was Phyllis's turn to look embarrassed. Which I interpreted to mean that she'd already started spreading the news.

She recovered her composure quickly, though. "Of course, Carol," she lied. "But I can't say the same for any of the other neighbors. I doubt that Bill and I were the only ones who saw what happened."

Nice save, Phyllis. That way, if I hear any neighborhood gossip featuring me as the star, I can't blame you.

"So, what about Will Finnegan?" I asked. "Would you recommend him?"

"Absolutely," said Phyllis and Bill at the exact same time.

"He's very reliable," Bill said.

"He's a real treasure," Phyllis added. "We were one of his first customers when he started Finnegan's Rakes. Now the company has more customers than Will can handle by himself. So he had to hire more people."

"He always does our work personally," Bill put in, daring to interrupt his wife.

Phyllis's face was getting a little pink. "Will promised that he'll never send anyone else to do our lawn. Because I'm...I mean, we're...special. Since we were one of his first official customers."

What an interesting way to talk about a business relationship. Or did prim and proper Phyllis also experience a *zing* where Will Finnegan was concerned? Food for my overactive imagination.

"Of course, Will's a local boy," Bill said. "His family lived in Fairport until he was twelve. Then his father got a new job and the family moved to the D.C. area."

I was surprised. "I wonder if Jenny or Mike went to school with him," I said.

"Not likely," Phyllis said. "Will is in his early forties now. He would have been several years ahead of both your children."

"He was in my Boy Scout troop years ago," Bill said.

"Oh, I didn't realize...."

Phyllis cut me off.

"None of this has anything to do with what you came to ask us, does it Carol?" She shot her husband a look.

"I'm sorry, Carol," Bill said. "Phyllis is right. I tend to go on about things too much. One of the curses of getting older, I guess."

Poor guy. I wondered if there was a special day of the week when Bill was allowed to speak without being criticized.

"So, what else do you want to know?" said Phyllis, making a show out of looking at her watch. "I have to start dinner now. We always make a point of eating at five o'clock sharp."

Bill nodded. "That way we're finished, and the dishes are all done, before our favorite television shows come on.

"Say, Carol, do you and Jim watch *Jeopardy!*? Phyllis and I would never miss it. Maybe sometime we could get together and have a neighborhood trivia party."

"There you go again," Phyllis said. "Boring Carol when I'm sure she has better things to do than listen to you."

Ouch.

Realizing that this time she'd gone too far, Phyllis reached out and patted her husband's hand. "You know I love listening to your stories, but Carol doesn't need to. That's what I meant to say."

Boy, I would *never* talk to Jim like that. I do tend to speak my mind, but my comments and suggestions are much gentler.

At least, I sure hope they are.

Note to self: Be cautious about your caustic comments. The man you hurt may be the man you love.

It was up to me to move this non-coffee klatch along.

"I don't mean to keep you," I said. "Jim will be wondering what's taking me so long. But he did have a question about Will Finnegan's rates. Is he reasonable? Does he charge by the hour, or by each job?"

I addressed these questions directly to Bill, implying I was merely the messenger between one guy (my husband) and another.

Of course, it was Phyllis who answered. No surprise.

"We may get a special rate," she said. "I don't think it's up to us to quote you any prices. That's something between you and Will."

Phyllis favored me with the look she had recently used on Bill. And stood up.

All righty, then. Don't let anyone tell you that I can't take a hint. I stood up and turned to leave. "I'll walk you out, Carol," Bill said, "so Phyllis can start cooking one of her delicious meals."

He gave me a wink. "You know the old saying, 'The way to a man's heart is through his stomach.' Right, Phyl?"

"To this man's heart, that's for sure," Phyllis said, turning and heading for the kitchen.

"I'm glad you're all right, Carol. And I'm sure that if you hire Will Finnegan, you won't be sorry," Bill said, ushering me toward the front of the house.

As he opened the door so I could leave, he leaned over and said, in a low voice that couldn't be overheard, "Don't pay any attention to Phyllis. She can be on the cranky side sometimes, but she has a good heart. And I know she was as concerned about you as I was."

In a louder voice, Bill said, "Come back and see us again, any time. And give some thought to that neighborhood *Jeopardy!* party. I think it would be a lot of fun. Give our best to Jim."

And then, to my complete shock, he gave me a quick kiss on the cheek.

Believe me, that smooch got my body moving toward my own house double quick. All I needed to complicate my life even more was a geriatric neighbor with a crush on me.

Chapter 7

My husband is always P.C.—my Personal Curmudgeon.

Since Jim still had the sniffles, I didn't fuss much with dinner that night. After all, he couldn't taste anything, so why bother?

I defrosted a container of homemade chicken soup—I bet that surprises you!—and added some extra vegetables and noodles to make it more of a substantial meal. Some whole wheat dinner rolls, fresh (almost) from the local supermarket and I was all set. And if Jim wanted dessert, I still had some of that mocha chip ice cream aging in the freezer.

Jim's sweet tooth never deserts him, no matter how sick he is. Me, too. When I'm down with a cold, the only things that taste good to me are ice cream, pastries, and chocolate. As you can imagine, I often gain a pound or two while I'm coughing and sneezing!

I hoped that Jim felt well enough to come to the kitchen table for supper. And I hoped even more that we wouldn't talk about my lawnmower fiasco while we were eating. Lectures impede my digestion, and I felt guilty enough about my adventure already.

And I do not take criticism well. At. All.

I was just about to ladle the soup into bowls when my phone beeped, indicating an incoming text. I was thrilled to see it was from the Miami branch of the family, our son Mike. His breakup with his possible wife Marlie (perhaps you know about that?), plus the added responsibility of running Cosmo's, a successful restaurant and bar, didn't allow for a lot of time to keep in touch with good old Mom and Dad. At least, that's what I always tell myself when we don't hear from him for a while. Since I've learned to text, though, the communications are more frequent.

By the way, Mike's the only one who ever calls me Cosmo Girl—a nod to my long-ago job at *Cosmopolitan* magazine back in the Helen Gurley Brown days. I've deluded myself into believing that he named the restaurant in my honor.

Mike: *Hey, Cosmo Girl! I see you've had another adventure!*

Me: *Hello to you, too. And what are you talking about? I'm here being a nurse to Dad, who has a cold.*

Mike: *Oh yeah? Then how'd you get a video on Fairport Patch 2day?*

Me: *What's that?*

Mike: *C.G., you gotta keep up with the times. Patch is latest way to ck out happenings in town. I ck it every day. And there u were!*

Oh, rats. That darn Phyllis. And she promised me she wouldn't tell anyone.

Me (typing furiously and making loads of typos): *Hjh? I mian, meea, mean, huh?*

Mike: *You did look darn cute chasing that ride-on mower. What did Dad have 2 say about that?*

Me: *A video? Oh, no!*

Mike: *U better check it out 4 urself. And cheer up. At least it's not on YouTube. That I know of. Gotta go. But be careful, Okay? Some of my customers are starting to wonder about u!*

And he signed off. The little devil. He always had to have the last word in these conversations.

Hmm. Wonder where he picked up that trait. Maybe it's genetic.

I turned around and almost tripped over Lucy and Ethel, who were in their "It's time to feed us so get going and no excuses" mood.

"That darn Phyllis Stevens," I fumed as I poured kibble into their bowls. Ethel raised her head briefly and made eye contact with me. Then, she went back to eating.

"Point well taken, Ethel," I said, interpreting her message. "Anyone who's never had at least one dog is not to be trusted. Even if Phyllis and Bill have allergies, there are medications for that."

I turned the soup on the stove to a low simmer, congratulating myself that I'd had the foresight to prepare such a simple meal that only got tastier the longer it cooked. Because I just had to look at

Fairport Patch and see what the heck Mike was talking about. And, even more important, try to figure out a way to get that video off the Internet right away.

I snuck a quick peek in the bedroom to check on Jim first. His glasses were perched on top of his receding hairline, and today's paper was in disarray all over our bed.

He was sound asleep and snoring softly. Thank goodness. Because that nap bought me a little computer time. Right after the dogs had a quick romp around the backyard on leashes, because part of the darn fence was down.

Imagine my surprise when we went outside and discovered that the damaged part of the picket fence had been repaired. It wasn't a perfect job, but at least it was standing up.

Maybe Phyllis was right. Will Finnegan was a treasure. If nothing else, he was certainly a man who kept his word.

And he was a very fast worker.

"No matter what's going on in Fairport, The Patch has you covered," I read. *"Visit Fairport Patch.com to keep up with news, business, and events in town. Check out photos and videos from your friends and neighbors. Stay in the know, even when you're on the go."*

Oh, boy. This did not bode well. And there was also an opportunity for people to comment on local posts.

I clicked on the *Today's Videos* link and there I was. Looking like an absolute fool, chasing that darn mower all over the yard. Although the clip seemed as long to me as a full-length movie, in reality it was less than thirty seconds.

I sat back in the desk chair and closed my eyes.

Breathe, Carol. In and out. In and out. Calm down. Maybe nobody but Mike has seen it. All your friends have better things to do with their time than spend hours on the Internet. And you're not identified by name.

Deep breaths. In and out.

Nobody's going to recognize that you're the jerk in this video. Mike did, but he's your son, for heaven's sake. Of course, he'd recognize his own mother.

I was definitely overreacting. I bet that doesn't surprise you, if you've known me for a while.

I clicked on the *Comments* icon under the video. And, to my horror, discovered a cyberspace conversation going on among a mixed group of total strangers, nervy neighbors, and so-called friends.

And most of the comments made me the butt (excuse me, but there's no other way to say it) of some pretty cheesy jokes.

I was pleased to see that Mike had posted a comment defending me—it was of the "This could happen to anybody" variety. Weak, but at least somebody was in my corner.

None from Phyllis Stevens, although if she was the one who posted the original video, she didn't need to. The damage had already been done.

The one from my former BFF Nancy really ticked me off. *I've known her for years, and she always has trouble driving. But she usually gets into the vehicle first! Ha ha ha.*

Traitor. Just wait until the next time she asked me for a favor.

I was desperate to find out if I could delete the video. The Patch had a *Contact Us* icon, so I clicked on it. Unfortunately, it asked for the usual identity information—name, e-mail, etc.—before it would let me into the site. There was no way I was going to share that I was the hapless female whose antics were currently garnering a load of comments on the website.

I was pretty sure that my own dear husband, the Andrews family's p.r. expert after years of working for Gibson Gillespie in New York City, would advise me to let the whole matter blow over.

If I told him about it. Which I had no intention of doing.

I bet that doesn't surprise you, either.

Chapter 8

The best way to forget all your troubles is to wear tight shoes.

By the time I got my aging body into bed next to a sleeping Jim, I was completely exhausted. And I ached in parts I never knew I had. Unexpected exertion can do that to a person. And in my case, any exertion is completely unexpected.

I flipped from my right side to my left, trying to find a comfortable position. Then I rolled over on my stomach. No go. I was equally uncomfortable no matter which way I lay. And I knew that, if I fell asleep on my stomach, I'd wake up with a pain in my neck in the morning.

You can take that remark any way you want.

I finally flipped over on my back again, forcing myself to lie still so I wouldn't wake Jim.

You should have taken a warm bath before you got into bed. That would have relaxed you so you could sleep. What a doofus you are.

I snapped my eyes shut and ordered them to stay that way. Big mistake. My imagination immediately presented me with a play-by-play rendition of the lawnmower debacle. It was like watching a rerun of a very bad television show when the remote control didn't work and there was no way to change the channel or turn the darn thing off.

Think of something pleasant, Carol. A view of the ocean. A spectacular sunset. Jenny announcing that she and Mark are expecting a baby.

Whoops. Maybe not that last one. My subconscious at work.

Will Finnegan. Now, that was a pleasant image. My hero. My new best friend.

I smiled and snuggled into my pillow.

I can't be sure, but I think that was when I finally dropped off to sleep. And I had a dream about Will riding the treacherous lawnmower, with me riding behind him, my hands clasped tightly around his waist to keep from falling off. We both had motorcycle helmets on, and Will was wearing a black leather jacket, no shirt.

Phyllis was running behind us, her face red from exertion. No matter how fast she ran, she couldn't catch up.

Faster. Faster.

"I'll take good care of you, Carol," Will said. "Forget Phyllis. You're my special client now. Trust me. You have to trust me."

And that's all I can remember. Darn it.

I stumbled out of bed the next morning feeling like I had been hit by a Mack truck. Well, in reality, even though the lawnmower didn't actually hit me, it did cause me huge emotional stress.

There was no sniffling husband beside me. I hoped that was a good sign.

The heavenly scent of perking coffee wafted into the bedroom. Now, *that* was a very good sign. Since his retirement, Jim usually made the morning coffee. And I let him think that he made it better than I did.

Hey, let the guy have his fantasies.

I pulled on a pair of bright pink Lilly Pulitzer sweats I found folded neatly near the back of my walk-in closet, along with a matching sweatshirt. Even if I don't feel my best, I try to look my best. Clothes that match, or at least complement each other, are one of my ways to compensate for the undeniable fact that the body wearing them is getting old and decrepit.

And the anticipation that hunky (there, I said it) Will Finnegan could, at this very minute, be outside in my yard had absolutely nothing to do with the fact that I also brushed my teeth, washed my face, and combed my hair before I hit the kitchen.

Adding blush and a touch of lipstick—well, why not? Anything to camouflage the new wrinkles that had undoubtedly popped up on my face overnight.

Nothing could disguise the bags under my eyes, though. Evidence of a restless night. Oh, well.

I followed the siren smell of coffee into the kitchen, expecting to see Jim hunched over the table reading the morning paper.

And instead found my darling daughter Jenny and her Fairport police detective husband Mark, heads bent so close together they were almost touching, conversing in low tones. Jim and the two dogs were nowhere to be seen.

Before they became aware of my presence, I distinctly heard Jenny say, "Let me handle this. She's going to be surprised. But I think once she has a chance to let it sink in, she'll be very pleased."

My mom-o-meter immediately ratcheted to high alert. Something was up. Most definitely.

Well, of course, I knew right away what they'd come to talk to me about. And why they'd come together, which is an unusual early morning occurrence. They were having a baby! Tears pricked my eyes. My baby girl was going to have a baby of her own.

Let them tell you the news, I cautioned myself. *For once, keep your big mouth shut. Don't rob them of the joy of seeing you surprised. And for heaven's sake, look surprised. And thrilled!*

"Well, good morning, you two," I said, leaning down to give each of them a kiss. "What a nice way to start the day. Which hopefully will be a much better one than yesterday."

Mark immediately jumped to his feet and pulled out a chair for me.

Jenny returned my smooch. "Hi, Mom," she said. "We're both on our way to work, but we thought we'd stop in to see how Dad's feeling." At my questioning look, she added, "We heard from Mike last night, and he said that Dad was down for the count with a cold. And that you were doing your Florence Nightingale thing." She paused for a millisecond, then added, "He caught us up on some other news, too."

She poured me a cup of steaming black coffee with just a hint of cinnamon, which I grabbed. "I really need this today," I said. "Thanks, honey."

Here we are, sitting around the same kitchen table where you two used to do your homework, so you can share your momentous news with me. Get to the point. Tell me your news. When are you due?

I didn't really say that, of course.

I suddenly realized that Jim should be here, too. Where the heck was he? If I was going to be a grandmother (at last!), that meant that he was going to be a grandfather.

"Where's your father?"

Jenny looked at her husband, who had an unreadable expression on his face. He nodded. *Go ahead.*

"Dad was up when we got here." She patted my hand. "He's feeling much better this morning. He's taken the dogs for a walk around the neighborhood. We've already talked to him."

What? Jim heard the big news before I did? That'll teach me to oversleep.

Not that I was jealous, so don't get the wrong idea.

"I see the way your mind is going, Mom. And that's not what we came to talk to you about. Sorry, but there's no baby news. At least," she looked at Mark fondly, "that we know of."

My face registered my obvious disappointment, despite my attempt to control my expression.

"You really are a piece of work, you know that, Mom? Don't worry. We'll make you a grandma one of these days, right, honey?" Jenny said. "But not at this exact moment."

Mark picked up the conversation. "So, Carol, Mike texted us last night. He's worried about you and Jim. He told us to check out the Fairport Patch video. He thinks you both need some help around the house, and he feels helpless because he's so far away."

I took another healthy swig of coffee to fortify myself. So this is how old age begins. The kids begin to take over their parents' lives and start telling them what to do, instead of the other way around.

No way, José. Not yet. Maybe, not ever.

Maybe I should go back to bed.

"I'll gladly surrender my license to operate a riding mower," I said. "That was a once-in-a-lifetime moment, and I've learned my lesson. But Dad and I aren't ready for matching recliners and remote controls yet."

Well, *I* wasn't.

"What exactly are you suggesting? I hope you don't think we're incapable of living here on our own and taking care of our house. Because that's simply not true." I glared at both of them, my imagination going into overdrive, down a completely different road.

Isn't it impressive, the way I can shift gears so rapidly?

"Relax, Mom," Jenny said. "We're not suggesting anything like that. But yesterday showed that you may need some help doing a few of the chores around here. It's a big house, and the property upkeep is enormous."

She beamed at me. "So Mike, Mark, and I have decided to chip in and give you an early Christmas present. We want to hire a landscaping company to take over the exterior work. Dad was resistant at first, but we convinced him that it was a great idea. So, what do you say?"

"Dad was resistant? That's interesting."

"You know how he is," Jenny said. "He hates any idea that he hasn't thought of himself. But eventually, he comes around. Although, come to think of it, this time he agreed much quicker than I expected."

I couldn't help but grin.

"Why are you smiling like that, Mom? You look like you're hiding something. Come on, give."

"Well, *kids*," I said, with just a tiny emphasis on the last word, "the old folks are way ahead of you on this one. Phyllis and Bill Stevens sent over their landscaping man to help me yesterday. Will Finnegan. He owns Finnegan's Rakes. His trucks are all over town.

"Dad and I have already hired him to do exactly what you're suggesting. In fact," I cocked my head at the sound of a leaf blower starting up, "if you look out the window, you'll see him right now. That's why Dad agreed so quickly. I think he was having some fun with you.

"So you can text Mike and tell him he doesn't have to worry about us. The old folks have this situation under control."

I hoped I didn't sound snippy. But I also hoped I made my point crystal clear.

Mark looked embarrassed. "We didn't mean to imply that you and Jim are old, Carol," he said. "It's just that…"

"It's just that we love you," Jenny interrupted. "And we want to make life easier for you."

The words *at this late stage of life* hovered, unspoken, over my kitchen table.

I softened. They meant well. And I was betting they had absolutely no idea how their "suggestion" had sounded to me. Like Jim and I were teetering on the edge of extinction.

"Do you have time for a real breakfast?" I asked. "I have eggs in the refrigerator and I can scramble them up in a jiffy. With a little cottage cheese, Jenny, just the way you like them."

Mark's smartphone beeped, indicating an incoming text. He took a quick glance and immediately jumped up. "I have to leave. I'm needed at the station. See you tonight, Jenny." He gave his bride a chaste kiss (after all, her mother was sitting right there), waved to me, and was gone.

"I hate it when he leaves so suddenly, like he just did," Jenny said. "I worry that, every time he goes out the door, he'll be hurt. Or worse."

Her blue eyes filled with tears.

"Oh, sweetie," I said, wrapping her in a mom hug. "That never occurred to me. I guess I figured that, now that Mark's been promoted to detective, he's spending more time behind a desk than outside arresting criminals. So he's a lot safer."

Jenny wiped her eyes on a napkin. "I suppose you're right. He is a lot safer. I don't claim I'm being logical about this. Like mother, like daughter, right?"

"Smarty pants," I said with a grin. "Now, how about those eggs?"

"I'll cook them, Mom," Jenny said, "in exchange for the whole truth about your riding mower adventure. And your buddying up with Phyllis and Bill Stevens. That's certainly a surprise."

"Deal," I replied. "I love being waited on."

Jenny howled when I told her about my visit to the Stevens house. "I'm not surprised that Mrs. Stevens was so inhospitable," she said. "Mike and I always skipped that house on Halloween. She probably would have given us a lecture about tooth decay instead of giving us candy.

"Mr. Stevens seemed nice, though. He always waved when he saw us."

Jenny handed me a plate of scrambled eggs. "Eat them now, before they get cold."

"You make me laugh," I said, picking up a fork and digging in. "That's what I always said to you.

"Oh, and by the way, when I was leaving the Stevens's house yesterday, Bill walked me to the door. And you'll never guess what happened next."

Jenny gestured me to hurry up. "I have a class to teach in twenty minutes, Mom. So you better just tell me."

"He kissed me goodbye," I said, my cheeks pink at the memory.

"Where?"

"At the front door. Phyllis was already in the kitchen, and couldn't see what was going on."

Jenny waved her fork at me impatiently. "No, Mom. Where on *you* did he plant the kiss? Did he sweep you off your feet and give you a passionate one?"

"Don't be ridiculous," I said. "He gave me a peck on the cheek."

"I think that's sweet, Mom," she said. "Just imagine. Mr. Stevens could have been harboring a secret yen for you all these years, and finally had the guts to let you know about it."

"Now you're really being ridiculous," I said, as I caught a glimpse of a shirtless Will Finnegan trying to bring some order out of yesterday's chaos.

Jenny followed my look. "That's the lawn man? He's gorgeous."

"I hadn't noticed," I lied. "He's the nice man who came to my rescue yesterday. And Dad met him and decided to hire him to do our outside work.

"He does snowplowing, too," I added.

"I'll just bet he does," my daughter said with a knowing look. "Now I know why you staged the riding mower incident yesterday. You wanted an excuse to hire Will Finnegan."

"Jenny! That's not true."

"Methinks my mother doth protest too much," Jenny said. "But I won't worry about you getting into trouble so much now. Or maybe," she added with a gesture in Will's direction, "I should worry more!"

Chapter 9

It always amazes me that if I keep something in my closet for a while, it shrinks at least two sizes all by itself.

"Stand up and applaud, Mary Alice," Claire said. "Our resident celebrity is here."

"Very funny," I said, sliding into a chair at The Admiral's Table, one of Fairport's most exclusive restaurants, and grabbing a luncheon menu.

"You know I said that with love, right?" Claire asked. "After all, it's not every day that someone I went to grammar school with is featured in an Internet video."

"I've had all the teasing about that horrible riding mower video that I can tolerate," I snapped. "I thought you guys, at least, would cut me some slack."

My face flamed. "Do you know that when I stopped at the Mobil station to buy gas, the smart aleck who works there asked me if I wanted extra gas for the mower so I could chase it around the yard again today? The nerve!"

"I'm sure Claire didn't mean anything, Carol," said Mary Alice in the soothing tone I was sure she reserved for her difficult patients. And being a nurse, she's had a lot of those over the years.

"I'm sorry, Carol," Claire said. "I guess I got a little bit carried away."

"Apology accepted," I said. I'm not one to bear a grudge,

despite what some people may have told you. Most of the time, that is.

"It's my turn to pick a subject," I said. I swiveled around in my chair to take in the spectacular view of Long Island Sound.

"How did we get to have lunch at The Admiral's Table? I thought it was only open to members of the Fairport Yacht Club."

"Nancy knows somebody," Claire said.

"Doesn't she always?" I said, laughing. "That woman has more connections than AT&T."

"Where is Nancy?" Mary Alice asked. "I'd hate to have some club employee figure out we don't belong here and tell us to leave. That would be so mortifying."

"I doubt that would happen," I said. "But let's behave ourselves, just in case. No dancing on the tables, like we usually do."

Mary Alice swatted me. "You are too much."

A cloud of Chanel Number 5 announced the arrival of our hostess, otherwise known as Fairport's most successful Realtor (her words, not mine).

Nancy slid into a chair and exchanged air kisses with everyone.

"I just love this place," she said, gesturing around the beautiful restaurant as though she'd designed it herself. "What a beautiful spot. Why did it take us so long to come here? I simply cannot believe that view."

She looked at all of us for confirmation, and being the obedient Catholic school girls we are, we nodded.

"It took us so long to come here because we're not members of the Fairport Yacht Club," I pointed out. "Unless one of us has been keeping a secret all these years."

Nancy laughed. "It's not necessary to be a full member of the yacht club to use the restaurant. There's an associate membership, which is priced very reasonably. I joined last week. I'm planning on bringing potential real estate clients here, if the food is as good as I've been told it is.

"You three are my guinea pigs."

"You certainly have a way of putting things, Nancy," Claire said. "I really feel special now."

Nancy ignored her.

"Sorry if I was a little late," she said. "I was on the phone with a seller, and she was going on and on and on. Refusing to make some of the minor tweaks I'd suggested to make her house more saleable. Honestly, most people really have an inflated view of what their house is really worth. Especially in today's market."

Since Nancy had represented Jim and me in a recent real estate transaction, which hadn't come to fruition thanks to the untimely death of the buyer, I tried not to take offense at her remark.

Besides, I had another score to settle with her.

"Thanks a lot for your comment on the Fairport Patch about my driving skills," I said, glaring at her. "I was humiliated enough without you putting in your two cents' worth."

"Sweetie, you know I was only kidding," Nancy said. "I'd never do anything to hurt you."

"Yeah, right. Why am I not convinced?"

"We've all apologized, Carol. We should know by now how hypersensitive you are," Claire said.

"It's time to order our lunch," Mary Alice said. "The server has been hovering a few feet away for at least ten minutes."

"Why don't you order for us, Nancy?" I suggested with a hint of malice. "Since you're the *member* and we're merely your guinea pigs. I mean, your guests."

"Oh, all right," Nancy said. She rattled off a series of appetizers and salads to the poor server, who was having some trouble keeping up with Nancy's wide array of choices.

"Why so many?" Claire asked. "We'll never finish all this food."

"We can always have the club pack up any leftovers and take them home," Nancy said. "That way, none of us will have to cook supper tonight. And we need to sample a lot of dishes to find out which are the best ones. After all, when I bring clients here, I want to look like I know what I'm talking about."

That made sense to me. Except for the part about the leftovers, of course.

"Leftovers? You must be kidding," I said. "You know that whenever we go out to lunch, we always protest that we can *never* finish what's been served. It's just too much food. We'll have to take some home."

"But by the end of the meal, all our plates are empty," Claire added. "I'm sure it's because of our Catholic school training. Remember, all the nuns told us it was a sin to waste food."

"You go ahead and tell yourself that if it makes you feel any better, Claire," I said. "Even though they also told us it was a sin to tell a lie.

"So, what's new with everybody?" I asked, not giving my tablemates a chance to revisit my video debacle again. "Or, in my case, what's not new."

I sighed. "Jenny and Mark stopped in this morning. I was so surprised to see both of them. Usually, Jenny stops in for a quick cup of coffee and a mother/daughter chat on her way to school. I assumed they'd come together to announce that Jenny was pregnant. But I was wrong."

Best pals that they are, all my tablemates shared my disappointment. And some unasked-for advice.

Notably, "Don't push them." *As if I ever would!*

"Don't jump to conclusions." *I know, I know.*

"When it happens, it will be perfect. And well worth waiting for." *I guess.*

"So why did they stop in, Carol? Any special reason?" Claire asked.

"Trust you to get right to the point, Claire," I said with a laugh. "That's what comes from being married to a lawyer."

"So…?"

I cleared my throat. "Unfortunately, the kids saw the Fairport Patch video, too. And speaking of jumping to conclusions, they decided that Jim and I need some help around the house. Or, to be exact, *outside* the house. They want to treat us to a landscaping company as an early Christmas present."

I omitted the fact that Jim and I had hired Finnegan's Rakes ourselves yesterday after my adventure with the riding mower. Or that Will Finnegan was a hunk. No sense in confusing my friends. I had an important point to make.

"I think that's sweet," Mary Alice said.

"I do, too," Nancy chimed in.

"Ditto," said Claire. "What the heck is your problem with it, Carol? Because, from the expression on your face, you've obviously got one."

"It's just that I resent the implication that Jim and I are getting too old to take care of ourselves. Or our house. I don't know. Maybe that's not what they meant, but that's what it sounded like to me."

"Good gracious, Carol, talk about looking a gift horse in the mouth," Nancy said. "Before Jim retired, you had someone to clean your house once a week, and also someone to take care of the lawn. And after he retired, Jim decided that the household expenses needed to be trimmed. So you got rid of the house cleaner and the landscaper. And complained bitterly about it."

I couldn't deny it. Nancy was absolutely right.

"And when Jim had his heart episode a while back, you talked him into hiring someone to do some outside work," Mary Alice reminded me. "Although that didn't last very long."

"That's just it," I said. "Exactly. Jim and I made those decisions. Not our kids. Don't you understand the difference?"

I looked at my three best friends, who are exactly the same age as I am. Despite Nancy's protestations that she's really several months younger.

"We're reaching the point in our lives where our kids think they should start making decisions for us, because we're not capable of making them for ourselves any more. What's next? Taking away our car keys and hiring a chauffeur, like in that movie, *Driving Miss Daisy*?"

Nancy looked shocked. Claire looked troubled. Mary Alice looked confused.

Finally, Claire spoke up. "I never thought of us as old before. But I guess we are. At least, in the eyes of younger folks."

It'll probably come as no surprise to you that, after my tirade, none of us had an appetite for dessert. We had enough food for thought—calorie-free.

Chapter 10

Just when I was getting used to yesterday, today came along and confused the heck out of me!

For the next few days, our yard was a beehive of activity. The number of workers varied. Sometimes, it was a crew of two or three guys, raking and mulching. One day, it was a carpenter, replacing the damaged section of our picket fence with a brand new one. When the carpenter left, a painter arrived to finish the job. All the workers wore tee-shirts with the Finnegan's logo—a rake and a snow shovel in the shape of the letter X.

I wondered how many people Will Finnegan employed. I never saw the same men twice.

I tried not to feel slighted that a lot of the landscaping and repair work was being done by other people, since Phyllis Stevens had bragged that Will always did their work personally. After all, it was a busy time of year, and Finnegan's Rakes had many other clients to take care of besides us.

Some days, the boss came by and did some of the work himself. Unfortunately for me, the weather had turned cooler, so the chances of a shirtless Will sighting would have to wait until spring.

Darn it.

I was surprised that Jim, completely recovered from his cold— which, as you may recall, is what started this whole chain of events in the first place—wasn't complaining about how much this was all costing. Nor did he complain that Will never got around to giving us the written estimate we'd asked for. Instead, Jim seemed to enjoy strolling around our yard when the workers were there, schmoozing and kibitzing and probably driving them all crazy.

Well, that was way better than driving me crazy inside the house. Now that the colder weather was coming, and we would be together inside more, I might have to resort to the Honey Don't list to save my sanity.

You remember that, right? Jim and I each make a list of what habits the other person has that annoy us. Naturally, the list of my own annoying habits is much shorter than Jim's.

Anyway, we put each habit on a small piece of paper and stuff them into two jars—one marked "His" and the other "Hers." And every morning (you don't have to do it that often—it all depends on how crazy your partner is making you) we draw a paper from the other person's jar. And that person has to refrain from that habit for the entire day. One point per day for good behavior. Minus a point for bad.

At the end of the week, add up the points. Whoever has scored the highest gets to choose the reward for best behaved.

I bet I don't have to tell you what Jim chooses. So, I won't.

Sometimes, I think he rigs it so he usually wins.

Smile.

Chapter 11

My house was clean last week. Too bad you missed it.

"I don't believe it!" I said. My hands were shaking so hard I almost dropped the morning newspaper.

"Jim," I yelled in the general direction of the bedroom. "Jim! Have you seen this morning's paper? Did you read the obituary page? You won't believe who died!"

No response.

Honestly, that man wouldn't hear a herd of elephants charging through the house. But let me whisper something to one of my friends that I don't want him to know about, and he doesn't miss a single word.

"I give up," I said, and headed toward the bedroom myself, newspaper in hand.

To be fair, Jim was in the shower with the bathroom door closed. No wonder he couldn't hear me.

Not that I let that stop me. No sirree. When you've been married as long as Jim and I have, you've seen it all. If you get my drift.

So I barged right into the bathroom. I know. I know. I probably shouldn't have done that. But I was so upset that proper etiquette went right out the window.

Jim turned off the taps and stuck his wet head out of the shower. "What are you yelling for, Carol? Can't a man have a little peace and quiet in here? Is that asking too much?" He grabbed the towel

I handed him and attempted to make himself decent.

"What the hell is so important that it couldn't wait until I was through with my shower?" he demanded.

I thrust the morning paper at him. "Look at the obituary page, Jim," I said. "You simply won't believe it."

Jim wiped his hands on the towel, then began to root around the sink top for his eyeglasses.

"Oh, for heaven's sake," I said, grabbing the paper back from him. "I'll read it to you."

My eyes welled up and threatened to spill over. Then I began to read, in a shaky voice: "William Finnegan, forty-eight, of Fairport, died suddenly Tuesday night at Fairport Memorial Hospital as the result of a cardiac incident. Mr. Finnegan, the owner of Finnegan's Rakes, a local landscaping and exterior maintenance company, leaves his wife of twenty-three years, Louisa, and two children, Brian, twenty-one, and Amy, nineteen. Calling hours will be Thursday evening from seven to nine p.m. at Mallory and Mallory Funeral Home, 323 Fairport Turnpike. At the request of the family, memorial donations in Mr. Finnegan's memory may be made to the American Heart Association."

I sank down on the edge of the tub. "I simply can't believe it. Will was so young. And he looked like he was the picture of good health. How in the world could this have happened?"

"It's shocking, all right," Jim agreed, finally finding his spectacles and reaching for the paper so he could read the obituary for himself. "Poor guy. I wonder if he had any warning at all. For all we know, he had a history of cardiac problems. Or a genetic predisposition. I've heard that's pretty common."

He handed me back the newspaper, then said, "And now, I'd like to get dressed. In private."

I blinked. "That's it? That's all you have to say about this, Jim?"

"Well, what do you want me to say? We hardly knew the guy. Yes, he did some lawn work for us. And helped us out of a jam after the riding mower debacle. But it's not like he was a personal friend or a member of the family. He worked for us, for crying out loud. And only for a short time, at that."

I glared at him. "I can't believe you're reacting this way. Will Finnegan was a good man who died much too young. You sound like he was someone you met once on a train ride into New York, had a brief chat with about absolutely nothing important, and that was it."

Jim sighed. "All right, Carol. You win. We'll make a donation to the American Heart Association in his name. Will that make you feel better and get me off the hook?"

"That's a little better," I said. "But I think we should go to the wake, too, and express our condolences to the family."

"Are you nuts, Carol? There is no way I'm going to do that. It's completely unnecessary."

I stuck to my guns. "I disagree. I think we should go out of respect."

"Respect for who?" Jim exploded. "The family won't know who the hell we are."

"Whom," I corrected automatically. "Respect for *whom*, not for who."

"Oh, for crying out loud," Jim said. "I think you want to go to the wake just because you're nosy. You want to see what his wife looks like. And his kids, too."

Well! I wasn't going to take that from Jim, even if a tiny part of it was true. I admit it, I am nosy. But I really did feel we should pay our respects. Writing a donation check was a real cop-out.

My mother had always impressed on me that attending wakes and memorial services brought comfort to the living. It was the right thing to do.

I stormed out of the bathroom and slammed the door. Real mature of me, right?

I sat down at the kitchen table and looked out at my now beautiful yard. The yard that Will Finnegan had saved. No, not just saved. Improved. Made better than it ever was.

In fact, Will had made my yard so gorgeous that, if the producers of HGTV's *Curb Appeal* saw it, they'd be hammering on my front door right now, begging me to let them film a segment here.

"Maybe Jim can satisfy his conscience by making a donation in Will's memory," I muttered. "But I can't. I'm going to the wake and pay our respects to his family. No matter what Jim says."

And I knew who'd go with me.

Phyllis and Bill Stevens.

Chapter 12

I decided to do nothing today. So far, I'm right on schedule.

This time, I didn't bother to make myself presentable. Either Phyllis and Bill took me in my natural state, sans makeup, or not.

For those of you who know me well, I'm sure this comes as a surprise. It seems that, the older I get, the vainer I get. Or maybe, as I age, more veins show on my body. My legs, hands, wherever.

You get the idea.

At least I'd brushed my teeth.

Then, I caught a glimpse of myself in the front hallway mirror. Yuck. I grabbed a baseball cap from the hall closet and smooshed it over my hair to hide my bedhead.

Note to self: make appointment with my super hairstylist, Deanna, asap.

I scurried across Old Fairport Turnpike, once again checking carefully for oncoming traffic. It would never do for me to be hit by a car when I wasn't looking my best. I do have a reputation in this town for always being well groomed.

When I arrived at the Phyllis and Bill's front stoop, it dawned on me that this visit was a very bad idea. After all, what was I going to say? I'm sorry for your loss? I'm sorry for our loss? Any suggestions for another landscaping company?

Nah, definitely scratch the last one.

I needn't have worried about how to begin the conversation.

Phyllis must have seen me crossing the street. She flung the front door open and threw her arms around my neck.

"Oh, Carol," she sobbed. "This is so awful. I can't believe Will is dead."

Gently, I extricated myself from Phyllis's embrace. And took a really close look at her.

I thought I looked bad. Truth to tell, Phyllis looked even worse. Her eyes were red-rimmed, evidence that she'd been crying for a long time. Her clothes were wrinkled, and her white hair, always tight against her scalp with the assistance of gobs of hair spray, rose around her head in peaks.

It reminded me of the meringue on top of a lemon pie.

"Who is it, Phyllis?" Bill asked from the direction of the kitchen. "Whoever it is, send them away. I don't want to see anyone."

"It's Carol Andrews," I called out. "I just read about Will Finnegan's death in this morning's paper." My voice cracked when I said the word *death*.

A slightly calmer Phyllis led me down the hallway toward the family room. I couldn't help but notice the hallway was littered with suitcases.

Phyllis gestured me to take a seat.

Now, under normal circumstances—which I hope will occur in my life one of these days—I would have asked, "What's up with the suitcases, Phyllis? Are you and Bill going on a trip?"

Definitely not appropriate right now.

So, instead I said, "I wanted to see how you and Bill are doing. I know how close you and Will were."

Big mistake. This produced a fresh round of tears from Phyllis. I felt terrible. Just when the poor woman had herself until control, I had to set her off again.

Bill appeared in the doorway with three coffee cups arranged neatly on a tray, along with some muffins. He had an apron tied around his middle.

He placed the tray on the table in front of me and sat down beside his now sniffling wife. "There, there, Phyllis," Bill said, patting her shoulder awkwardly. "It'll be all right. Will's at peace."

"How do you know he's at peace?" Phyllis demanded. "You must have some inside information that Carol and I don't. And it's the absolute worst time for this to happen."

It certainly was for Will. I didn't really say that, of course.

Bill nudged the plate of muffins in my direction. "Help yourself, Carol. I apologize if they're not the freshest you've ever had. We're cleaning out the pantry and the refrigerator today."

"I was planning on letting you know later this morning," Phyllis explained. "But when I saw the obituary page…." Her voice trailed off.

Bill took up where Phyllis left off. And it was testament to how upset Phyllis was that she let him.

"We're taking a cruise to celebrate our fiftieth wedding anniversary," he said. "We leave tomorrow morning from New York. But we're going into the city this afternoon and staying overnight at a hotel, so we won't have to rush in the morning. It's a trip we've been planning for a long time."

"And Will was going to take care of our house while we were gone," Phyllis said. "He was supposed to come over this morning to pick up the key. And now, well, I don't know how we can even go. Or if we should."

"Now, Phyllis," Bill said again. "Of course we're going. Will would want that."

His eyes misted up. "I'm really going to miss that boy."

Sometimes my mouth has a life of its own. And this was one of them.

I heard myself saying, "Jim and I would be glad to take care of the house while you're away. You shouldn't miss this trip. It sounds like the vacation of a lifetime. And celebrating fifty years of marriage is a wonderful thing."

"We couldn't ask you to do that," Bill protested. "It's too much."

"Nonsense," I said. "That's what neighbors do. Help each other out."

"If we leave on our cruise, we won't be able to attend Will's service," Phyllis said. "I'd never forgive myself if we weren't there."

"I had already planned to go," I said. "I'll be glad to pay respects on your behalf, too. In fact, if you'd like to write a sympathy note and drop it off at our house before you leave, I'll be sure that the Finnegan family gets it."

"That's a perfect solution," Bill said. "We'll write the sympathy note right now and give it to you, if you don't mind staying a few more minutes."

I nodded. "I'll be glad to wait, Bill. Take your time."

Phyllis brightened up for the first time. "Oh, Carol, would you really take care of our house? You're sure Jim won't mind?"

"Of course Jim won't mind," I said.

He may divorce me, but he certainly won't mind.

I didn't really say that last part. Of course.

Chapter 13

The secret to a long marriage is knowing when to keep your mouth shut.

"Thanks for coming with me tonight, honey," I said to Jenny. "I can always count on you."

My stubborn husband had flatly refused to attend Will Finnegan's wake at Mallory and Mallory Funeral Home, even though I insisted that we would also be representing the absent Phyllis and Bill Stevens.

"No way, Carol," Jim had said at the end of our umpteenth "discussion." His voice was getting dangerously high, a sure sign that he was upset. He dangled the key to the Stevens house in front of me. "While you're paying your respects to the deceased, I'll do a good deed for the living. Which was all your idea, in case you've forgotten."

I sighed at the memory. I really do hate arguing with my husband. Especially if a small part of me thought he could be right.

But I can be stubborn, too. And, besides, I'd promised Phyllis and Bill.

I sighed. "I hate wakes. And I especially hate wakes for someone who died so young."

"You just missed a parking spot, Mom," Jenny said. We were cruising around the funeral home parking lot, looking for a place to park my car where I could drive straight out, and not have to back up. Or, worse, parallel park.

I drove around the lot one more time, then eased my way into a parking spot near the exit. Perfect position for a quick get-away.

"Nobody likes wakes, Mom," my daughter pointed out. "It's more for the living than for the deceased, anyway.

"And you're welcome for my coming with you. Mark is working again tonight, so I would've been alone, anyway. Although that's probably preferable to being here.

"And, by the way," she said, her blue eyes (so like mine!) locked on me, "I think Dad is absolutely right. You didn't have to attend this. You won't know anyone."

"Well, we're here now," I said, not wanting to argue with Jenny, too. I checked my watch. "It's a few minutes after seven o'clock. Let's go inside, pay our respects, and skedaddle out to get a quick dinner."

I grabbed Jenny's hand and propelled her toward the funeral parlor's main entrance.

The sign inside the front door announced that the Will Finnegan wake was in Slumber Room A.

I headed in the direction of the guest book, resting on a pedestal near the slumber room entrance. "No one's signed the guest book yet," I said as I picked up the pen and wrote "Mrs. James Andrews" in my best Catholic school cursive. "And there's no place to leave sympathy cards and notes." I fingered the note Phyllis had instructed me to give to the family. "I was hoping to just drop this off, and not get into a big conversation."

Truth to tell, I was getting more and more uncomfortable. Why did I feel compelled to come, anyway? I could have just looked up the Finnegan family's home address and sent a note. Or, even better, signed the funeral home's online guest book. Assuming that there was one.

In the background, I could hear organ music playing. It creeped me out.

I snuck a quick peek inside Slumber Room A. Yup, the guest of honor was in the prime spot, resting in an open casket.

But there was nobody else in the room. No grieving family. Nobody at all.

"Are you sure you have the time right?" Jenny whispered in my ear.

"Of course I'm sure," I whispered back. "The obituary said seven o'clock. But I certainly didn't expect we'd be the first ones here.

Where's the family?"

The sounds of the organ grew fainter, and I heard low voices coming from the next room.

"They must be in there," I said to Jenny. "Composing themselves. I'm sure this will be a real ordeal for them."

The organ music started up again. Louder.

"I'm going up to the casket now and say a little prayer for Will," I said. "We'll wait for a few minutes and see if anyone else comes in. If not, we can give the sympathy note from Phyllis and Bill to someone in the funeral home office and get the heck out of here."

Jenny nodded. "Good plan."

I forced myself toward the casket, knelt down, and closed my eyes.

"Good bye, Will," I said. "Jim and I will miss you. God bless."

I opened my eyes and looked at Will's handsome face, now waxy in death, despite the best efforts of the mortician.

As I started to get up, I caught the glint of something shiny on Will's chest. At first, I thought it was a strange-shaped medallion. I wasn't wearing my bifocals, so I had to squint to get a better look.

And I immediately wished I hadn't. It wasn't a medallion. There was a scissors in Will's chest.

I fought back the scream that was bubbling up in my throat.

No way. I had to be mistaken.

I looked again. I wasn't.

A hundred thoughts jumbled through my brain:

Maybe it's some sort of obscure burial ritual that you don't know about.

Maybe it's a joke. Yes, that could be it. Somebody's idea of a sick joke.

Maybe somebody wanted to be sure Will was really dead. Can a man be murdered after he's already dead?

Oh, God, Carol, you are really losing it now!

No matter what, I didn't want to be around when the family discovered the scissors. Jenny and I had to get out of here. Right now.

Chapter 14

I'm retired. I was tired yesterday, and I'm even more tired today.

I scrambled back to my chair and grabbed my daughter's hand. "Come on. We're leaving."

"What? I thought we were going to wait for the family."

"Change of plan," I said. "Grab your purse and let's get out of here. I'll explain when we get outside."

As we turned to make our escape from Slumber Room A, I saw a handful of people heading out the door of the funeral home. I shrank back. No way did I want to get into any conversation with anyone.

Especially since one of them could have left the shiny souvenir in Will's chest.

There was a crying woman, dressed in black, in the middle of the group. She seemed to have trouble walking, and two young men were helping her.

Please, God, don't let it be the widow.

I blinked, then looked again. I knew that woman. I recognized her immediately. Only one woman had spiky hair like that.

It was my hairstylist, Deanna.

I flattened myself against the wall, pulling Jenny with me. "We can't leave now," I hissed.

"What? Mom, you're not making any sense."

"You're going to have to trust me," I said. "We have to find some place quiet for a few minutes. I have to think."

Up the hallway on the right blinked the most welcome sign I'd ever seen. *Restrooms.*

Believe me, I never needed a restroom more than I did at that exact moment. And like most women of a certain age, I need restrooms frequently.

"Come on. I need to use the women's room."

"Oh," Jenny said, following my lead. "Well, why didn't you just say that instead of being so mysterious. Honestly, Mom. You are the limit."

Fortunately, the women's room at Mallory and Mallory could accommodate more than one patron at a time. And there was even a loveseat and wingchair in a separate lounge area. A box of tissues was discreetly placed on a nearby lamp table.

I scanned the lounge to be sure we were alone. Then, all the emotion I'd been holding in for the last several minutes rose to the surface, and I began to cry.

Jenny, of course, completely misinterpreted the reason for my unexpected outburst.

"Mom, I'm so sorry you're this upset. I didn't realize you felt so close to Will Finnegan."

"No, Jenny, that's not why I'm crying." In a few short sentences, I filled her in on what I'd seen in Will's casket, ending with, "and that's why I wanted to get out of here. I don't know if it's a crime, but I didn't want us to be involved. And then, just as we were leaving, I saw my hairstylist, Deanna, right ahead us in that group of people. I didn't want her to see me. I can't explain it, but I instinctively ducked her."

Jenny reacted as the wife of a Fairport detective, and whipped out her smartphone to call the police.

"No, Jenny. Don't do that. Not yet, anyway," I said, grabbing her hand.

"But, Mom, this has to be reported."

"You're right, Jenny. But I'm tired of being linked with every suspicious death in Fairport. Let someone from the funeral home call the authorities. Or a family member. Anybody but us."

The next thing we heard was a piercing scream. Followed by running feet outside the women's room door.

"Now what, Mom?" Jenny asked. "We should have left when we had the chance. You could have explained everything to me in the car."

"There's no reason why we can't just walk out the door," I said. "Nobody knows who we are. Or that we've already been inside Slumber Room A."

"You must be delusional, Mom," Jenny said. "There's no way we can just melt away unseen."

I could have been angry at Jenny's choice of words. Delusional, me? Hopeful, yes, But not delusional.

Until I opened the door of the women's room. And came face to face with my least favorite Fairport police detective, Paul Wheeler. His usual partner, my daughter's husband and my favorite son-in-law, Mark Anderson, wasn't with him.

"You again!" Paul snarled at me. "Why am I not surprised to see you here? Every time a dead body shows up in town these days, you always seem to be there, too."

He looked behind me at my daughter and his voice softened. "Hello, Jenny."

"Well, Paul," I countered in the most reasonable tone I could muster up on such short notice, "we are in a funeral home, after all. It's the logical place to find a dead body."

Jenny leapt into the conversation before my mouth got me into more trouble. "Will Finnegan did landscaping work for Mom and Dad, Paul. So when we found out that he had passed away, naturally we came to pay our respects."

"Naturally," Paul said with a hint of sarcasm.

"Did you know Will, too, Paul?" I asked. "Or is something wrong?"

"That's what I'm here to find out," Paul said. "We got a call from one of the funeral home staff about some weird irregularity at the Finnegan viewing. The person who called wasn't making any sense. I was doing a ride-along in the neighborhood with one of the students from our Community Police Academy, so I got the assignment."

I realized it was a lucky break that Paul was here instead of Mark. I was used to handling hostility—Paul's immediate reaction whenever he saw me. And he wasn't the brightest bulb in the chandelier, that was for sure.

I tucked "Community Police Academy" into the front file folder of my brain, to be referred to if necessary. If Paul was asking me questions I didn't want to answer, maybe I could divert him.

But Mark knew me far too well. I didn't need my son-in-law peppering me with questions. And I wasn't sure how Jenny would react if she was also on the receiving end of a police interrogation. Especially from her own husband.

Things like that can really put a strain on a marriage. Or so I've been told.

Of course, Jenny hadn't actually seen the scissors. But I had.

Careful, Carol. Don't reveal too much information. You know how Paul loves to make you squirm every chance he gets. And if he finds out you've already visited Slumber Room A, who knows what conclusions he'll jump to?

Our conversation was mercifully cut short by the arrival of a dignified man whom I figured must be the mortician-in-chief, followed close on his heels by a young woman who looked so much like him that she had to be related.

"Are you from the police?" the man asked Paul. "I'm Richard Mallory, the funeral home director, and this is my daughter, Melinda. She's the one who called you. Nothing like this has ever happened in all my years as a mortician."

Mallory turned to his daughter and said, "Go back to the family living room and try to keep everyone calm."

"I don't know how you expect me to do that," Melinda said, looking as frazzled as she must have felt. "The widow has already seen her husband and is freaking out."

Her father frowned. "You'll think of something. Just go," Mallory said through tight lips. "Now."

Then to Paul, Jenny, and me, Mallory said, "There's an irregularity with the client in Slumber Room A. Follow me, please."

OMG, he thinks Jenny and I are with the police, too.

Under other circumstances, I would have been thrilled to be mistaken for a member of Fairport's finest, to say nothing about sitting in on an official questioning that didn't have me on the hot seat. But since I was the first person to view what Mallory referred to as an "irregularity," I certainly didn't want to let that fact slip out by mistake.

Just in case I was accused of causing said "irregularity."

Paul pointed his thumb at Jenny and me and said, "They're not part of the Fairport police force."

I, of course, immediately had to jump in and explain why we were at the wake in the first place.

"My husband and I were customers of Mr. Finnegan's

landscaping company," I said. "My daughter and I," gesturing to Jenny, "came to pay our respects to the family. We're not involved in any way with whatever the 'irregularity' might be. In fact, we hardly knew the man."

I was babbling, but I didn't care.

I grabbed Jenny by the arm. "So I guess we can leave now. We already signed the guest book. Come on, sweetie. Let's go."

"Stay here," Paul ordered. "Until I find out what this is all about, nobody's going anywhere."

Rats.

Chapter 15

I don't lie. I speak creatively.

"You got home much later than I expected last night, Carol," Jim said as I poured out a bowl of granola, topped with some fresh blueberries and skim milk (yuck!), and set it down in front of him.

We're trying to eat healthier these days. And for someone whose breakfast of choice is high fat and high calorie content, like me, it's torture. But I try hard not to complain. After all, when a person reaches a certain age, and a heart attack or stroke may be in the not-too-distant future, well…you get the idea.

I considered my possible responses as I prepared my own breakfast— fresh fruit and yogurt, topped with granola. I knew I'd be starving in about an hour, but I could always have an apple. Or an apple muffin.

"Jenny and I were delayed," I said, choosing my words with extra care.

Oh, what the heck. Jim was going to find out about the Finnegan wake one way or the other. He might as well hear my version of events first.

"Did you two have a girls' night out after the wake?" Jim asked. "If you went out to dinner, I hope it was our treat."

"We never met the Finnegan family," I said. "In hindsight, I wish we hadn't gone at all. You were right, Jim. I should have stayed home and we could have sent a donation to the American Heart Association in Will's memory."

"Give me a minute or two to commit this to memory," Jim said.

"I'm not sure I heard you correctly. After all these years, you're finally admitting that I was right about something?"

Normally, I would have had a snappy comeback to my husband's teasing. But this morning, I wasn't up to it. I pushed my breakfast bowl away, my appetite suddenly gone as I remembered poor Will.

"Something unexpected happened before the wake actually began," I said. "Jenny and I were the first ones to sign the guest book, and we waited a while, but no one else came. So we went to the women's room. While we were in there, we heard a scream. And the next thing we knew, that odious Paul Wheeler from the Fairport police came and shut the wake down."

"What? You're not making any sense, Carol. Why would the police shut down a wake?"

I took a fortifying sip of coffee and prayed my stomach would accept it without complaint. And then I told him about the scissors in Will's chest. Of course, I left out the fact that I had seen the scissors myself. No sense in confusing the guy.

And I hadn't shared that information with Paul Wheeler, either.

In my defense, lest you think that I deliberately misled the police, I took a hint from all those Perry Mason television shows. Perry always told his clients not to offer any extraneous facts. Just answer the questions.

So that's why I didn't tell Paul about seeing Deanna, either. Because, well, maybe I was mistaken, and it was just someone who looked like her.

"That's why the wake was shut down," I said. "Until the police can figure out if a crime was committed, there won't be any wake. Or funeral."

Jim sighed. "And you, of course, are right in the middle of this thing. Once again."

He waggled his finger at me. "I know you, Carol. I bet you want to nose around and find out who did this to poor Will. Don't you dare try to 'help' the police this time, Carol. Promise me."

Jim had asked one of the questions that had been rolling around in my brain since last night. Who'd done this? And, even more intriguing, why?

Honestly, I had no intention of, as my husband so quaintly put it, "nosing around." But it wasn't a bad idea. I did, after all, know more of the key players than the police.

So I changed tactics and went on the offensive.

"That was uncalled for," I snapped back. "It's not my fault if I just happened to be at the wrong place at the wrong time. How was I supposed to know that something like this would happen?"

"That may be true," Jim said. "But I bet you're the only one who secretly harbors a yen to be an undercover detective. So, I repeat, stay out of it."

"Of course I will, Jim," I said. I hoped he didn't notice that my fingers were crossed underneath my napkin.

Chapter 16

I never nag. I offer helpful suggestions.
Repeatedly.

What I'm going to tell you next is guaranteed to surprise you. Heck, it even surprised me.

After my initial childish fit of pique, I thought long and hard about what Jim had said. Not the "Don't get involved" part, which made my hackles rise every time I thought of it. The part about my secretly harboring a yen to become an undercover detective.

Because I really didn't have a secret longing to become a detective. At least, not consciously.

But SJR (Since Jim's Retirement), bad things just seemed to happen which involved me, whether I liked it or not. To friends of mine. And immediate family members, in case my dear husband forgot that particular incident. And I'm a very helpful person. A fixer. I want to make everybody happy. Peace on earth and everything right with the world and all that stuff.

I'm also a very curious person. Some may call me nosy, but I'm sure they're just jealous because I have the nerve to ask the questions they'd love to, but never would.

I'm also an excellent judge of character (most of the time), and people talk to me. In fact, sometimes complete strangers tell me things about their personal life that I'd rather not know.

And when I really thought about this "incident," I realized that I didn't know Will Finnegan well at all. He'd done some work for

Jim and me, but we weren't exactly close buddies.

Yes, what happened at his wake was horrible. But just because I happened to be there did not mean I had to figure out who did the deed.

Especially because, if I did decide to nose around, I might find out some nasty things about a very important person in my life, Deanna. I had already worked very hard to convince myself that the person I saw leaving Will's wake was a Deanna lookalike, not Deanna herself.

My rational side (the one I never listen to) told me that was impossible. Nobody else in Fairport looked like her. So I turned that side of my mind completely off. Click.

And I succeeded, too. For about an hour.

I needed a distraction, and for me, retail therapy often does the trick. Just getting out in a crowd of people, overhearing some incredibly intimate conversations from other shoppers shared via cell phone, and spending a little money, is a guaranteed pick-me-up. It doesn't even matter what I'm shopping for—clothing, something for the house, dog food, people food.

Yes, that was it. Food shopping. Because when I'd checked the larder earlier today, the pickings were pretty slim. In fact, I hadn't done much of anything in the domesticity department since Jim's battle with the sniffles.

I took a quick shower, then it was time for me to make a grocery list. I found myself humming as I wrote: "Eggs, milk, whole wheat bread."

I realized I was humming a song from *South Pacific*, the beloved musical by Rodgers and Hammerstein, and one of my all-time favorite shows.

I added shampoo to the shopping list. And then it hit me.

My sneaky subconscious was playing games with me. I was humming "I'm Gonna Wash That Man Right Out Of My Hair." Which, of course, brought me right back to the Deanna dilemma.

What if it turned out that she was really at the funeral home? On the face of it, that wasn't so problematic. After all, I didn't know who Deanna's friends were. In fact, I didn't know much about her personal life at all. When I'm at the hair salon, I'm the one who shares all my secrets, and Deanna responds when she feels it's necessary.

Maybe she knew the Finnegan family. Maybe Will's widow was

another client of hers. Or—and this was really a stretch—maybe Will Finnegan was. I've read online (so you know it must be true) that more and more men these days are turning their backs on traditional barbershops and frequenting hair salons, instead. The male ego—especially when it comes to looking younger—can be just as fragile as the female's.

Not that I know this from personal experience, understand. My own dear husband's hairline receded so quickly, so early in our marriage, that I can't remember when he ever had lush locks.

My mind was racing now with even more questions. Questions I didn't dare ask. Like, if Deanna did know Will or the Finnegan family, why did she leave the funeral home before the official wake began? And who was that group of people leaving with her?

Was she making a hasty exit before any of the family arrived and saw her?

It wasn't up to me to point a finger at her. *J'accuse!*

But I couldn't deny that the instrument which had inexplicably found its way into Will's chest was a scissors. An integral part of every hairstylist's tool kit.

I hadn't talked to Jenny since I dropped her off at home after the wake. I value her opinion—she takes after the level-headed side of the family. I wondered what her take on last night's disaster was.

Only one way to find out. I knew that, if she was already in class, my call would roll over into her voice mail and she'd call me back when she could.

I had my hand on the telephone, prepared to punch in her cell number, when I realized this could be a very bad idea. Jenny was married to a police detective, after all. And I didn't want to know if they'd had a conversation about Finnegan's wake. Because if they had, I was sure that Jenny would have told Mark that I had seen the scissors myself. In fact, except for the person who put them there, I had seen the scissors before anyone else.

And Mark-the-detective would want to know why I hadn't told Paul Wheeler that.

Rats. I could be in trouble already and not even know it. Perry Mason may have given me bad advice if I were accused of deliberately hiding evidence from the police. And he wouldn't be around to take my case, either, since his television show had been cancelled a long time ago.

AARGH. I was driving myself crazy. Not much of a stretch.

The house was very quiet, and I suddenly realized that, except for Lucy and Ethel, I was all alone. Where the heck was Jim?

Don't get me wrong. Under normal circumstances, I'm thrilled to have some alone time. SJR, even though we have a large house, Jim and I often seem to be in the exact same space—usually the kitchen—reaching for the exact same thing at the exact same time.

I folded the shopping list and jammed it into my purse. It was time to get out of here.

I scribbled a note for Jim and propped it up against the microwave, where I was sure he'd see it. Because, even though he could disappear without a word to me, he had a fit when he didn't know where I was. Especially around mealtime.

Gone food shopping. Yes, I have coupons with me.

Jim never minds supporting the local economy as long as he thinks I'm being thrifty.

"You behave yourselves while I'm out," I warned Lucy and Ethel. "No jumping on the bed to take a snooze. I can always tell when you've been there. You rearrange the pillows."

I made sure there was fresh water in their bowls, grabbed my car keys and headed out the door.

Where I came face-to-face with Will Finnegan.

Chapter 17

We got married for better or for worse. He couldn't do any better, and I couldn't do any worse.

I screamed loud enough to be heard in Canada.

Well, can you blame me? I'd just seen the guy at Mallory and Mallory Funeral Home the night before, and he was not looking his best.

And now the ghost of Will was standing here, wearing a grey sweatshirt and jeans, looking as healthy and handsome as he always did.

In my very own driveway. In broad daylight.

I do believe in reincarnation, but I never realized it could happen so fast.

The man and I took a step back from each other. He seemed just as startled as I was, although, to his credit, he didn't scream. But he didn't speak, either. He just stood there, looking at me.

"Will? Is that you?" I squeaked. "But, you're dead."

At least, you sure looked that way last night.

The man offered me his hand and I shrank back. No way did I want to touch an apparition.

"I'm so sorry I frightened you, ma'am," he said. "I should have knocked on the side door first, to tell you I was here."

What? Do ghosts knock first? I mean, I'd heard of things that go bump in the night, but not during the day.

"I'm not handling myself very well," he said. "I'm not Will Finnegan. I'm his younger brother, Jack."

The man offered me his hand again. "You can shake my hand, and you'll know I'm real."

I flushed with embarrassment. How stupid could I be?

Please, don't answer that. It was a rhetorical question.

"That's not necessary," I said. "I can tell you're a live person. But you look so much like Will. You gave me a real fright!"

"I'm sorry, ma'am," Jack repeated. "Will and I do look enough alike to pass as twins." His face saddened. "I mean, we *did* look enough alike. We were only ten months apart. Our parents called us Vatican twins. Do you know what I mean?"

I nodded. I didn't have sixteen years of Catholic school education for nothing!

"Sometimes, we even fooled our teachers. At least, we did when we were little kids. That came in very handy sometimes." Jack smiled at the memory.

I took a closer look at Jack and realized that, while the resemblance to his deceased brother was striking, there were subtle differences. While Will had the lean torso of a man who regularly worked outdoors, Jack was fleshier. Paunchier around the middle. Not that he was fat, mind you. Just, softer. And while Will's eyes were a dark brown, Jack's eyes were more hazel.

I realized suddenly how rude I was being. And that I hadn't introduced myself, either.

"It's my turn to apologize to you," I said. "I'm Carol Andrews. Your brother's company does landscaping work for us."

A sudden, selfish thought struck me. "Will the company still be in business?" I asked. "I mean, now that…." My voice trailed off.

Sheesh, Carol. That's the least of Jack's problems. He doesn't care about doing your lawn, for heaven's sake.

I recovered my wits enough to say, "I'm so sorry for your loss. My daughter and I came to the wake last night to express our condolences to the family, but we never got the chance."

"Yes, that sure was something," Jack said. "Somebody wanted to make extra sure that Will wouldn't be coming back."

Like the cherry on top of a hot fudge sundae.

I didn't really say that, of course. Give me some credit.

"How is the rest of the family holding up?" I asked. "His widow must be devastated. I know I would be, knowing someone hated my husband that much. And it must have been horrible for you, too. Seeing your brother…'interfered with' like that."

Yes, I was being nosy. But the opportunity was too tempting for me to pass out.

"I didn't actually see Will," Jack said. "By the time I got to the funeral home, the police were already there and had shut the wake down. Louisa is hanging tough. But she's very anxious to get this whole ordeal over with. We all are."

Which told me absolutely nothing.

"But since we don't know how long the police will take with their investigation, the wake and funeral are both on hold." Jack's face mirrored the frustration he was feeling.

"This morning, I realized I had to find something to keep myself busy. The uncertainty and the waiting were driving me crazy. I decided to go to Will's office. I figured I could find something to do there.

"It was closed, of course, but I was able to find a key. The week's work schedule was posted, and I saw your address. I thought working outside would keep me focused on something besides Will's death. And help me lose a little of the extra pounds I've managed to attract over the years." He patted his belly for emphasis.

I could definitely identify with that.

"And here I am," Jack finished. "But I should have knocked on your door first and introduced myself."

"None of us are thinking straight this morning," I said. "I'm very glad you came to finish the yard work," I said. "Jim will be, too. Jim's my husband," I clarified.

"Well, I should let you get back to work now. I'm sure you'll be needed back at the house before too long to help with the arrangements. Whatever they may turn out to be. And just be with the rest of the family. I know how important it is for family to be together during traumatic events."

I put out my hand and he shook it. "It's nice to meet you, Jack. Although I'm very sorry about the circumstances."

Then I had a sudden thought. "Is there anything at all you need? Food, for instance? I'm sure that the last thing your sister-in-law needs is to worry about feeding people. I'd be glad to put a casserole together and drop it off later today."

Not that I was trying to intrude on the family at such a traumatic time. No way. I was just being polite. Neighborly. Sympathetic. Kind and caring. The way I was raised.

Jack looked unsure of how to respond.

"I would love a home-cooked casserole," he said. "But I don't know how Louisa would react, receiving food from a complete stranger. As you can imagine, she doesn't trust too many people right now, after what happened to Will at the funeral home."

It was hard for me to ignore the implication that I could be the person responsible for the delay in Will's funeral proceedings.

So I didn't.

Instead, I drew myself up to my full height—five feet three and three quarters, in case you were wondering—and gave Jack one of my famous withering looks. The kind I frequently use on Jim these days when he's acting up.

"For your information, Jack," I said, measuring out each word deliberately and clearly, so there was no possibility of him misunderstanding me, "my son-in-law, Mark Anderson, is a detective on the Fairport Police force. It was his partner, Paul Wheeler, who was the responding officer last night at your brother's wake. In fact, I've personally been very helpful to the Fairport police during some of their investigations. They often turn to me for help with particularly difficult cases. My husband and I have been upstanding citizens of Fairport for over thirty years.

"Your brother came to my rescue when I was in trouble. I feel terrible that he's dead, and will miss him. I made the offer to deliver food because I am a good person and I wanted to help. And that's all. To suggest that I had any other reason for volunteering to prepare a meal for your family is downright insulting."

I was breathing heavily now, and I was sure my face was beet red. But I was livid. And for once I didn't care how terrible I looked.

Which ought to show you how upset I was.

Jack moved a step back from me and held up his hands. "Whoa, Mrs. Andrews. Hold on. I didn't mean to provoke you. And I certainly didn't mean to imply that you had anything to do with the funny business about Will. I was just trying to explain that Louisa's a little suspicious right now. I'm sure you can understand why."

He waited for me to answer him. But I just stood there and didn't say a word. I was waiting to see what else Jack had to say.

Finally, I couldn't stand the silence any longer. No big surprise there. And I had gotten a little carried away.

Particularly with that bit I threw into the conversation about my association with the Fairport police. Mark would ream me out if he knew I'd said that, even though I was the grandmother of his future children.

"We're certainly getting off on the wrong foot," I said. "First I scream at you because I think you're a dead man come back to life, and now I scream at you because you imply that I'm not to be trusted."

Jack was obviously embarrassed. I figured he didn't have a lot of experience dealing with hysterical women.

Jim could give him some suggestions after all these years of living with me. In fact, he could probably teach a course about it at the local community adult school. I bet the class would be packed.

"How about this?" I said. "I'll pick up a tray of wrap sandwiches at Fancy Francie's Market and deliver them to the house. Everyone in town loves Francie's sandwiches. You go back to the house and let Louisa know that I'll be coming, so she won't be surprised."

Or suspicious that the sandwiches could be poisoned.

I didn't really say that last part, of course.

"If she doesn't want to see me, that's fine. But I'll feel better, knowing that I've helped out."

"You know," Jack responded, "that's a great idea. And I'm betting Louisa will want to talk to you, too."

Huh? I tried not to look surprised.

"Because of your close association with the Fairport police," Jack continued, looking at me like I was dense, "you can find out who added the scissors to Will at the wake last night."

Chapter 18

My mouth and my brain are never on speaking terms.

Fancy Francie's has been a fixture in our town since the mid-1960s. The market has gone through a series of owners since then, but the store name remains the same. Despite the siren call of upscale food emporiums like The Particular Palate (nicknamed by some wise acres as The Peculiar Palate, since some of its over-the-top specialties are better suited to a sophisticated New York City gourmet), or big box stores like Shopper's Paradise, Francie's has retained a loyal customer base for eons.

One of the charms of the store is that it offers free delivery within the town limits. Needless to say, Jim loves that.

About five years ago, a new owner, Helen Konisburg, took over the store, and that's when things really started to cook. Literally.

Helen came from a big city background, and because Fairport is a commuter community to the Big Apple—that would be New York City, for the benefit of you out-of-towners—she realized right away that a catering service would provide an added bonus to the bottom line. I'm talking about basic comfort foods, like meatloaf, macaroni and cheese, pot roast, and southern fried chicken. The kind of things Mom used to make. And Helen also added a hot and cold salad bar.

Francie's always had a deli department, of course. But Helen expanded that, too. She added a wide variety of sandwiches named after celebrities. So it was possible to have lunch or dinner with Robert Redford one day, and Brad Pitt the next. The place was wildly popular and lived up to its slogan, "The Freshest Food in Fairport."

Don't tell anyone I admitted this, but I have Francie's on speed dial. And I always order more than we'll eat in one meal, so I can freeze the leftovers.

Jim hasn't caught on yet about how much I use Francie's. In fact, he's complimented me much more frequently on my cooking than he used to, and I try not to take offense.

The market also started a frequent buyers club, with discounts. Of course, I was one of the first customers to sign up. I'm such a regular customer there that I asked Helen for a reserved parking space in front of the market. So far, that hasn't happened, but I remain hopeful.

I was confident that Helen had come through for me again and prepared a tray of wrap sandwiches for me to deliver to the Finnegan family on very short notice. Especially since she was used to my last-minute food crises, which happen more frequently than I care to admit.

Even to you.

Timing is everything. And today, my timing was off. I usually don't venture onto Fairport Turnpike, the main commercial artery in town, until late in the afternoon. From noon to two o'clock, the center is jammed with workers on their lunch hour, trying to grab some food or do a quick errand before heading back to the office. Forget about going to the bank or the post office then. Unless you have an extra hour or two to wait in line.

And from two-thirty till about four o'clock, it's dominated by school children of all ages, crowding the sidewalks, darting across the street on skateboards or on foot, never looking where they're going or at any possible obstacles that could be in their path.

But I was in a hurry to make my sandwich delivery to the Finnegan home, so I broke my own rule and ventured to Fancy Francie's at a little after one o'clock.

Big mistake.

I should have realized that the place would be a madhouse when it took me forever to find a parking space. The good news was that I finally found a spot four blocks from the market. The bad news was that I had to parallel park, never one of my fortés even when I was younger and could turn my neck to see where I was going.

The worst news—I was saving this for last—is that when I was parallel parking, I backed up and *thump*. I had misjudged how much room I had to maneuver and had an unplanned encounter with another car's bumper.

This is what happens when you're rushing, you idiot. You get all stressed out and do stupid things.

And I really did say that! Of course.

I put my head down on my car's steering column and prayed to whomever was the patron saint of aging automobile drivers. I would have prayed to St. Christopher, but he got bounced off the official saints' roster a long time ago.

Please don't let there be a lot of damage. To my car or the other vehicle. I promise I'll be more careful in the future. I'll never try to parallel park again. Amen.

I couldn't put it off any longer. It was time to survey the wreckage.

OMG. It was worse than I thought. Not the damage I had caused, but the vehicle I had backed into.

It wasn't an ordinary car. It was an emergency response vehicle from Fairport Ambulance.

Boy, when I make a mistake, I make a big time mistake.

Of course, the vehicle was huge, like a supersize SUV, but even sturdier. I bent down to inspect its front bumper, and was relieved to see that there was only a small dent on the left side as evidence of my unexpected visit. And—I had to squint to see this—a tiny particle of gray paint on the otherwise pristine bumper.

Big phew. I'm ashamed to admit that my first thought was, maybe the driver wouldn't even notice. Or think the dent happened a while ago. After all, emergency vehicles responded to, well, emergencies. I would bet that caring for a person in distress took precedence over parking skills.

I know. I know. I can be a weak person. But judge not. Etc. etc.

I checked out my own car, and it was no surprise that its damage was more significant. And more evident. Unfortunately. I'd never get away with pretending it never happened. Jim had an eagle eye for stuff like that.

After a brief wrestling match with my conscience, I left a scrap of paper under the vehicle's windshield wiper with my name and contact information. And scrawled a huge "SORRY!" at the bottom of the note.

I hoped this incident wouldn't be documented on the Fairport Patch, too!

Then, to atone for my carelessness, I hiked the four blocks to Fancy Francie's without changing from my high-heeled shoes into sneakers.

I hope Whatshername The Driving Saint noticed my suffering and gave me extra points.

With all this lollygagging around, by the time I got to the market, the lunch rush had subsided.

Helen looked up from behind the deli counter where she was slicing cold cuts and gave me a wave. "Your order is ready to go, Carol. It's in the refrigerator. Can you wait until I finish with this customer?"

I couldn't help but notice that the normally unflappable Helen was looking frazzled today. Her auburn curls were escaping from the cap she always wore, and her face was pale and dotted with beads of perspiration. I hoped she wasn't ill.

Especially if she'd prepared my wraps herself.

Helen held up five fingers, which I assumed meant a five-minute wait.

"No problem," I said, forcing myself to think healthy thoughts. I ordered myself to mosey around the take-out area and see what I could pick up for supper that might put Jim in a good mood.

Before I gave him the bad news about the car.

Hmm. Francie's Famous Pot Roast sounded good. With a side order of mashed potatoes and fresh carrots. Jim loves carrots. In any form. I kid him that he eats so many, he's beginning to hop and his ears are growing.

Done. I loaded tonight's supper into a shopping basket and headed back to Helen.

This time, she was ready for me. And I was happy to see that she seemed more composed than when I'd first come into the market.

Of course, the wraps looked yummy, but I resisted snitching one before she could cover the tray.

"What's going on at your house today, Carol?" Helen asked. "You better not be having one of your famous bunco parties during working hours, when I can't come. You promised I'd be invited to the next one. It's the stuff of legends here in town."

I laughed. Which felt extra good after the day I was having.

"Don't worry, Helen," I said. "This tray isn't for me. I'm bringing it to the family of a friend of mine who's just died."

I thought for a second, then corrected myself. "Will wasn't really a friend of mine. I only knew him for a short time. He did some landscaping work for Jim and me."

Was it my imagination, or did Helen's eyes suddenly well up with tears?

Nah. My mistake. When I looked again, her face was filled with concern, but her tears were non evident.

"Do you mean Will Finnegan?" she asked. "The man who owned Finnegan's Rakes?"

I nodded. "Why do you ask? Did you know him?"

"Only as a customer," Helen said very quickly. "He came in here every day at noontime, just like clockwork, and bought sandwiches for his crew. And sometimes, he even paid for other people's lunches, too. Especially if they worked for the police or fire department, or the Fairport emergency squad. He said it was his way of thanking the ones who keep us safe."

"Wow," I said. "I had no idea he was so generous."

"Will could be a very nice guy," Helen continued with just the hint of a smile. "Very helpful. If he realized a person had a problem, and he could fix it, he was always there. Do you know what I mean?"

"That's exactly right," I said excitedly. "In the short time I knew him, he was very helpful to me."

Helen gave me a look I couldn't interpret for the life of me. But I felt compelled to add, "What I should have said was, Will was helpful to *Jim* and me. Our yard is beautiful now, thanks to him."

"So, you're going to pay a condolence call on the Finnegan family?" Helen asked, carefully placing the plastic bubble top over the tray of sandwiches and snapping it into place. "You must know them."

"I've never met them," I admitted. "But bringing some food seemed like the right thing to do."

I realized Helen was hanging on my every word. I figured that she had no life except for Fancy Francie's and her customers. So, I couldn't resist giving her a little more information.

"Did you hear what happened at the Finnegan wake?" I asked. "You won't read this in the newspaper, but...." I leaned toward Helen and whispered to her about the police closing down the wake and why.

The next thing I knew, Helen disappeared from my view and I heard a *thunk*. I wasn't tall enough to peer over the counter to see what happened, but it sure sounded like Helen had fainted.

"Helen," I said. "Are you all right?"

I know. What a stupid question. But in the stress of the moment, it was the first thing out of my mouth.

I looked around for someone else to help, but now that the lunch crowd had gone, Fancy Francie's was pretty much deserted. Two elderly women were in the produce section of the store, discussing the pros and cons of a head of lettuce. And the check-out person was busy with an order for a harried young mother who was trying to bag her own order while keeping a toddler from climbing out of the shopping cart.

So, that left me.

I scurried around the back of the deli counter and Helen was lying in a crumpled heap on the floor. Fortunately, she was breathing. Thank God. I've had a few experiences when that hadn't been the case.

But clearly, she had hit her head when she fell, and head injuries are always dangerous.

I knelt down beside her. "Helen," I said. "Can you hear me?"

Her eyes fluttered open and she tried to sit up.

"What happened? How did I end up on the floor?" She reached for my hand. "Can you help me up? I'm so embarrassed."

I got her to a sitting position, and then Helen managed to right herself completely.

"I think you fainted," I said. "I'm sorry if what I told you about the Finnegan wake upset you."

"I *never* faint," Helen snapped. "There must have been a wet spot on the floor, and I slipped." She took a deep breath. "I'm fine now. Really. Just mortified that you witnessed my little misstep."

"I'm glad you're okay," I said. "But head injuries should always be checked by a doctor. Maybe you should go to the emergency room. I'd be glad to take you."

Helen waved me off. "I'm perfectly fine." I started to hand her a credit card, but Helen said, "Pay me the next time. Do you need any help getting the sandwiches into your car? I have more orders to fill before the next rush of customers starts."

So it's time for you to leave, Carol. We're done here.

Helen didn't actually say that, of course. But she certainly implied it.

"I can manage, thanks," I said, taking the tray and hurrying out the door.

As I made my way down Fairport Turnpike, I was occupied with three things: Not dropping the food, hoping the emergency vehicle I backed into was gone, and wondering what the heck was up with Helen.

Because something certainly was.

Chapter 19

Victoria's secret is an elasticized waistband.

Remember that old saying, "No good deed ever goes unpunished?" That's exactly what I was afraid of.

So far, my track record for doing a good deed for the Finnegan family was a big fat zero. If my unlucky streak continued unbroken, the widow Finnegan would probably dump the tray of sandwiches over my head and throw me out the door on my keester.

Or, even worse, accuse me of planting the scissors in Will, and call the Fairport police to come and arrest me.

I was tempted to forget the whole thing, go home, and have the sandwiches for supper. And probably for lunch the next day, too. Which was especially appealing since, with the excitement of Helen fainting, I had forgotten to buy the pot roast for Jim's dinner.

Oh, grow up, already. You can always leave the sandwiches on the front steps and vamoose before anyone sees you. And besides, Jack Finnegan asked you to stop by. Hopefully, he conveyed that information to his sister-in-law.

On the other hand, if you get any negative vibes, you don't have to introduce yourself at all. You could just pretend you're a delivery person from Fancy Francie's. Or doing a favor for a nameless friend.

Now, that was a great idea.

Comforted by my new escape plan, I headed toward the Finnegan home, which was located in one of Fairport's priciest areas—and there are many—the beach.

After a few wrong turns, I found myself at the far end of Fairport Beach Road, a series of small bungalows and cottages interspersed with some mega mansions. Although most of the older homes looked like they could use a major facelift, they fronted directly on Long Island Sound, and the land alone was worth a fortune.

I knew that some of these homes were only used by their owners during the summer months, and rented out to college students during the fall and winter. The annual Clam Jam rite-of-spring party, held on that stretch of beach in early April, was always a magnet for hundreds and hundreds of students to party hearty until the Fairport police came to shut it down.

The Finnegan home was on the opposite side of the road from the beach, so the view of Long Island Sound wasn't as good. A small blue bungalow style, its major attempt at curb appeal was a wraparound porch rather than the knock-your-socks-off landscaping that Will could have used to advertise his company.

Odd. But maybe I noticed this because of all the years living with a p.r. professional, who used to drill into my head that clients often lost major marketing opportunities that were right under their noses. This was a perfect example. Will could have taken "before" and "after" pictures of his front yard and used them to attract new clients. If he'd bothered to fix up his own yard first, of course.

There were no cars in the driveway, so I hoped I'd gotten lucky and nobody was home. I could just leave the tray of sandwiches with a quick note and get the heck out of there.

Feeling braver than I had before, I headed for the front door. Balancing the food tray in the crook of one arm, I rang the doorbell.

No answer. Things were looking up for me to make a speedy getaway. But just to be sure, I forced myself to ring the bell one more time.

Rats. I could definitely hear the sound of footsteps coming in my direction. Then the door swung open, revealing a petite brunette in her mid-forties who seemed vaguely familiar. "Can I help you?" she asked. "What address do you want?"

The woman eyed the tray of sandwiches, then me. "You don't look like a typical delivery person."

"I'm not a delivery person," I said quickly. Then I corrected myself.

"Actually, I'm delivering these sandwiches to the Finnegan family, so I guess that does make me a delivery person."

Carol, you are such a dope. Introduce yourself, express your condolences, give her the food, and leave. Why are you complicating things so much?

"Do I have the correct address?" I asked. "Are you Mrs. Finnegan?"

"Technically, I guess I am," the brunette said. "Although nobody's called me that in a long time."

She gestured me to follow her down a long hallway toward the back of the house. "The kitchen is this way. Come in and I'll put the tray in the refrigerator. We can have them for supper, which will save me from cooking."

A woman after my own heart.

"Is there a delivery slip for me to sign?"

"No delivery slip, Mrs., ah…." I stammered. "I came to express my condolences on your loss. Well, my husband sends his condolences, too, but I'm the one who picked up the food. The tray is a gift from both of us to your family."

I couldn't tell if the woman was grateful or not. She had the strangest expression on her face.

"I'm sorry," I said. "I should have introduced myself when you answered the door. I'm Carol Andrews. Will Finnegan did landscaping work for us. I took it for granted that you were his… ah…widow." I stopped myself, completely embarrassed.

This encounter was even more uncomfortable than I had imagined. And you all know that I have a very vivid imagination.

"I'm the one who should apologize," the woman said. "Technically, I am Will's widow. Although I don't think of myself that way."

My face must have mirrored my confusion. And I was plenty confused.

"I'm Louisa," she said. "You were very kind to bring us food. This whole thing has been such a shock."

Of course, I was now dying of curiosity, which under the current circumstances was very inappropriate. But I couldn't understand how someone could "technically" be a widow. In my universe, either you were or you weren't.

"The rest of the family is out right now," Louisa said. "Would you like a cup of tea? Even though you're a total stranger, I want to tell you about Will and me. It's quite a story."

She paused, then continued. "Maybe I want to talk to you because you are a total stranger. Do you have a little time to spare?"

At this point, it would have taken a herd of elephants to drag me out of Louisa's cheerful kitchen.

"I'm a very good listener," I said, settling myself into a chair and taking off my coat. *When I let other people get a word in edgewise.*

I didn't really say that last part, of course.

Louisa placed two cups of green tea on the table, sat down opposite me, and took a deep breath.

"Here's the abbreviated version of my so-called marriage to Will Finnegan," she said. "I hadn't seen the creep for more than ten years. Not since he walked out on me. And then I got a call from the hospital on Tuesday night that he'd had a heart attack and I was listed as his next of kin."

Chapter 20

Guilt is the gift that keeps on giving.

I had no idea how to respond to such a bombshell. So I picked up my teacup, preparing to take a sip. Then, I noticed my hands were shaking, so I put the cup back on the saucer before I dropped it.

Louisa didn't notice. Her eyes were closed, and a few tears were leaking down her face.

"Damn it," she said, taking a napkin and drying her cheeks. "I thought I'd used up all the tears I had for that rat years ago. I'm sorry to break down in front of you, Carol. If the kids could see me like this, they'd both give me hell, that's for sure. They have no use for their father, either."

Silence. From both of us. And Louisa's tears continued to flow.

Finally, I handed Louisa another napkin—the one she'd been using was a crumpled mess—and started to get up from my chair.

"I think it's best if I go," I said. "I never realized...."

"No!" Louisa said, grabbing my hand and pulling me back down into a sitting position. "Don't go. I need to let this all out, once and for all. And then, maybe, I can finally find some peace in my life. I've been pretending for too long."

She took a deep breath. "When I met Will Finnegan twenty-two years ago, I thought he was the handsomest man I'd ever seen."

No argument from me on that point.

"He had a way of making me feel so special," she said. "Like I was the only person in the world he cared about. Every time he'd hold my hand, even when I suspected he was being unfaithful, I'd feel a *zing*, like an electric shock. And he'd convince me that I was wrong. That I was the only woman in the world for him. And I believed him. Does that make any sense to you?"

I nodded. Even though I'd never seen the cheating side of Will, I could certainly relate to the *zing* part.

"When I first met Will, I was singing in the chorus of a Broadway musical," Louisa continued. Her face lit up at the memory.

"Although the competition was fierce, the director chose me to be an understudy for the female lead. I was so excited. It was going to be my big break, and I was on my way to becoming a Broadway star. Which is all I ever wanted to be, ever since I was a little girl.

"And then, Will asked me to marry him. He made it clear that he wanted a stay-at-home wife, and forced me to make a choice. It was either him or the theater."

Louisa laughed bitterly. "Boy, did I ever make the wrong choice. And by the time I figured out what a sap I'd been, my moment had passed. So now I sing in local amateur performances. And churches. Anything I can get."

"That's how I know you!" I exclaimed. "I've been trying to figure it out. I knew you looked familiar when you opened the door, but I couldn't place you. You're the choir director at St. Ambrose."

Louisa nodded. "That's one of my regular jobs. Are you a member of the parish?"

I didn't want to admit that Jim and I have only a nodding acquaintance with St. Ambrose, so instead I responded, "You have a gorgeous voice. And you play the organ beautifully. The music there is so wonderful, it's like going to a concert."

She beamed. "That's nice to hear. And I give music lessons, too. Anything to add some extra money to the family coffers. Although I have to say that, even though I hadn't laid eyes on Will in years, he always provided child support.

"I never told the kids that, though. If Brian and Amy found out that I was taking money from their father, they would have had a fit. When he walked out on me, he walked out on them, too. And they've never forgiven him."

I had to wonder why Louisa and Will didn't get a divorce. It seemed like the easiest solution to a complex problem.

As if reading my mind, Louisa said, "I suppose you're wondering why we didn't get a divorce."

"It's really none of my business," I said. "You don't have to explain anything to me."

In fact, you've told me too much already.

I didn't really say that, of course.

"You may find this hard to believe," Louisa said, "but Will didn't believe in divorce. He said divorce was a sin. That when two people were married, they were married for life. Isn't that rich? He thought divorce was a sin, but having extra-marital affairs wasn't.

"And I was so stupid, I didn't argue with him. I guess I was in shock when he walked out. Or maybe I thought that, one day, he'd come back. And I would probably have taken him back, too."

Louisa shook her head. "I was so naive and trusting! Always waiting for my happy ending, just like in the fairy tales we read when we were kids. You know what I mean?"

I started to respond, but Louisa wasn't quite finished.

"Have you met Jack?" she asked me. "Will's brother?"

I nodded. "He came to my home this morning to finish up some of the landscaping work Will had started. When I first saw him, it freaked me out. He looks so much like Will, they could be twins. In fact, Jack was the person who suggested I stop by to see you."

Notice that I left out the part about my supposed association with the Fairport police. No sense confusing the poor woman. And heaven knows I had no desire to go sleuthing again. Even if I frequently unearth evidence that the entire police department has overlooked. And thereby solve the case. Not that I'm bragging, mind you.

"Jack's a doll," Louisa said. "As a matter of fact, he's been more like a father than an uncle to Brian and Amy since Will deserted us. I often think that he's the Finnegan brother I should have married. And he's made no secret of his feelings for me. Oh, well. No sense going into all of that now. It's over and done with."

Louisa glanced at her watch and said, "Oh, golly, I didn't realize it was so late. I have to go to the funeral home to see what arrangements can be made for another memorial service. And when. I just want this whole thing to be over with, for my sake and for the kids'.

"Or maybe I should be asking the police about that, not the funeral director. Did you hear what happened there last night just as the wake was about to start?"

I started to admit that I had been there, but stopped myself in time. No sense going down that particular road right now.

Instead of answering the question, I started for the front door. "I hope the food will be a hit with the family."

Louisa gave me a hug. "Thanks so much for the sandwiches, and especially for letting me unburden myself to you like I did. I hope I didn't bore you with my troubles. I'm sorry I kept you here so long."

"No apology necessary," I said. "I was glad to be a friendly ear. Please let me know if I can do anything else to help. I really mean that."

I rattled off my cell number and headed down the driveway to one of my favorite thinking places, the solitude of my car.

As I drove in the direction of Old Fairport Turnpike, it should come as no surprise that my brain was more confused than usual. So much so that I drove right by my own house, and had to go to the corner, make a U turn (there was no oncoming traffic, thank goodness), and head back in the right direction.

I hate to admit it, but I have a very suspicious nature. I had an awful feeling that there was another mystery to be solved. Don't get me wrong, the scissors incident was grisly. Horrible. I shuddered when I remembered the sight of Will in his casket.

But I couldn't help but wonder why had Will had died so suddenly, when he appeared to be in the best of health. Did Will have a history of heart problems? Or was it possible that he didn't die of natural causes?

Louisa would probably know. But even I didn't have the nerve to ask her about Will's health history.

I wondered if the police would take a closer look at Will's actual death. With Paul Wheeler on the case, any real detective work was doubtful, or even nonexistent.

I couldn't stop myself from imagining a terrible scenario, one that Louisa herself had inadvertently given me. Maybe she got tired of waiting in marital limbo and wanted to be free. Or maybe Jack got tired of waiting to marry the woman he loved. But now that Will was out of the way, the coast was clear for Louisa to marry the other Finnegan brother.

And Louisa wouldn't even have to change her last name, or the initials on her guest towels.

Chapter 21

I'm not old. I'm timeless.

"More au gratin potatoes?" I asked, passing the casserole dish across the table in the direction of my darling daughter and her husband. "And there's more baked ham, too." I handed the empty meat platter to Jim. "How about cutting the rest of the ham while it's still warm, dear? That way, anyone who wants seconds can have them, and I'll be able to use the rest for leftovers."

It was Sunday night, and our turn to host the Andrews family dinner. It's a tradition I started right after Jenny and Mark were married, and a way for us to keep in touch as a family.

Yes, I actually cooked the meal myself. Just in case you were wondering.

And if you're thinking that Sunday dinner is also an excellent opportunity for me to casually get information from my son-in-law the police detective about a case I might be interested in, you'd be absolutely right.

Mark attempted to take the platter away from Jim, but I stopped him. "Let Jim do it, Mark," I said. I gave My Beloved a squeeze on his knee. Under the table, of course. We're not into overt displays of affection at our age.

"You don't mind doing it, do you, dear?" I asked. "You know exactly how to slice the ham so it's thin enough to be used for sandwiches." I gave him my most winning smile.

With Jim safely occupied in the kitchen, I turned my winning smile in the direction of my son-in-law.

"So, Mark, how are things?" I asked, once again passing the au gratin potatoes in his direction. "Have some more potatoes. I remember these were one of your favorites when you were a kid."

Mark patted his washboard stomach. "That was long before I joined the Fairport Police," he said with a rueful grin. "Keeping in shape is a requirement for being on the force. So I better pass on seconds."

"You're always in perfect shape as far as I'm concerned," Jenny said, gazing at her husband of almost one year adoringly.

It was hard to believe it had taken Jenny and Mark so long to figure out what I had known from their pre-puberty days—that they were made for each other. I silently congratulated myself on giving them the necessary nudge in the right direction during an Andrews family crisis that brought Mark back into our lives after a prolonged absence.

Unfortunately, Mark came back into our lives in an official police capacity, since he was the investigating officer in the death of Davis Rhodes, Jim's late retirement coach. And at first, poor Jim was number one on the police suspect list.

I, of course, straightened the whole thing out and unmasked the real culprits. Which began my unofficial sleuthing career.

I hope I'm not boring you by telling you something you already know, but some folks have difficulty remembering things after a certain age.

I'd been thinking most of the day about whether or not to bring up the subject of Will Finnegan's death—and its unusual aftermath—at our family dinner.

Lord knows, although I'd skimped on the details with Jim, I got another lecture about how I shouldn't have delivered food to the Finnegan family. That now I was involving myself even more in another mysterious death. When would I learn to mind my own business? Blah blah blah.

But I'll bet you'll be surprised when I tell you that Jim's eruption about the damage to my Jeep's rear bumper after my close encounter with the emergency vehicle didn't happen. Why? Because I'd had it fixed before Jim could see it, thanks to our local body shop, Fairport Auto Repair. Its owner, Skip Clark, makes a fortune providing extra quick, discreet service for repeat customers like me. So I dodged that particular bullet. Figuratively speaking.

And I paid the car repair bill in cash from a secret stash I keep hidden in my lingerie drawer. I always plan ahead. Pretty smart, right?

Some folks (not saying who) criticize me for not being entirely forthright with Jim all the time about my adventures, retail-wise or otherwise. I usually turn my baby blues onto these people and ask these folks if they're married. And, if the answer is yes, how long they've been married.

The married ones are *always* newlyweds. So, what do they know? The ink isn't even dry on their marriage license yet.

A little knowledge is a good thing. A lot of knowledge leads to nothing but trouble. Trust me—I know what I'm talking about.

Since my own daughter fell under the category of the newly married, I wasn't sure how much of our funeral home adventure she'd shared with Mark. But I decided to test the waters with a few innocent questions and another offer of food.

"Here, Mark," I said, passing my Waterford salad bowl in his direction. (I always use the good stuff for Sunday dinners. After all, at my age, why wait?) "You can't say no to fresh vegetables."

"Mom's right, honey," Jenny said. "According to the latest health reports, a person's supposed to eat at least five portions of fresh fruit and vegetables a day. And a jelly doughnut doesn't count as fruit."

Mark laughed. "Maybe not, but where would a cop be without his daily dose of doughnuts and coffee? That's what keeps us going."

"Speaking of the police, Mark," I said, "how's the investigation into Will Finnegan's death going? Any suspects yet?"

See how I oh-so-naturally segued from salad to sleuthing? I hope you're all impressed.

"Do you mean the guy whose wake was shut down because of an irregularity? Paul's handling that one, not me." Mark speared a tomato, then said, "I shouldn't tell you this, but...."

I leaned forward in my chair, trying not to appear too eager. Any time someone says they shouldn't tell me something, I know they should.

"Around the Fairport Police Station, we call Will Finnegan 'Double Dead Will.' "

Jenny smacked Mark's hand. "That's terrible!"

"I know. I'm sorry."

"So, you do know something about the case," I continued, not letting him off the hook.

"I told you that Mom and I were at the funeral home for that wake," Jenny reminded him. "Will used to do landscaping work for Mom and Dad. So it's natural that she'd want to know what's going on. In fact, I'm wondering, too."

"All I've heard is that an official burial is on hold until Paul can figure out what happened the night of the wake. He's continuing to interview people," Mark said.

"If Paul's the only one on the case, that might take forever," I said. "I don't have a lot of faith in his detective ability."

Mark bristled at my criticism of his colleague. Even if he knew it was true. "I know you and Paul got off to a rocky start, but he really is a good guy, Carol. And a darned good detective, too. Otherwise, he wouldn't still be on the force."

"I'm sure you're right, Mark," I said. "My crack was way out of line." I didn't believe that for a second, mind you, but sometimes it's more important for me to keep peace in the family than to share my usually on-target, but unasked for, opinions.

I sighed. "It's just that I feel so sorry for the Finnegan family. I'm assuming Paul's talked to them. Not that I'm suggesting how he should do his job, of course."

Mark mumbled something I didn't quite catch. It could have been, "When are you going to mind your own business?"

But I'm sure I misunderstood.

I cocked my head in the direction of the kitchen. The sound of the electric knife indicated that Jim was still hard at work, slicing the remains of the ham.

"I met the widow when I delivered sandwiches to the house Friday afternoon," I said, watching Mark's face to see his reaction, which was predictable. A cross between aggravation and admiration.

"She didn't act particularly broken up about Will's death. In fact, he walked out on her years ago. Will was quite the Fairport Romeo, according to her.

"I got the sandwich tray from Fancy Francie's. The owner, Helen Konisburg, seems to be a very close friend of Will's. Lots of avenues for Paul to explore."

If you've been paying attention, you'll notice I left one name off my interrogation list: my hairstylist, Deanna. I still hadn't figured out her connection to Will Finnegan. And I wasn't sure I wanted to try.

"What's the normal procedure in a case like this?" I asked, probing for more information. "I mean, when the police figure out who…did the deed in the funeral home, then what happens?" Bile rose in my throat as an image of poor Will flashed into my brain.

"That's a good question, Mom," Jenny said. "I know this isn't appropriate dinner conversation in most households, but when Paul figures out who…did the deed, what would that person be charged with? Murder?"

"Not murder, Jenny," Mark said. "Maybe criminal interference. I'm not sure. I have to look that one up. We've never had a case like this in Fairport before. And I'm not sure the police academy covered it, either."

In for a penny, in for a pound, as my late mother used to say.

So I took a deep breath, then said, "I'm wondering if the police should take a closer look at the cause of Will's death, under the circumstances. Which, you must admit, are bizarre. I mean his actual *death*, not what happened later. Maybe someone really wanted him out of the way. Or more than one person did."

Mark gaped at me. "What are you suggesting, Carol?"

The buzz of the electric knife had stopped, indicating that I had to talk fast. Before Jim returned with the sliced ham and accused me of sticking my nose into something that wasn't my business.

Again.

"I'm suggesting that perhaps Will didn't die of natural causes," I said. "Maybe he was murdered."

Chapter 22

I was at the beauty shop this morning for nearly two hours. And that was only for the estimate!

I woke up grumpy Monday morning.

No, I don't mean Jim. I could hear sounds of him already puttering around the kitchen, hopefully conjuring up some extra strong coffee to open my eyes and clear my fuzzy brain.

I woke up grumpy because I realized I had put my foot in my mouth big-time at last night's family dinner. My helpful suggestion that the police should investigate into the cause of Will Finnegan's sudden death was greeted by a variety of negative responses.

Jim, overhearing me as he was carrying the platter of ham into the dining room: "Have you lost your mind, Carol?"

Jenny: "Mom, usually I'm impressed with your deductive skills, but this time you're way over the top."

Mark: Stony silence. Then, "Don't tell me how we should do our job. Stay out of this, Carol. I mean it."

Me: Big sigh.

But I wasn't giving up that easily.

"Maybe you'll all think differently when I fill you in on what I discovered about the widow Finnegan and her brother-in-law, Jack."

Quickly (for me—I do tend to take a long time to get to the point of a story, one of my worst faults), I filled the doubting trio in on my conversation with Louisa, emphasizing once again her long-time-separation-but-not-divorce from her husband. And her admission of love for her brother-in-law.

"So if Will didn't want a divorce," I said, "and Louisa and Jack were in love and wanted to be married, Will stood in their way. They could have gotten tired of waiting around, and decided to speed up Will's demise."

I thought I made a pretty impressive case.

Unfortunately, nobody else did. "Your overactive imagination is in overdrive again," Jim said. "I've seen it too many times. Drop it, Carol. Mark agrees with me, don't you?"

"Let the police handle this, Carol. I really mean it this time," Mark said. He grabbed Jenny's hand and pulled her to her feet. "Come on. Let's go home."

And that was it. The end of what should have been a cozy family dinner. All because of my big mouth. Remembering the expression on Mark's face as he and Jenny left last night made me cringe.

What if I'd completely ruined our relationship? What if I never saw them again?

A fat tear rolled down my cheek as I thought about Jenny, in labor having my first grandchild, without me there to comfort her. And the little girl (I just knew her first child would be a girl) growing up without the love and support of her grandma.

I was beyond grumpy. I was now inconsolable.

And my feet hadn't even touched the bedroom floor yet.

Get up and get moving, I ordered myself.

While performing my morning ablutions, I couldn't help but notice that my hairline was starting to sport telltale white hairs. Yuck.

Time for a visit to the hair salon?

No way. I wasn't ready to see Deanna yet. She always knows when I have something on my mind, and for some reason, I find myself telling her things I haven't told anyone else, even Jim.

Oh, whom am I kidding? Especially Jim!

I jammed a baseball cap ("Fairport Police Do It Better!") on my head and padded out into the kitchen. Lucy and Ethel had obviously been fed, because neither so much as lifted a head when I made my appearance.

For a brief moment, I wished I were a Blue Roan English cocker spaniel, too. Their furry mixture of black and white hairs always looks perfect. Except when it's on my furniture.

Jim lowered his newspaper and commented, "Nice touch, Carol. I didn't realize we were dressing for breakfast this morning."

"Very funny," I snapped back, heading in the direction of the coffee pot. "I haven't taken a shower yet, and I have 'bed head.' I was trying to spare you the sight first thing in the morning."

"Very thoughtful," Jim said, reaching over and pulling out a chair for me at the kitchen table. "Too bad you weren't as thoughtful last night at dinner."

"What? I looked perfectly presentable at dinner last night. Even Mark complimented me on my outfit."

"I'm not talking about what you wore last night, Carol. As you very well know. I'm talking about how you didn't think before you spoke. Your outrageous theory about Will Finnegan's death being murder was absolutely ridiculous. And to make the situation even worse, you wouldn't let it go. Once again, you're meddling in a situation that's none of your business. It's a good thing that our son-in-law is such a good guy. He could have you arrested for interfering with a police investigation."

I sat there, fuming. And trying to come up with a snappy defense, even though I knew that Jim was right on target.

Not that I'd ever admit that.

Fortunately, he hadn't thought about our being boycotted from seeing our grandchildren-to-be, as punishment. And I hoped he never did.

"Well, what do you have to say for yourself, Carol?"

I searched my repertoire of possible comebacks and came up empty. But I wasn't giving in without a fight.

"You'll be happy to know that, just this once, I have absolutely nothing to say, dear. In fact, I'm willing to concede that I may have been overzealous in presenting my case to Mark last night." I held up my hand to forestall Jim's response. "I still believe that there's something suspicious about Will Finnegan's sudden death. But since I've shared my theory, and been rebuffed, what more can I do?"

"I'm glad you've come to your senses, Carol," Jim said. "I apologize for coming down on you so hard. I know you have a good heart, and you always mean well. You can't help being super inquisitive, I guess."

Too true.

Now, if you've been paying close attention to this husband/

wife exchange, perhaps you've noticed something important. A clue, if you will.

At no time in our discussion did I promise Jim that I wasn't going to continue my so-called investigation. What I said was, "What more can I do?"

This could be interpreted by someone who doesn't know me at all as my asking Jim for advice about what he thought my next step should be.

It wasn't that at all, of course

I already knew what I was going to do. I was going to pick up the phone and make a hair appointment with Deanna.

Chapter 23

Sometimes I talk too much and say too little.

Normally, a visit to Crimpers, the upscale Fairport hair salon owned by my super hairstylist, Deanna, is a sure way to improve my spirits. And improve my looks, too. Which, at my advancing age, is no easy task.

Not today, though. How does one begin a very sensitive conversation with someone who has the power to shave one's head, or turn one's hair a bilious green if provoked?

Very, very carefully.

Since I shrink from any kind of confrontation, I decided the direct approach was definitely out. I would be so subtle that Deanna would never figure out that she was being interrogated by Fairport's Number One amateur sleuth.

Which would be me, in case you didn't understand that reference.

And I wouldn't begin my questioning until way into the appointment, after Deanna applied the glop she uses on my hair to bring back my dormant blonde highlights. Which seem to have turned into more than fifty shades of gray and white, all on their own.

There was a new receptionist at the desk when I breezed into the salon. Who frowned at me and said, "Mrs. Andrews, I presume? You're ten minutes late for your appointment. And Deanna worked you into her very busy schedule as a favor. Please don't make a habit out of this, or you'll be charged a late fee."

Say what? I'd been coming to Crimpers for years and no one had ever talked to me that way. And I make a point of being on time for all my appointments. Mostly.

The nerve of this little snip. Who the heck did she think she was talking to anyway?

I smiled sweetly and said, "You're new, right? Well, I'm not. I've been a client of Deanna's for more than ten years. And I'm always right on time for my appointment. In fact, I'm frequently early. You can check that out with Deanna herself. Is she ready for me now?"

And I sailed back to the Crimpers inner sanctum.

Deanna glanced up from the sink, where she was vigorously shampooing a customer, and nodded in the direction of her station. "I'm running behind today, Carol. I hope you don't mind waiting a bit. I told you on the phone that my schedule was pretty tight."

"Not a problem," I said, plopping down in a chair. "I appreciate your working me in on such short notice. But you might tell your new watchdog at the front desk to be a little more customer friendly. She bit my head off when I came into the salon, accused me of being late myself, and threatened to charge me a late fee if I did it again. Who the heck is she, anyway?"

Deanna rinsed her customer with a spray of warm water before replying. Handing the person a towel to drape around her shoulders, she said, "Head over to my station and I'll be right with you."

Then, to me, "I apologize if she was unfriendly. I'll have a talk with her. Lisa's never worked with the general public before. She can be a little rough around the edges."

Thus pacified by Deanna's apology, I settled down in my chair, hunted in my purse for my bifocals—never easily accessible for some reason I will never understand—and prepared to entertain myself with some lurid tabloid fiction.

The salon atmosphere, and the sound of a blow dryer, soothed me into such a relaxed state that I could feel myself nodding off. I figured it couldn't hurt if I closed my eyes for just a few minutes. Just resting my eyes, so to speak. Not really sleeping.

I was in that halfway state between awake and asleep when I heard Deanna say, "Lisa, you've got to be more polite to my customers. Carol Andrews has been a loyal customer for years. In fact, because of her and her friends, I've been able to afford that fancy private school you've been going to for the past three years.

As long as you're working here, you'd better watch what you say."

I was definitely awake now, but kept my eyes closed. It didn't take a genius to realize that this conversation wouldn't be happening if Deanna thought I was listening.

I heard someone crying softly. I immediately felt guilty, assuming that my complaint was to blame for the tears.

"I'm sorry for what I said to Mrs. Andrews. I was just trying to help. And you always say that time is money. I didn't mean to insult her. Or upset you any more than you already are."

I heard some mumbled conversation and strained to decipher what was being said. But it was useless.

And then I heard Lisa's voice again. "You know I love you. And I'm so grateful for everything you do for me. I'd do anything to help you, Mom. Anything."

Mom? Did I just hear Lisa call Deanna "Mom"?

Although my nosy side wanted to continue listening to what was, essentially, a very private conversation, the angelic side insisted that was not playing fair.

The angelic side won—just this once—and I feigned moving around in my chair and stretching, so Deanna would think I was just waking up from a quick nap. Just for good measure, I rustled the newspaper in my lap, too.

In a flash, Deanna was beside me. "Have a good snooze, Carol?" she asked.

"I'm so embarrassed," I said.

Well, that part, at least, was true.

"I don't normally drop off to sleep in public. I haven't been sleeping well the last few nights. I hope I didn't snore."

Deanna laughed. "I didn't hear a thing," she said.

I certainly did.

I didn't really say that, of course.

"I had a talk with the receptionist while you were dozing," Deanna said, handing me a black smock to wear over my clothing. "I told her in no uncertain terms what a good customer you are, and that she should be more polite when she talks to you."

"It's not just me," I protested. "For all you know, she may be rude to some of your other customers, too. Has anyone else mentioned it?"

Deanna shook her head. I couldn't help but notice that her hair color, usually a bright shade of red, was much more subdued today. Nor was it styled in the spiky style she usually favored.

Before I could continue my surreptitious interrogation, Deanna asked, "Why aren't you sleeping well, Carol? Is there something bother you? Would it make you feel better to talk about it?"

Rats. This is the way my hair appointments always went. I used them as an excuse to unload my latest crisis on Deanna, she offered wise counsel—or perhaps, just a series of hmms—and I left the salon feeling and looking much better than when I walked in. In other words, I spilled my guts about my personal life (figuratively speaking, of course) and she told me zip about hers.

I had to figure out a way to turn the conversation around to her.

"I figured out that I can't have regular coffee at dinner," I said. "It keeps me awake. I had decaf last night instead, and I slept like a baby."

Of course, this was a total lie, but it sure sounded good. I will never give up my high test coffee, no matter what.

"That's very smart of you, Carol," Deanna said. "I had a customer once who…."

Before she could launch into one of her stories, I interrupted her. I know, I was rude. But it had to be done.

"So, tell me more about Lisa," I said. "Where did she come from? An employment agency? I can't imagine an agency sending someone out on a receptionist job with no customer service skills whatsoever. Don't they screen applicants these days?"

Deanna flushed. "Lisa didn't come from an agency, Carol. She's only here temporarily. By the time you come back for your next regular hair styling appointment, she'll be back at school."

I pounced.

"School? Hairdressing school?"

"No, Carol." Deanna stopped applying color to my hair and gave me a piercing look. "Why do you ask?"

I opened my baby blues as wide as possible, feigning innocence. "I just wondered."

I focused on the newspaper on my lap, pretending to read it. But since I didn't have my bifocals on any more, even the headlines were blurry.

After a pause of about ten seconds, I said, "How old is she?"
"Who?"
"Lisa. That's who we're talking about, right?" I said.
"That's who *you're* talking about," Deanna corrected. "I'm just

trying to get all your color on before my next client comes in. I worked you in as a favor, remember?"

I started to nod in agreement, but Deanna stopped me. "Don't move your head, Carol. You need to keep very still right now." She continued applying my base color, then said, "I hope you don't want foils today, because I don't have time to do them. If you really want them, you'll have to make an appointment to come back next week."

She glanced at the large clock on the wall. "Time for you to move to a new chair. I have another client coming in about five minutes from now. I'll set your timer for thirty minutes." She gestured to a chair on the other side of the salon, well out of potential eavesdropping range.

Rats.

"I'm glad to see your business is doing so well these days," I said as I allowed Deanna to lead me across the salon. "Especially in such a down economy. You're very lucky."

Deanna looked at me. "You must be kidding, Carol. My business isn't that great."

"But you're extra busy today," I said. "I just figured that you had loads of new clients to take care of."

"I only wish you were right," Deanna said, handing me a slew of magazines to keep me occupied while the hair color did its thing. "I've been closed for a few days, and now I have to scramble to make up the time with all those clients I had to cancel."

I gave it one last shot.

"Vacation?" I asked.

"No," Deanna snapped back. "If you must know, there was a death in the family." And she walked away.

Chapter 24

Experience is a wonderful thing. It enables you to recognize a mistake right away when you make it again. And again.

It's a good thing I was already sitting down. Otherwise, I'm sure my derriere would have hit the floor in response to Deanna's announcement, followed immediately by the rest of me. And who knows what damage I'd have done to my aging body? After a certain age, I've read that a woman's bones are much more brittle and subject to fractures. No matter how much calcium she takes every day.

I sat in my chair at the opposite side of the hair salon, straining to hear whatever tidbits Deanna might be sharing with her other customer. And pretending to be leaf through a few of the magazines Deanna had given me.

I finally gave up trying to eavesdrop and sat back in my chair. More than anything, I wished I had something to write on. Sometimes making a list helps clear my brain, which was now whirling with all sorts of possible scenarios.

I'll let all of you take a minute and work out a few of them for yourselves. Let's see how good you are at sleuthing. Believe me, it's a lot harder than it looks.

Here's how my thought process went:

I saw Deanna at the funeral home the night of the Finnegan wake. Why was she there so early, way before the wake was supposed to begin? And who were those people with her?

Deanna and Lisa are mother and daughter.

Was Lisa at the funeral home with her mother?

Deanna is a hairdresser. She uses scissors all the time. Did she use the scissors on Will? And if she did, why?

Lisa told Deanna she'd do anything to help her. And she's working temporarily in the hair salon. Therefore, she also had access to the tools of Deanna's trade. Like scissors.

Which meant that Lisa could have used the scissors on Will. Assuming she was also at the wake. Big assumption. And again, why?

Deanna told me that she's running way behind her appointments today because the salon had been closed due to a death in the family.

OMG! Could Will Finnegan be Lisa's father?

I had to think of a way to continue my conversation with Deanna. But it was clear that asking her direct questions was making her angry with me. Something that had never happened before, in all the years we'd known each other.

In a flash, I had a new strategy. Deanna loved to hear about other people's problems. And she always had a helpful suggestion to offer. So I needed to come up with an imaginary problem for her to advise me on.

A problem that, if I was very clever, might also make Deanna reveal something about her own personal life.

I whipped through my mental filing cabinet and came up with something I hoped would do the trick. I was so caught up in my plan that I jumped a foot when I heard Deanna say, "Come over to the sink, Carol. It's time to wash your hair."

Obediently, I did as I was told, allowing a single tear to leak from my eyes in the process.

Yes, like Nancy, I can whip up tears pretty easily. Which comes in very handy when certain household bills arrive.

There was no reaction at all from Deanna. Rats. I'd have to do it again. I hoped my eye makeup didn't run.

I waited until I was settled in her styling chair, then squeezed my eyes shut and—just like that!—produced another tear. And added a heavy sigh to my performance.

This time, Deanna saw me. And was concerned. Just as I'd expected.

"Oh, Carol, I'm sorry for the way I acted earlier. I didn't mean to upset you."

I looked around the salon and realized it was now empty of other clients. Even the lovely Lisa had left.

I gave Deanna a weak smile, then said, "I'm not upset about you, Deanna. It's Jenny. I mean, it's my relationship with Jenny. Since she and Mark have been married, Jenny and I aren't nearly as close as we used to be. I suppose that's natural, but Jenny came up with a pretty outrageous suggestion recently that, well...."

Not my best story, I admit. But I didn't have a lot of time to come up with one. As extra emphasis, though, I allowed a few more tears to appear.

It's a gift.

"I've heard from so many clients that the mother-daughter relationship can be a rocky one," Deanna said, looking at my hair critically. "What happened between you and Jenny?"

"I really don't want to go into it," I said. "It's too upsetting. I'm worried that someone will walk in and overhear me."

"Don't worry about that, Carol," Deanna said. "You're the last appointment of the day. But if you're really concerned about being overheard, I can fix that."

In a flash, she had locked the salon door and put up the "closed" sign.

"Now we can talk privately about what's really on your mind. And it's not Jenny, so don't think you're fooling me."

"I don't know what you mean, Deanna," I said, trying to look innocent and hoping I was successful.

"I'll make it easy for you, Carol. When you saw me at Will Finnegan's wake, I saw you, too. And knowing you as well as I do, I bet you want to know why I was there."

Deanna reached into her equipment drawer and pulled out a pair of cutting shears.

"And I'm just dying to tell you all about it."

Chapter 25

I took a course in speed writing. Now I can write for an hour in only ten minutes.

Have you ever heard that expression, "a frisson of fear"? I never knew what it meant until Deanna came at me, scissors in hand.

I was alone in the hair salon. Which was closed for the day.

And nobody knew where I was. I didn't even leave a note for Jim.

OMG. I was going to die. My hairstylist was going to kill me for nosing into her private life.

"Deanna," I said in a shaky voice, "can't we discuss this like two rational people? We've known each other too long to have our relationship end like this."

To say nothing of my life.

"I really did want to talk to you about Jenny and me. I don't know what you mean about Will Finnegan's wake."

My favorite hairstylist and possible killer looked at me in disgust. "That is so typical of you, Carol. It's always all about you. But this one time, when I need so desperately to trust someone, to talk to someone about the mess my life is in, you turn your back on me."

She waved her scissors around my head for emphasis, and I flinched. It was an automatic reaction, but Deanna saw it.

"What the heck is wrong with you, Carol? Are you afraid I'm going to scalp you?"

"Don't be silly, Deanna," I said. "I was just shifting my position in the chair. To ease my lower back."

"Yeah, right," Deanna said. "Why don't I believe you?" She whirled me around in the chair so I was facing the mirror. "Let's see if I can get this done quickly. I assume you want the same style."

Same style? What difference does it make how my hair is styled if I'm dead?

I started to respond. Well, beg for my life, actually. When I heard banging on the salon door. And a familiar shrieking voice.

"Deanna, let me in. It's Nancy. I came right over after I got your text. And Claire is with me."

I was giddy with relief. Saved by the knock. So to speak.

While Deanna dealt with the front door, I took a minute to compose myself. Both Claire and Nancy knew my facial expressions far too well—that's what happens when you've been best friends since grammar school.

And I realized, now that reinforcements had arrived, how absolutely ridiculous my fears were. There was no way that Deanna would have harmed me. The whole thing was just a series of... unfortunate coincidences. Yes, that was it. Coincidences that propelled my imagination into overdrive. Again.

I really should write some of this stuff down. If I ever get a free minute.

Nancy leaned down and gave me a quick kiss, being careful not to smudge her makeup by getting too close to my damp hair.

"Thanks for coming so quickly," Deanna said to Nancy and Claire. Then, to me, "I'll finish your haircut in a little while. And there's no charge for today's appointment. You've been very patient. All things considered."

I knew Jim would be thrilled when I told him that. Especially since Crimpers doesn't take credit cards, so there was no chance of racking up those extra bonus points he's so crazy about.

"So," Claire asked, getting straight to the point as usual, "what's your big emergency, Deanna?"

"Mary Alice was sorry she couldn't join us," Nancy interrupted before Deanna had a chance to reply. "She has a hot date with a new guy." She grinned. "Lucky her."

"Someone she met on that Internet dating site?" I asked, my demon curiosity once again getting the best of me.

"I hope she's not seeing someone she met online," Deanna said. "That's how all my troubles started."

"I think it's someone she met at the hospital," Nancy said.

"She says all the guys she's met through the Internet have been real losers."

"Mary Alice is certainly right about that," Deanna said. "She must be a better judge of character than I am."

"All right, Deanna," I said. "Let's forget about Mary Alice's romantic life for a minute. What the heck is going on with you? This has easily been the longest hair appointment of my life. And the most confusing. I feel like I've been on a roller coaster ever since I walked in here…" I checked my wristwatch… "four hours ago. Good grief. Jim will think I've been kidnapped!"

"Are you having man troubles?" Nancy asked. "Is that what this emergency is all about?"

Deanna laughed. It was a very odd laugh. Then she said, "I guess you could call it 'man troubles.' Or, to be accurate, 'dead man troubles.' The man I've been in a relationship with for years is dead. And I'm afraid I'm going to be accused of killing him."

Claire just gaped at Deanna, shock written on her face.

"That beats any man troubles I've ever had," Nancy said. "And I've had a lot of them."

Even I was surprised.

"I guess I'd better start at the very beginning," Deanna said.

I couldn't help it. Julie Andrews singing, "Doe a deer, a female deer," from *The Sound of Music* popped into my head. Fortunately, I didn't try to make it a duet with Julie.

"His name was Will," she continued, her voice trembling. "Will Finnegan."

"You mean the guy who ran Finnegan's Rakes?" Nancy asked. "His trucks are all over Fairport. In fact, I think Dream Homes Realty has used his company to spruce up some of our real estate listings. There's nothing like eye-catching curb appeal to draw in a potential buyer."

"Nancy, just this once, spare us the real estate lecture," Claire said.

Nancy sniffed. "I just wanted to be sure we were talking about the same man," she said.

"It's the same man," I said. "He's been doing some landscaping work for Jim and me. And Phyllis and Bill Stevens, across the street from us, have used him for years."

"Will and I became involved several years ago," Deanna said. "I fell hard for him. I thought he was the man I'd been waiting for all my life. And he said I was his soul mate. That fate had brought us together, and we were destined to be together forever. And I believed him. Every word. For ten years."

"But Will was married," I interjected. "Did you know that?

"I delivered a tray of sandwiches to the family," I explained to the group. "And I met his widow."

"Will told me he was still married right at the beginning of our relationship, Carol," Deanna said. "He said his wife didn't believe in divorce, so he would never be free to marry me. But that we were married in spirit, and that was all that counted."

"Wait a minute," I said. "That's not what his widow told me. She said that Will was the one who didn't believe in divorce."

"Carol, for crying out loud. Just this once, don't interrupt," Claire said. "Let Deanna talk."

"As it turned out, Carol's right," Deanna said. "But I didn't know that until the night Will died." Her eyes clouded over. "That was the worst night of my entire life."

It wasn't such a great one for Will, either.

I didn't really say that, of course.

"I got a call from Will about nine o'clock on Tuesday night. He sounded awful. He said he had terrible pains in his chest and begged me to come to his condo right away. I told him to call nine-one-one and I'd be right over."

Deanna pressed her lips together to stop them from trembling.

"I got to Will's just in time to see him being loaded into an ambulance. The paramedics wouldn't let me ride to the hospital with him. One of them handed me Will's iPhone and told me Will wanted me to call someone named Louisa and tell her what happened. I had no idea she was his wife. I made the call, and she said she'd meet me at the hospital. Even when she came into the emergency room, I had no idea who she was."

Deanna took a deep breath.

"She identified herself as Will's wife to the doctor. I was so shocked. Can you imagine the scene? Me on one side of the bed, and her on the other. And Will in between us, all hooked up to tubes and monitors, breathing so shallowly. It was horrible."

Nancy reached over and patted Deanna's hand. "I'm so sorry you had to go through this. You don't have to tell us any more if it's too hard for you."

I shot Nancy a look. *Don't tell her to stop now. Are you nuts?*

"Thanks, but I have to finish telling you what happened," Deanna said. "Maybe by talking about it, the whole thing will finally make some sense to me.

"So, there we all were, the wife, the girlfriend, and the husband/ boyfriend, in one of those small curtained cubicles in the emergency room. I finally had the chance to confront the woman who'd prevented me from marrying Will and wrecked my chance at happiness. And when I called her on it, you know what she said?"

"She told you what she told me!" I said. "That it was Will who didn't want the divorce, not her."

"Bingo," said Deanna. "That's exactly what she told me. And you know what else? She also told me she hadn't seen the louse in years. And that he'd never even made an attempt to see his kids."

"What a creep!" Nancy said.

"At first, I didn't believe her. You have to remember, she was talking about the man I loved. I called her a liar. I said that Will had made it a practice to see his kids every Sunday night. And he always spent holidays with them, too. And she had the nerve to laugh at me. Can you imagine? She said I must be the biggest sucker on the face of the earth.

"By this time, we were both yelling. I'm sure other people in the emergency room heard us. And I stormed out. But not before I said that if the creep wasn't already dying, I'd kill him myself."

"Everybody says things they regret when they're angry," I said. "I certainly do."

"Nobody's going to think you really meant it," Nancy said.

"Why in the world do you think the police are going to arrest you for what you said?" asked Claire. "That's just plain crazy."

"Because there's more," Deanna said in a small voice.

Somehow, I was afraid there would be.

"After I left the hospital," Deanna continued, "I drove around for a while. I was a mess, crying and cursing and screaming. But then, I calmed down. I realized that Will's wife could be lying. No matter what, I had to give Will a chance to explain. That was the only fair thing to do.

"So I went back to the hospital one more time. Will was in the same cubicle, but this time, he was alone. He looked so peaceful lying there. And then I realized that he wasn't breathing. He was dead."

"Didn't anyone from the hospital realize Will had died?" Claire asked. "That makes no sense."

"It may not make sense, but that's the way it happened, Claire," Deanna snapped. "You weren't there. I was. I figured that everyone in the emergency room had heard me threaten Will earlier. I panicked. I'm not proud of myself, but I knew I had to get out of there as fast as I could. Before someone at the hospital blamed me for his death.

"So I ran away."

Chapter 26

Money isn't everything, but it sure keeps the kids in touch.

"I must be missing something," Nancy said. "People die in hospitals every day.

"Well, they do!" she insisted, reiterating her point. "You know I'm right. I don't see how in the world Deanna could possibly think she'd be blamed for Will's death."

It was almost 6:00 on the day of The Longest Hair Appointment Ever, and the Nancy, Claire, and I were huddled together in the parking lot of Crimpers, trying to make some sense of what we'd just been told.

"Keep your voice down, Nancy," I said. "Deanna might hear you. And I, for one, have no desire to continue a conversation with her right now. I just want to go home."

"At least your hair looks nice," Nancy offered.

We could see from our vantage point that Fairport Turnpike was clogged with commuters and traffic was at a standstill.

"It's going to take us a long time to get home," Claire said. "I don't know about the two of you, but I could use a nice glass of white wine."

"Why don't we go to Maria's Trattoria?" Nancy suggested. "We could have dinner there, too. And maybe Mary Alice could catch up to us. She can fill us in on her hot date. It'll make a nice change of conversation. What do you say?"

"It's tempting," I agreed. "But Jim's expecting me home. And

I'm sure Larry's waiting for Claire, too. Neither of us has the flexibility that you do, Nancy. We're married to our husbands twenty-four/seven, not dating them, the way you are yours."

"Oh, for heaven's sake, Carol," Claire said. "This is the twenty-first century. Let's just call Jim and Larry and say we'll be late." She pulled out her phone and punched in numbers.

Nancy and I walked away to give Claire some privacy. It could be a long phone call.

But it wasn't.

"Well, that was easy," Claire said, clicking her phone off and heading in our direction. "Larry was relieved that he didn't have to suffer through the third night of the same tired leftovers. He's going to call Jim and suggest they get together tonight. So we can have a girls' night out."

"Perfect," Nancy said. "I'll text Mary Alice and tell her what we're up to."

"Text? Why not just call her?" I asked.

"I don't want to take a chance on interrupting anything important," Nancy said with a wink. "I'll see you two at Maria's."

Honestly, that Nancy!

"I can't remember the last time we went out to dinner together," I said, sliding into a booth at Maria's Trattoria.

"Try, never," Claire retorted. "We always meet for lunch. So we can hustle right back into the kitchen and get dinner started. Lord forbid that it's late for the guys."

"I keep telling you two that dating your husband instead of living with him is the way to go," Nancy said. "Bob's always on his best behavior these days. And I don't have to pick up his dirty socks off the bedroom floor, either. I call it 'married but dating.' You should try it yourselves."

"Ha!" said Claire. "I don't think so, not for us. Larry and I are too used to each other's foibles by now. We cohabitate just fine, thank you very much."

"It was nice of Maria to put us in this quiet corner," I said, deciding a change of subject was definitely in order. "Although I did feel guilty about her waving us in ahead of everyone else waiting in line for a table."

"Honestly, Carol. Will you ever get over your Catholic guilt?" Claire asked. "For all those other people knew, we had reservations. And Maria always treats us well. Of course, when she was teaching our kids way back when, I never thought we'd become such good friends."

"New career, new life," Nancy said. "I give Maria a lot of credit for what she's accomplished since she retired from teaching."

"So, did Mary Alice text back?" I asked. "Is she going to meet us?"

"I think I see her now," Nancy said, craning her neck in the direction of the front door of the restaurant. "Yep, that's her. And from the big smile on her face, I'd bet that she had a great first date."

Mary Alice was positively glowing. I was glad somebody had a good day today. It certainly wasn't me.

"I hope I didn't make you wait too long," Mary Alice said, sliding into the booth so she faced me. "I came as soon as I could. This is such fun, going out to dinner together. Are we celebrating something special?"

Turning to Nancy, she said, "I bet I know. You sold an expensive property today. That's what we're celebrating, right?"

Nancy shook her head. "From your mouth to God's ears," she said. "Not in today's real estate market. Those expensive houses just sit on the market forever."

"Well, then why are we here at dinnertime?" Mary Alice asked. "Something is definitely up. I can see it on your faces. What have you been up to today? Have I missed anything important?"

We three burst into a chorus of nervous laughter.

"Thanks, I needed that," I said when the laughs trailed off. "Even more than the glass of chardonnay I ordered."

"What in the world are you all laughing about?" Mary Alice asked. Then, looking at me, she said, "Carol, your hair is fabulous. Did you just have it done?"

That provoked another chorus of nervous tittering.

"What did I say that's so funny?" Mary Alice asked. "How long have you been sitting in this booth, and how much wine have you had?"

"It's not what you're thinking, Mary Alice," I said. "No, we haven't been here drinking all afternoon. And, yes, I did have my hair done at Crimpers today."

"And Carol got a lot more than she expected," Nancy chimed in. "Claire and I ended up there, too. And Deanna had more to share with us than what shampoo was best for our hair. A lot more."

"I'll say she did," I said. "Poor Deanna."

"You got that right," Claire said, shaking her head. "What a mess."

Mary Alice looked at all three of us in turn, then burst out laughing. "I know you all so well. You know how gullible I can be. I bet you're all just trying to make me extra curious because I wasn't there, too. Don't think you can fool me. Deanna has never shared anything about her personal life with any of us. Even though we've been going to the salon for years."

"We're not trying to fool you, honestly," I said. "It's just that...."

"It's just that you were all dying of curiosity about my date today, and you decided we should meet for dinner so you could ask me all the details, right?" Mary Alice asked. "Am I right?"

Without waiting for any of us to answer, our shy friend continued, "Well for your information, I had a great time this afternoon. And yes, Isaac and I have made another date for later this week. So there."

"Isaac?"

"That's his name. Isaac Weichert. He's a very nice man."

I have to confess that my insatiable curiosity is on automatic response, no matter what. And Nancy and Claire, although not in my league, are pretty close. So, of course, we spent the next few minutes grilling Mary Alice for more information.

Claire: "Did you meet this guy online?

Mary Alice: "No. I met him at the hospital."

Nancy, sounding hopeful: "Is he a doctor? Oh, that's wonderful!"

Mary Alice: "He's not a doctor."

Me: "Is he a nurse? Physical therapist? Technician?"

Mary Alice, shaking her head and laughing: "This is like 'Twenty Questions.' No, no, and no. Who's up next?"

Claire: "How old is he?"

Mary Alice: "I don't know. I didn't ask him that! But he's... mature."

Me: "Has he ever been married? Is he divorced? Widowed? Come to think of it, can a man be widowed? Maybe he's widowered? Is that a real word?"

Mary Alice, impatiently: "He was divorced. Years ago. And then his ex-wife died. So figure out a word to describe that, Carol. If you can."

Claire: "Does he have any children? Grandchildren?"

Mary Alice: "I don't know. We didn't talk about that."

Nancy: "Does he have his own hair?"

Claire: "Does he have his own teeth?"

Me: "Does he still drive at night?"

That did it.

"Enough, you guys!" Mary Alice said, laughing. "You're all terrible. But I know you won't stop until I give you all the details, so here goes. His name is Isaac Weichert, and he's originally from upstate New York. He moved here ten years ago when he was recruited by a medical research company in New York City. Fairport was an easy commute to his job, and he liked the combination of small town charm and big city access. He took early retirement— he referred to it as a golden parachute—and then decided to try something he's wanted to do all his life. He took courses and now he's a paramedic. So, even though he's not a doctor, Nancy, he is helping people in medical crisis. He works for Fairport Ambulance."

She took a deep breath. "And I really like him. So, please, back off and let me enjoy myself a little. It's been a long time. And being a lonely widow is not the way I want to spend the rest of my life. I want to have some fun."

I couldn't speak for Claire and Nancy. But the reference to Fairport Ambulance immediately conjured up visions of the hospital emergency room. And patients being wheeled in on stretchers, frequently battling life and death issues.

Just like poor Will Finnegan.

Chapter 27

At my age, getting lucky is finding my car in the supermarket parking lot.

One quick look at Claire and Nancy and I could tell they were both picturing the same scene I was.

We three fell silent.

A rare occurrence for us.

Mary Alice, immediately misinterpreting the reason, jumped into and tried to apologize. "What did I say? Oh, gosh. If I hurt your feelings by what I just said, I'm so sorry. I shouldn't have insisted you back off. That was unforgivably rude of me. I know you all love me and only want the best for me. You're trying to protect me from being hurt. And you're right. I haven't had much experience in the dating game lately.

"I didn't mean to come on so strong. It's completely unlike me. I don't know what came over me." Mary Alice's voice trailed off.

I looked at Claire. And nodded my head. *You take it from here. I just can't.*

Bless her heart, she did. And she proved that she hadn't been married to an attorney for all those years for nothing.

Claire laid out what had transpired at the hair salon in an orderly way. Just the facts, ma'am. Very little emotion to color the story.

She was brief, and to the point. Clear about what Deanna had told us about her relationship with Will Finnegan. And how the relationship had ended.

"Wow, Claire," I said, "that was amazing. You should have been a lawyer, yourself. If I'd been the one doing the talking, I would have taken twice as long."

Claire said, "Correction, Carol. If *you* had been the one doing the talking, it would have taken at least four times as long, and you would have interrupted yourself several times to go off on a tangent or two, and probably cried as well."

Well, really! I was insulted, and my face showed it.

"Of course, I say that with love, Carol," Claire said. "But that's just the way you are."

I was mollified. Slightly. Especially since I knew in my heart that what Claire said about me was true. Exaggerated, but true.

"So, Mary Alice," Nancy asked, "what do you think? You work in the hospital. Is there any way that Deanna could be blamed for Will Finnegan's death?"

Mary Alice seemed lost in thought. Then, she said, "There's no way I can answer that question, Nancy. I wasn't there. And it seems pretty farfetched to me. Assuming Deanna told you the whole story, of course. I'd say that she's letting her emotions rule her head. She's grieving, even though she doesn't want to. She feels guilty for what she said, even though she was justified, from what you've told me. And she never had the opportunity to talk to Will, to hear his side of the story."

We were all quiet for a minute, mulling over what Mary Alice had said. Then, she spoke again. "I bet Deanna is suffering from survivor's guilt. I know all about that, believe me. Remember, the morning that Brian died in that car accident years ago, we'd had a terrible argument and he stormed out of the house. Within an hour, I got a call from the police that he was dead. I never got the chance to tell him I was sorry."

Claire covered Mary Alice's hand with her own. "Oh, honey, I'm so sorry. I never expected that telling you about Deanna would bring up all these painful memories."

"It happens when I least expect it, Claire," Mary Alice said, dabbing her leaking eyes with a napkin. "Even after all these years. Don't blame yourself. But at least, because I was Brian's wife, I was able to have a wake and funeral for him. Since Deanna had no legal relationship with Will Finnegan, she couldn't even do that."

I cleared my throat. My turn to speak.

"You're wrong, Mary Alice. Deanna did have a wake for Will. I was there. Sort of."

"What in the world are you talking about?" Nancy asked. "That's not logical at all. How could you be 'sort of' anywhere? You're either there, or you're not."

This from a person who flunked Logic when we were in college. And it's none of your business what my grades were for that same course, so don't bother asking.

"You didn't mention this when we were hashing things out with Deanna," Claire said. "Why not?"

I started to squirm in my seat, even though I had nothing to feel guilty about. But the way Claire asked the question made me uncomfortable.

"I wasn't trying to hide it," I insisted. "Deanna and I had talked about it before you got to the salon. Although I'm still not completely clear on all the details."

Like, most of them.

"And besides, Deanna was doing all the talking when we were together, in case you've forgotten. She needed to unburden herself. So, I kept quiet."

"Okay," Nancy said. "You kept quiet at Crimpers. But now, tell us what happened. And don't leave a single thing out."

As if I would.

"Be brief and stick to the point," Claire said.

As if I wouldn't.

I had a brief flash of how I could shock all three of my best friends by describing the lurid scene at the funeral parlor. Finishing with my discovery of the …um…scissors. But we were in a public place, after all. About to have dinner. And my mother, and the nuns, had raised me with good manners.

Besides, talking about that terrible sight was bound to make me lose control. Something I was determined not to do, if only just this once.

So instead, I motioned for everyone to come a little closer to me. Then, I leaned over and said in a low voice, "Jenny and I went to Will Finnegan's wake to pay our respects because he'd done landscaping work for Jim and me. We got there a little early, and Deanna was just leaving. We didn't get a chance to speak. That's it."

True, yet not, if you get my drift.

Nancy eyed me. "No, that's not it. There's something more

you're not telling us. There has to be. I can tell by the way you didn't look any of us in the eye when you were talking."

I took a sip of water. My eyes filled up. Damn it. Automatic sprinklers, for sure.

"You're right." I glared at Claire. "But *someone* told me to be brief. I'm doing as I was told."

"Oh, for Pete's sake, Carol. Grow up, already," Claire said.

"What else happened," Mary Alice asked. "Something did. And it upset you terribly. Am I right?"

I nodded my head. "It was horrible. We were the first ones to arrive at the funeral home. We sat and waited for a few minutes, but no one else came. So I went up to the casket to say a prayer. There was a…scissors…in Will's chest."

"What?" Nancy shrieked. "That's unbelievable."

"SSSHHH," I said. "Keep your voice down. We don't want everyone to hear what we're talking about."

"Who would do such a thing?" Mary Alice asked.

"Who indeed?" mused Claire. "That's a very good question."

"And then what happened?" Nancy asked.

"I hustled Jenny out of there as fast as I could. But we only got as far as the women's room when a group of people came out of another part of the funeral parlor. Deanna was one of them. I didn't want to talk to her, so we ducked inside the bathroom."

"I don't get it," Mary Alice said. "Do you mean Deanna was there before the wake started? Why?"

"More to the point, why didn't you want to talk to her?" Claire asked, cutting to the chase as usual.

I chose my words carefully. "I can't explain my reaction to seeing Deanna there. It was just a gut response. But now, after hearing about her relationship with Will Finnegan, I'm wondering if maybe there were two wakes for him that night."

"You're losing me, Carol," Nancy said.

I held up my hand. "Just give me a minute to think more about this."

I passed out the menus. "Decide what you want for dinner while I think about this scenario and see if it's possible."

"I don't think I can eat a thing," Nancy said, scanning the menu, no doubt for the most low-fat item on it.

I didn't believe her for a minute. No matter what, Nancy can always eat.

Me, too.

The more I thought about the two-wakes idea, the more it made sense to me. Which explained why Deanna and the folks with her were leaving the funeral home just as the official wake—the one that had been mentioned in Will's newspaper obituary—was about to start.

"I know this sounds nuts," I said, "but I really think I'm right. Deanna must have had an earlier wake, so the friends she and Will had made as a couple could pay their respects. And then there was probably a half hour lapse, so that group could leave and the Finnegan family could come in and have their own wake. And sometime during that half hour, someone…added the scissors."

"Unless," Claire said, her expression thoughtful, "Deanna did it as a parting gesture to the man who had, as the song goes, 'done her wrong.' "

Or perhaps someone who loved Deanna, and who thought she had been treated badly by Will, was the guilty party. Like Deanna's daughter, Lisa. Whom I'd overheard telling her mother that she would do anything to help her.

Don't go down that road, Carol. None of these people suspect Deanna has a daughter. And maybe you misheard. For once, keep your mouth shut.

"This is a somber group of patrons," I heard a familiar voice say. "You're not a good advertisement for my restaurant, that's for sure. I hope the service and the food aren't why you all look so unhappy."

"Oh, no Maria," Mary Alice said. "We haven't even ordered yet."

"Have you been waiting long?" Maria asked. "I'll send a server over to you right away. You're all very good customers, and deserve to be treated well."

"Honestly, Maria," I said, trying to spare the restaurant's serving staff from Maria's wrath, "there's nothing wrong with the service." I had heard horror stories about her temper from my kids when she was a teacher.

"And besides," Nancy put in, "the restaurant's very busy tonight. We don't mind waiting a little while. Especially since it's a rare occurrence that we're out to dinner on our own."

Maria relaxed. A bit.

"Then you must let me send you over a bottle of Prosecco," she said. "To make the waiting more enjoyable. On the house."

Well. Sounded good to me.

Maria snapped her fingers and two servers immediately

responded. "A bottle of Prosecco for my friends," she said. "And when you deliver it, be prepared to take their orders immediately."

Golly, it sure was fun to have friends in high places.

Maria leaned over the booth to continue our conversation. "I have to get back to the kitchen, but before I leave, I feel I have to ask you what's wrong. You all look like you've lost your last friend."

She straightened up. "I'm sorry. It's probably none of my business."

Claire jumped in. "We were talking about the death of someone here in town," she said by way of explanation. "I didn't really know him, but Carol did."

"So I was right, then," Maria said. "You were talking about someone who died. Who was it?"

"He was a local landscaper, and did some work for Jim and me," I said. "His name was Will Finnegan."

I thought I saw a quick flash of recognition on Maria's face. But it was gone in an instant, so perhaps I was wrong.

"I don't think I know the name," she said. "Every death is always sad. Enjoy your Prosecco." And she hightailed it back to her kitchen as fast as she could.

Chapter 28

I had amnesia once. Or, was it twice?

I don't know if it's a sign of age or not, but I have more and more trouble falling asleep at night. Jim's out like the proverbial light within five minutes after he climbs into bed, but not me. I toss and turn, turn and toss. Sometimes for more than an hour.

Hmm. I wonder if that counts as an aerobic exercise. I could be burning fat and not even know it.

Anyway, when I dragged my weary bones to bed that night, I expected to fall asleep immediately. Just this once. I was sure that the combination of the longest, most stressful hair appointment known to womankind, plus the rich food and Prosecco I'd overindulged in at Maria's Trattoria, would send me to dreamland in an instant.

Not that I expected to sleep through the night, mind you. I haven't done that in at least ten years.

Of course, I was the last one in bed. Jim was on the left side— where he always is. The center and right half of the bed had been completely commandeered by two sleeping English cocker spaniels.

It was hard to figure out which of the three was snoring the loudest. And Lucy—who was in my spot—refused to budge. The little stinker.

That'll teach me to stay out so late.

I didn't want to have an argument with Lucy. Especially since I knew I'd lose. And truthfully, I wasn't that sleepy. Darn it.

I turned and made my way, as silently as possible, into the kitchen, so as not to awaken my sleeping prince and his two canine bedmates. Of course Lucy, little dickens that she is, immediately roused herself followed me. For a split second, I debated racing her back to the bedroom. If I got there first, maybe I could jump into bed and she'd have to sleep on her dog bed. For a change.

Of course, she'd probably beat me, and there was no way I was sleeping on her dog bed.

"How about a midnight snack?" I asked my fellow insomniac. "Dog biscuits for you, and a cup of chamomile tea for me. And I'll tell you all about my day. And the World's Longest Hair Appointment."

Lucy wagged her stubby tail. Any sentence that includes the words "dog biscuits" is a guaranteed hit with her.

"It's a deal," I said. "But you have to promise me you won't interrupt while I'm talking.

"Oh, wait a minute. I can't make tea because the kettle will shriek when it comes to a boil. And if I use the microwave to heat the water, it'll ding when it's done. Either way, I'll wake Jim."

I sighed. "Well, I guess I have to settle for a few cookies instead."

See how I justified substituting something fattening for something healthy? Try it for yourself sometime, and you'll find out how easy it is.

Just don't do it right before a cholesterol test.

Lucy and I padded into the family room and settled on the coach, each munching on our respective treats.

"We have to stop this midnight snacking routine," I said. "Your waistline is getting bigger." My dog gave me a dirty look, and I sighed.

"You're right. So is mine. So, do you want to hear about my day?"

Big yawn from my sofa mate.

"Well, tough, because you're going to hear about it, anyway. It's the price you have to pay for your late night snack. And besides, maybe if I talk about everything out loud, it will make more sense to me."

Another yawn. Then, Lucy pulled herself up to a sitting position, facing me, which I took as a sign to go ahead and start talking.

"I'll keep this brief," I promised. "Claire says I take too long to get to the end of a story. Here goes."

I don't plan to go over my day again with you, so I hope you were paying attention while it was happening. There's no quiz, though, so if you weren't, you can always flip back a chapter or two and refresh your memory.

By the time I was reaching the end of my story, I was starting to feel sleepy. Maybe I had discovered a new solution for my insomnia—talking so much that I put myself to sleep.

I yawned, then said to Lucy, "I hope this guy Mary Alice is dating is a good one. She deserves some happiness in her life. She's been alone too long. But you already know that."

I yawned again.

"Oh, there's one more thing I want to tell you before we go to bed, Lucy."

She opened one eye and gave me a sleepy look.

"I'll be quick," I said. "I'm tired now, too. But Nancy had a funny thing happen to her that she shared at the end of dinner. It made all of us laugh, which was a good way to end the meal. It seems that she had an online friend request from someone named Alison Green. She didn't recognize the name, but accepted the request because she's always looking for new real estate clients. You know how she is. Well, you won't believe this. It turns out that Alison Green is a dating site for people to cheat on their spouses. She started getting all sorts of weird e-mails, even though she claims she never officially registered. Isn't that hilarious?"

Lucy got up from the sofa, stretched, then turned to look back at me.

"Okay, I get it," I said. "I agree. It's time to turn in. I just hope we can sneak into the bedroom without waking Jim. Or Ethel."

No worries in that department. They were both deep in slumber, and Ethel had shifted her bed of choice to the official doggie bed in the corner. Leaving more room for me and You Know Who.

But I had the darndest dream when I finally got to sleep. Lucy and Ethel were at the Pray Farm in Rehoboth, MA, where they were born. I always take both dogs there when they need grooming, even though it's a long drive from Fairport. Their mommy-in-chief, Lynn Pray, and daughter Courtney Cherico, were busy clipping their coats and combing them out after their baths.

And what were my two canines doing while they were being beautified? Spilling all the Andrews family secrets to every other canine in the place! In doggie language, of course.

You don't think that's really possible, do you?

Chapter 29

I went to San Francisco and found somebody's heart. Now what?

I'll tell you a secret. I don't wait until New Year's to make resolutions I'll probably break anyway. I make them on a regular basis, so I can break them and not feel an avalanche of guilt on January 2.

The following morning, I decided to try something I'd resolved to do way back in June. Yoga.

Nancy gave me an exercise CD for my birthday—Yoga with Yolanda. My BFF is a real exercise nut, and starts every day with an hour or so of ritual torture at a local fitness center.

She's been on my case to come with her for a long time. I know exercising will do me good. But I also know that I will never stick to a regular routine. I have no self-discipline whatsoever.

You can check that fact out with Jim, should you happen to see him. I'm certain he'll agree.

Anyway, Nancy finally figured out that there was no way I was going to join her, so she gave me this CD. She knows I'm always complaining that I can't turn my neck very well, and assured me that yoga was the answer.

Of course, I hadn't taken the CD out of the plastic wrapper yet. But today was the day. Come on, endorphins! I need you to do your stuff right now!

I loaded the CD into my computer. Yolanda and I had a date.

I could hardly wait to start. I pressed "play."

And the darn phone rang.

Wouldn't you just know it? Here I was, all pumped up to pump iron (well, not really, but close enough), and someone had the nerve to interrupt me.

I considered yelling for Jim to answer it, but then I remembered it was his Fairport Merchants Association morning. He loves going to those weekly meetings so he can pick up some local gossip for the State of the Town column he writes for our weekly newspaper. And also, I was sure, so he could enjoy a high calorie, high cholesterol breakfast without my trying to stop him.

Yolanda would have to wait. I hoped she was patient.

The instant I picked up the phone, I heard a male voice. An angry one.

"Mrs. Andrews? Carol Andrews? Is that you?"

"Who is this?" I demanded, prepared to slam the phone down in the caller's ear.

"This is Detective Paul Wheeler of the Fairport Police. I hear you're up to your old tricks, snooping around something that's none of your business. And you had the nerve to criticize the way I'm handling the Finnegan case. Back off. This is a police matter. Don't interfere. I mean it."

The next thing I heard was the dial tone.

"I have never been so insulted in my life!" I proclaimed to Lucy and Ethel, both of whom looked at me without trying to hide their skepticism.

"You're right," I admitted. "There've been a few other times.

"But the nerve of that…little twerp…to call here first thing in the morning and ream me out like that. Wait'll I tell your brother-in-law what's happened."

Then it occurred to me like a bolt of lightning that, perhaps, that's how Paul found out about my sleuthing in the first place. Maybe Mark said something to Paul directly, or maybe he suggested to his superior at the police department that the Finnegan death should be looked into more closely, beyond what happened at the funeral home.

Either way, I had to be very careful about my next move. I didn't want to antagonize my son-in-law any more than I already had, and I certainly didn't want to try anything that might result in a personal visit from the odious Paul Wheeler.

However, I had information about the Finnegan case that Paul Wheeler probably didn't. Which I should share with him. As any upright citizen would.

But I figured that, assuming he'd even deign to see me, Paul would brush off all my information about the widow and her long-time, stalled romance with her brother-in-law. That was the primary motive for Will's death. I was sure of it. They just got tired of waiting to be together, and hastened things along.

Assuming Will had been murdered. And I had no idea if he actually had.

Hmm. I also knew about Deanna's involvement with Will. And how he had lied to her for years. Did that make her a possible suspect, too?

Oh, God, what if she were guilty? Or, if she didn't actually kill him, what if she'd plunged the scissors into his chest at the funeral home?

Where would I go to have my hair done if Deanna went to prison? I didn't think she'd be able to see clients if she were behind bars.

Stop it, Carol. You're really being ridiculous.

Then, another possible scenario occurred to me. Maybe Will's estranged wife and his brother knocked off Will, and the lovely Lisa, Deanna's daughter, added the scissors to make a point (sorry!) about how badly Will had treated her mother.

Hmm. I liked that one. Except that Deanna's heart would be broken if her daughter were implicated.

Or, maybe Deanna suspected Lisa, and was trying to protect her by taking the blame herself. For Will's death, not the scissors. Or the other way around.

If you're confused, you can imagine how I felt!

I needed to step back and stop thinking about this. Give my mind a chance to de-clutter. Maybe a date with the waiting Yolanda and her yoga CD was the answer.

Nah. Who was I kidding? I was treating myself to some heavy duty retail therapy.

And I'm not going to tell you about that. After all, you might squeal to Jim.

Especially since I don't always shop with coupons.

Chapter 30

Protons have mass? I didn't even know they were Catholic.

"What do you love doing more than anything else in the world?" My Beloved asked me at dinner that night.

Hmm. So many options to choose from.

Or, maybe I was busted! Yes, that must be it. I'd stupidly left evidence of my shopping spree in a place where Jim had found it.

"Is this a loaded question?" I asked, smiling so he'd think that I was joking. Which I most definitely was not.

"Don't be silly, Carol. I have a surprise for you, and you're going to love it. Because it involves something you love to do. And lately, haven't done nearly as often as you used to."

Ah, I got it now. I knew what Jim was up to. I hadn't been married to him all these years without being able to read his mind. Especially when it came to this particular activity.

And the fact that my dear husband still found me attractive after all these years, well, I was a lucky woman.

I gazed at my husband fondly, and replied, "I think I know what you're talking about, Jim. But let's wait until I at least clear up the dinner dishes."

Jim wiggled his eyebrows suggestively. "That's not what I was thinking of, but it's a damn good idea.

"How'd you like to get all gussied up in a fancy dress and go to a dinner dance with me? I'll even wear my tuxedo."

"Why, Jim, I'd love that. When? Where? Are we going to New

York? Oh, how I've missed those black tie events we used to go to before you retired from the agency. This is great!"

I jumped up and planted a big smooch on Jim's cheek.

"Well," Jim hedged, "it's not exactly a New York party. It's more of a New York suburbs party."

My face must have shown my disappointment, because he immediately added, "But it is a chance for us to go out on the town for a night. The town of Fairport, that is. The Fairport Merchants Association is holding a dinner dance next month and the newspaper has bought a table. The editor's given me two tickets. What do you say? Want to be my date?"

"Of course I do," I said. "It sounds like a lot of fun. Where's it being held?"

Then, I had another thought. Why not go for broke? Figuratively speaking.

"You know, Jim, I'll have to buy something new to wear to this dinner dance. I haven't gotten dressed up for a long time."

Jim sighed. "I figured that'd be part of the deal," he said. "Oh, go ahead. I know how you like to shop."

Major understatement. I *love* to shop. Almost more than I like to snoop. I mean, sleuth.

Of course, I've had years of practice to perfect my shopping technique. The sleuthing is a new addition to my repertoire.

"Actually, Jim, this could be helpful to the Merchants Association," I said as the wheels in my brain continued to turn.

"You mean, you'll be helping the bottom lines of stores all over town?" Jim asked with a smile. "That's really noble of you."

"No, silly. That's not what I meant."

Not exactly.

"But you know how you're always after me to go after some freelance writing and editing jobs? Well, how about if I document my shopping in a story for the Fairport Merchants Association? You know, like a promo piece. About all the wonderful stores we have right here in Fairport, so there's no need to go to the mall, or New York City, to find fabulous buys. Does the Association have a marketing person?"

Jim shook his head. "It's an all-volunteer organization, Carol. Individual members do their own marketing. Nobody's ever done it as a group."

"Why, Jim Andrews, I'm surprised at you. After all your years doing public relations in New York. Why haven't you suggested it?"

I was on a roll now. There was no stopping me.

"I'd call it 'Shopping With Carol.' Or maybe 'Carol's Fabulous Finds.' Why, it doesn't have to be just about my shopping for a dress for the dance. I could write a shopping column for the local paper, and feature a different business each week. I bet it'd be a real hit. Why, I could do restaurants, and stores, and beauty salons...."

Wait a minute. I suddenly realized I could include all kinds of local businesses in this kind of column. Even landscaping companies. And nobody would think anything of my showing up and asking nosy questions. It would all be on the up and up.

Brilliant, Carol. One of your best ideas yet.

I'd use researching a shopping column as a cover for my real purpose. Solving the mystery behind Will Finnegan's death.

This time, I ignored the little voice inside my head when it told me in no uncertain terms to let the police do their job. Especially since I knew how helpful I'd been in previous investigations, pointing out little clues that that had been overlooked.

Besides, people talked to me. I was...unthreatening. Nosy, yes. Devious, sometimes. But always unthreatening.

"So, what do you think, Jim?" I asked. "Would your editor go for the idea of my writing a shopping column? It may even boost the paper's advertising revenue. Will you talk to him for me? Or, even better, make an appointment for me to go and talk to him?"

I frowned. "That might be a better idea. I don't want you to be in the middle of this."

Jim laughed. "I've been in the middle of this ever since we said 'I do.' " He held up his hand. "Not that I'm complaining. Life with you is never dull, that's for sure.

"I'll tell you what. Why don't you do a little informal research and put together a sample column for me to bring in to the newspaper? Where would you start? With your shopping for a new dress to wear to the dance? And what about the 'Shop Local' angle? Isn't that the point of your idea?"

"I'd certainly stress 'Shop Local.' But I want the column to appeal to men, too," I said. "So I think it would be better if I started with something more generic than my shopping for a dress."

I thought about my answer for a millisecond.

"Maybe the first column should be about food. And not just Fairport restaurants. Local markets, too. Especially the ones with takeout sections. I'm sure the owners would love some free publicity."

"Sounds like a great start," Jim said. "And an easy sell to my editor. Everyone needs to eat, after all."

The more I thought about this idea, the more excited I became. I realized that I could cleverly work in a few questions about the importance of curb appeal to bring in customers.

Then I'd toss in an innocent question about the importance of patronizing other local businesses.

Like, say, Finnegan's Rakes.

Chapter 31

If the world were a logical place, men would be the ones who ride horses side-saddle.

It didn't work out that easily, of course. Few things that are worthwhile seldom do. Just ask any woman who's in labor at Fairport Hospital, and I'm sure she'll agree with me.

The first thing I did the next morning, at Jim's suggestion—he was the in-house newspaper expert, after all—was to write a quick, one paragraph synopsis of what the column would be about. He called it an "elevator speech," though I had no idea why. Since we don't have an elevator in our antique house.

Once I was satisfied with what I'd written, I decided I was ready to try it out on my first suspect. I mean, subject.

I planned to start with Helen Konisburg from Fancy Francie's, because I figured I could accomplish several things at the same time: column research, sleuthing, and tonight's dinner.

A perfect trifecta!

I practiced my opening lines on the dogs, and we all decided that I should use the subtle approach. It hadn't worked for me with Deanna, but Helen didn't know me nearly as well. And besides, practice makes perfect, right?

So, instead of making an appointment to see Helen, I called the store and placed an order for the special take-out dinner of the day with Cathie, my new telephone friend/culinary consultant. It was beef stroganoff, one of Jim's favorites, so I ordered four portions, two for tonight and two more for leftovers. Which I sincerely hoped I'd have, but with Jim's appetite, that might not happen.

I arranged a pick-up time, and just as Cathie was about to hang up, I said, "Oh, by the way, will Helen be there when I come into the store? I'd like to say a quick hello."

Cathie snorted. "She'll be here. I don't think she ever leaves this place."

Perfect.

I was just congratulating myself on how well I'd pulled that off when my cell phone started to chirp, indicating a text was on the way.

I squinted to read the message. It was from Deanna.

I need u. Can u come 2 Crimpers right now?

Double rats. I wasn't up to more Deanna drama this morning. Although she'd put herself high up on my list of suspects. Truthfully, even higher than Helen K.

Me, by text: *Y?*

Deanna: *Police came 2 talk 2 me. Help!*

Me: *Will be there asap!*

I dashed into the bedroom and headed for the closet, trying to find a pair of clean sweats to put on. No time to beautify myself. This was an emergency.

Lucy followed me into the bedroom and positioned herself in the center of our unmade bed.

"Get off, Lucy," I said. "You know that's not allowed. You have to wait until I pull up the comforter. I don't want dog hairs all over the sheets. That'll make Jim sneeze all night."

My canine companion didn't budge. And gave me an unblinking doggy stare.

I sank down on the bed beside her. "You're right, as usual, Lucy. This is probably all my fault. Paul would never have had the brains to dig a little deeper into the Finnegan case if it weren't for my big mouth. I should have realized that once he started looking, he'd find out about Deanna's relationship with Will Finnegan. What a mess."

Lucy yawned, a sure sign that she was bored. She's heard me blame myself for too many things over the years. Including some that I hadn't even been responsible for.

But maybe this wasn't my fault after all, I thought as I pulled a sweatshirt over my head. I wasn't worried about mussing my hair.

After all, Deanna could fix it in a second. Assuming she would.

"You may have something there," I said to Lucy. "It would have been natural for Paul Wheeler to go back to the funeral home and question the staff. Someone there must have told Paul about the first wake."

I felt better now. A little. I just hoped that Paul wouldn't get around to asking me any more questions about that night. Because I had absolutely no idea what I could say without implicating Deanna. Who had means, motive, and opportunity for both Will's death and the wake incident. In spades. But was she the only one who did?

I sighed. "I guess it's up to me to find out, Lucy," I said. Then, remembering my dream, I added, "You have to doggie swear to keep this to yourself."

A hastily scrawled "Closed until noon" sign had been taped to the Crimpers' front door, and all the window blinds were shut tight. Deanna must have been watching for me, though, because the door flew open before I had a chance to knock.

"I got here as soon as I could," I said. "How are you doing? Was it terrible for you? The questioning, I mean."

"Thanks for coming, Carol," Deanna said. "I was pretty frantic when I sent you that text. I'm doing a little better now."

I followed Deanna to the rear of the shop. "I made a fresh pot of coffee," she said. "Caffeine always helps me think more clearly."

Me, too.

"How do you take it, Carol?" Deanna asked me, handing me a mug. "There's sugar on the shelf, and some milk in the refrigerator. Help yourself."

I was momentarily flummoxed. I couldn't count the number of times Deanna and I had shared coffee over the years. She knew I always drank it black.

Then, I realized that she was stalling for time. So, instead of chastising her for forgetting, I said, "Black is fine. Thanks."

"Why don't you let me style your hair, Carol?" Deanna said as we walked into the main part of the shop. "It looks like it could use a little help."

I sat down in my regular chair at Deanna's station and turned to face her. "Okay, Deanna. Yes, my hair needs some help. But that's not why I'm here, and you know it. Quit stalling. What happened with the police?"

"Do you mind if I fuss with your hair while I talk?" Deanna asked, turning me around so I faced the mirror. "That'll calm me down. Give me something to do with my hands."

"Sure. Now, talk."

"It didn't go at all well," Deanna admitted, misting my hair so she could style it better. "I wasn't expecting a visit from the police. I guess I was naive. After all, the funeral home people would have told them that I'd made arrangements for an earlier wake for Will. My name was bound to come up."

She combed my hair and tskd. "I just did your hair, Carol," she said. "How did it get so messy so fast?"

"I didn't have time to do anything with it this morning," I said. "Because you sent me that urgent text. So I have 'bed head.' "

"That's for sure. Don't worry. I'll fix it.

"Anyway, someone knocked on the shop door around eight this morning. I figured it was one of my clients, on the way to the train, who needed to make an appointment. But instead, it was a police detective. Paul Wheeler. And he proceeded to ask me a whole lot of questions about my relationship with Will Finnegan. What a horrible little man."

"I know Paul," I said. "He's pretty full of himself. Unfortunately, he's my son-in-law's partner on the Fairport police force. I don't know how Mark puts up with him."

"I resented the way he questioned me," Deanna said. "Although I guess it's pretty unusual for someone to have two separate wakes. When he asked me about my relationship with Will, I implied that we'd been good friends for years, and that was the extent of our relationship."

"Oh, Deanna, you never should have done that," I said. "Especially since so many people knew about you and Will. All Paul has to do is talk to one person who came to the first wake, and the truth will come out. And then, he'll want to know why you lied. You've made things even worse for yourself."

"You're right, Carol. And I could tell that Paul didn't believe me. I was stupid."

Deanna took a deep breath. "Then Paul noticed the collection of scissors at my station. I had cleaned them the night before, and didn't have a chance to put them back in my drawer. Paul suggested I could have planted one in Will the night of the wake. Just to make sure that he was really dead.

"I really lost it then. I told Paul that I'd never do anything to hurt Will. I admitted that I loved him. And that we'd been together for years.

"Of course, then Paul wanted to know why I hadn't been honest with him in the first place. At that point, I stopped talking. I said I wasn't answering any more questions without a lawyer present.

"He finally left the shop," Deanna said, "but said he'd be back. I texted you right away. I knew you'd figure out what to do."

"Don't give me too much credit," I said. "It's true that I've pointed the police in the correct direction a few times...." I let my voice trail off, remembering how Paul had told me, in no uncertain terms, to butt out of this investigation. My face burned at the memory.

"I think you really should call a lawyer. Larry McGee, Claire's husband, is a very good one. Even though he's semi-retired, I bet he'd be glad to help you."

Deanna ignored my suggestion.

"Oh, God, Carol, what if Paul finds out that I was also at the hospital the night Will died? And what his wife told me? What a mess."

"Give me a few minutes to think," I said. Or a few days.

I was afraid that Deanna was now numero uno on Paul's short list of suspects. Not for what happened at the wake. But for murder. All thanks to my suggestion that the police take a better look at how Will died.

Me and my big mouth. I said it before any of you could.

"I understand why you're so frightened," I said. "Believe me, I really do. I've been on the receiving end of Paul Wheeler's interrogations, too. It's not a pleasant place to be. Especially if you're innocent."

I glanced up at my favorite hairstylist and confidante. "You are innocent, aren't you? I'm sorry, but I have to ask."

Deanna's face turned stormy. "Of course I'm innocent, Carol. How the hell could you even ask me that?"

"I was sure you were innocent," I said, backpedaling as best I could. "I just wanted to hear you say it. But...."

"But what, Carol? What?"

I cleared my throat. Deanna wasn't going to like this next question.

"What about Lisa?"

"Lisa!" Deanna exploded. "What does she have to do with this?"

"Don't be angry, Deanna," I said, "but I overheard you and she talking the other day. I know she's your daughter."

Deanna stiffened. "I never figured you for an eavesdropper, Carol."

Ha! That surprised me. All my friends know that I'm a shameless eavesdropper.

"Since you're already mad at me," I said, "I might as well go for broke. Was Will Finnegan Lisa's father?"

"No," Deanna spat. "Will wasn't her father. But he was more like a father to Lisa than the rat who is. That's why Lisa was so devastated when she found out how Will had lied to me. But she would never hurt Will. Never."

Deanna paused, then added, "In case you're going to ask me who Lisa's father really is, let's just say he's someone who was in my life years ago, and now he's not. I don't even know if he's still alive. And I don't care."

"Does Paul Wheeler know you have a daughter?" I asked.

"Of course not, Carol. He didn't ask me about my family, and I certainly didn't offer the information on my own. I don't want Lisa involved in this mess."

"Deanna, I understand your desire to protect Lisa. After all, I'm a mom, too. But you have to realize that she's already involved. Especially if she was at the wake with you that afternoon. Which I'm sure she was, so don't deny it."

"I can't believe how hard you're being on me, Carol," Deanna said. "I called you because I thought you were a good friend as well as a client. Someone I could trust to help me. I can see that I was wrong."

Well, that last part made me mad. After all, I'd come flying over to Crimpers as quickly as I could when I got Deanna's text. No matter how inconvenient it was for me. I had a life, too. And important things to do today.

Come to think of it, all the items on today's to-do list involved my investigating the Finnegan death.

Carol, you are such a dope. You have a golden opportunity to ask Deanna some nosy questions, and you're letting it slip by because your feelings are hurt.

"I am your good friend," I said. "I wouldn't have come this morning if I weren't. And it's much better that I'm asking you these questions than the police."

Long silence.

Finally, Deanna said, "You're right. I'm sorry. It's just that...."

"It's just that you're a mother trying to protect her child," I finished for her. "But from what I overheard Lisa say the other day, she wants to protect you, too. So, was Lisa with you at Will Finnegan's wake?"

Deanna nodded. "I called her at school the night Will died, and she came home the next morning."

"And she was with you at the wake?" I asked again. "The entire time?"

"Why, of course she was," Deanna asked. "She sat right next to me."

"What about at the end of the wake?" I asked. "When I got there, Slumber Room A was empty, except for the casket. You and your group had gone into another room, although I didn't figure that part out until later. Lisa didn't leave you for a brief time then, maybe to use the rest room?"

"No," Deanna answered. "We were together the entire time. I swear we were."

I hope it doesn't come to that. In court.

I didn't really say that, of course.

Instead, I asked, "Where's Lisa now?"

"She went back to school yesterday afternoon. I have no intention of telling her about my police interview this morning. It would just upset her."

Deanna gave my hair one last spritz of hairspray. "Done. You look much better now than when you came in."

She gave me a hug. "Thanks for coming over on such short notice this morning. I'm sorry I lost my temper when you asked me about Lisa. I know you're just trying to help me."

"I don't want to alarm you any more than you already are," I said, "but I really think you should talk to a lawyer. Especially if Paul comes back with more questions. You need to protect yourself."

"You don't think that hiring a lawyer will make it seem like I did something criminal?"

I shook my head. "Just talk to Larry. He'll tell you what to do."

"But you'll help me, too, won't you, Carol? It's so much easier talking to you. And I'm sure you'll be the one to get me out of this."

"I'll do my best," I said, not sure exactly what I meant. It was a lame answer, but it seemed to satisfy Deanna.

"There's one more thing I have to show you, Carol." Deanna reached in her pocket and pulled out a cell phone. "This was Will's. He gave it to me in the ambulance, and with everything that happened afterwards, I forgot I had it. . Maybe there's something on it that will help clear this whole thing up. I want you to check the phone and see, Carol. I can't face doing it myself."

Oh, boy.

I had a brief vision of myself, in handcuffs, being hauled in front of a judge by Paul Wheeler, charged with concealing evidence in a crime. And both my favorite son-in-law and my beloved husband reading me the riot act for getting even more involved.

I couldn't do it. I shouldn't do it. I won't do it. I'm going to be sensible for once.

I backed away. "No, Deanna. I can't. You need to turn the phone over to the police right away."

She pressed the phone into my hand. "You have to, Carol. I don't trust anybody else."

I swear, holding that darn phone felt like I was holding a loaded gun.

Then I flashed back to another incident with a cell phone, a few years ago. When Jim had been accused of causing the death of his retirement coach, Davis Rhodes.

He was innocent, of course. I'm sure you already know that.

But someone—not saying who—found my own cell phone in this very hair salon. And mailed it to the police anonymously, to implicate Jim for the crime.

And Deanna helped me prove Jim was innocent. In fact, she gave me the information that cracked my first foray into the sleuthing business.

So, of course, I said, "Okay. I'll check it out for you. But if I find anything on the phone that I think the police should know about, I'm taking it right to the police station. Agreed?"

"Agreed," Deanna said. "And thanks."

I squinted at the cell phone number. "I don't think this is the same number I used when I called Will about landscaping work at our house."

Deanna looked at me like I was the stupidest person in the world. "Of course it isn't, Carol. This is his personal cell phone. I gave it to him last Christmas."

She flushed. "We used it for very private messages."

"And you want me to check it out? Are you absolutely sure?"

I was embarrassed. And darned uncomfortable. I'm nosy, but I'm not a voyeur. Sheesh.

"Please, do this for me, Carol," Deanna insisted. "I'm afraid of what I might find on the phone. Or maybe I should say, who."

Chapter 32

Someone told me once that I was gullible, and I believed him.

"You really are nuts," I told myself as I drove back toward my home. "Do you know what a chance you're taking? You're asking for big trouble. You should have stuck to your principles and refused to take Will's phone from Deanna."

I hate it when I'm mad at myself. I never can figure out which side I'm on.

Of course, I'd be lying if I didn't admit that I was a wee bit curious about what/who was on the late Will Finnegan's private cell phone.

Okay, I was burning with curiosity.

Oh, all right! I cannot tell a lie. I could hardly wait to get home and spend the rest of the morning seeing what secrets it held. And if any of them hinted at why Will's life ended so abruptly.

I turned into my driveway and slammed on my brakes, narrowly missing a car parked smack in front of me, blocking my way to the garage.

I realized Jim must be having a meeting with one of his cronies. The nerve of whomever it was to park that way. I stormed across the back yard, hell bent on chewing him out.

Imagine my shock when, instead of one of Jim's buddies, I found Mary Alice sipping a cup of tea at my kitchen table. Lucy and Ethel were snoozing at her feet.

"Mary Alice," I said, trying not to show my annoyance at the cozy domestic scene, "what are you doing here? And where's Jim?"

To her credit, my friend Mary Alice blushed. "I hope you don't mind my making myself at home, Carol. Jim heard me knocking and suggested I wait for you in the kitchen. I haven't been here very long. He asked me to tell you he'll be home in time for dinner."

Oh, joy.

Then, I took a closer look at my friend. Something was most definitely up.

"Of course, I'm always glad to see you, Mary Alice," I said. "In fact, you're one of the few people I'd allow to see me in this condition. I ran out of the house this morning on an emergency mission. I barely had time to shower."

"At least your hair looks good," Mary Alice said.

"Thanks for the compliment," I said. "But never mind about that. What's up with you? Are you working at the hospital today?"

Mary Alice smiled. I suddenly realized how long it had been since I saw my friend this happy.

"I'm not working today," she said. "In fact, I've decided to take the rest of this week off. I'm lucky that I have the freedom to do that. It's time I had a little fun. That's where you come in."

"I'm flattered that you think I'm such fun to be with," I said, fingering the cell phone that I was sure was burning a hole in my purse. "But this week is kind of jam-packed for me. What did you have in mind?"

"Not the whole week, silly," Mary Alice said. "I just want you to have lunch with me today."

"Well, of course I can do that. You know that I've never turned down a chance to eat out in my whole life. Are Nancy and Claire coming, too?"

Mary Alice shook her head. "No. It's just you, me, and one other person. I want you to meet Isaac Weichert and tell me what you think of him. Because I think he's a really special guy."

Wow. I didn't know what to say.

"I know it's a lot to ask," she said. "Especially on such short notice. But he's asked me to meet him for a late lunch today at Fancy Francie's. That's where a lot of the paramedics go for a quick meal. I really want to go, but I also know that my dating radar is pretty rusty. He seems nice, but I'd be more comfortable if somebody else was there, too. Someone whose opinion I value."

"You flatter me, Mary Alice," I said. "But why me instead of Claire or Nancy?"

"Claire is too critical," Mary Alice said. "I love her dearly, but you know that's true. And Nancy can be such a flirt. You're my friend of choice. So, will you come?"

"Well, sure I will," I said. "But won't Isaac think I'm horning in on your date?"

"I have a plan," Mary Alice said. "I'm supposed to meet him at one-thirty. I figured you could just happen to be there at the same time and I'd introduce you as one of my best friends. And suggest you join us for a quick bite."

"Why, Mary Alice, that's positively devious," I said, laughing. "Your plan sounds like something I'd come up with myself.

"Of course I'll be there."

Fancy Francie's was still busy by the time I arrived at 1:45. I decided to show up a little later than Mary Alice had suggested, to make it seem more like an accidental encounter than the setup it really was.

Instead of scouring the restaurant section for my friend and her lunch date, I kept my eyes straight ahead and headed toward the take-out section.

And also to be sure Helen was around, for future grilling. I mean, chatting. I am a mistress of multitasking when I set my mind to it.

Helen, deep in conversation with another customer, acknowledged my presence with a quick wave.

"I'll talk to you later," I mimed. And she nodded.

"Carol, is that you?" asked Mary Alice from the other side of the store.

I turned around, a phony look of surprise pasted on my face. I'd never win an Oscar for my performance, but hopefully, Isaac wouldn't catch on.

"Why, Mary Alice," I said, "how nice to see you. I'm just here to pick up my take-out order."

"Come say hello," Mary Alice said. She turned to her two companions. "I'd love to have you meet Carol Andrews. She's one of my very closest friends."

When I took a closer look at the table, I really was surprised. It was a table of three: Mary Alice, a man who appeared to be in his late fifties, and a knockout brunette. Both the man and the brunette were wearing uniforms identifying them as paramedics with Fairport Ambulance Services.

"I can just stay a minute," I said.

The man jumped to his feet and pulled out a chair. "Please, sit here. You may have to squeeze in, though. I hope you don't mind. "

I was immediately charmed. Good manners have that effect on me.

"This is Isaac Weichert," Mary Alice said, looking at him fondly. "And his partner, Pam Augustine."

Pam acknowledged me with a quick nod. "Let me move over a little to give you more room," she said. "Put the chair next to me, Isaac."

"I believe we already know each other," Isaac said, once I was comfortably seated. "Although this is the first time we've met face to face."

Huh?

"You and our emergency vehicle had a brief encounter on Fairport Turnpike last week."

I was mortified. Then I noticed that Isaac had a big smile on his face. Was he teasing me?

"You've become something of a legend at the department," he said. "You're the first person to hit one of our vehicles and actually own up to it. I'm happy to meet a person who takes responsibility for her own actions."

"You didn't do any real damage," Pam hastened to assure me.

My cheeks were burning. I felt I had to explain myself.

"I was in a terrible hurry that day," I said. "Of course, I'm always in a hurry. Mary Alice can attest to that."

"No comment," said my friend, trying to keep from laughing. I was positive this wasn't exactly the way she'd expected this accidental/on-purpose meeting to go.

"I was picking up a tray of sandwiches, and I had a devil of a time finding a place to park. I was paying a sympathy call on Will Finnegan's family. He was our landscaper, and he died very suddenly a few days before."

I thought I felt a tiny movement to my immediate left. But when

I snuck a quick glance at Pam, her face betrayed nothing.

Don't see suspects everywhere, Carol. You have enough to concentrate on already.

I looked at my watch, then at Mary Alice. "I'm really sorry, but I have to talk to Helen about my order."

"Can't you stay and have something to eat with us?" Mary Alice said. "You just got here."

At that moment, Pam's beeper went off. "I guess we have to leave, too. We're on call. Come on, Isaac. Let's go."

Mary Alice tried not to look disappointed. "Of course. I understand."

"This wasn't much of a lunch date," Isaac said. "How about if I make it up to you tomorrow? It's my day off."

"That would be wonderful," Mary Alice said, beaming.

Just then, a brilliant idea popped into my head. "Why don't you two come for dinner tomorrow night? Jim would love to meet you, Isaac." *Once I tell him who you are.*

Then I realized my gaffe. "I'm sorry, Pam. You're welcome, too. If you're free."

"Four's company, five's a crowd, Carol," Pam said. "But thanks, anyway."

"I'd love to come, Carol, if it's all right with Isaac," Mary Alice said. "I can tell you from personal experience that a home-cooked meal at the Andrews home is always a treat."

"Sounds great," said Isaac. "I haven't had a real home-cooked meal in a long time."

Neither has Jim. I didn't really say that, of course.

"Then it's all settled," I said. "Be at our house at six o'clock. Mary Alice knows the address. Oh, and Isaac, there's one condition that'll guarantee you second helpings. No mention of our vehicle close encounter to my husband, Okay?"

Isaac laughed. "It's a deal."

We all said our goodbyes, Mary Alice mouthing, "I'll call you later." I nodded, then headed in the direction of my next quarry: Helen Konisburg.

But she was nowhere to be seen. Like Elvis, she apparently had left the building.

Chapter 33

Teach a child to be polite and courteous, and when he grows up, he'll never be able to merge his car onto the freeway.

After I had carefully tucked four containers of Fancy Francie's beef stroganoff in my insulated tote bag for safekeeping—I do try to plan ahead whenever possible—I sat in my car and, lacking Lucy and Ethel to talk to, had an in-depth conversation with myself.

I did get a few funny looks from some passersby, but I ignored them.

The clerk who waited on me explained that Helen had an emergency dental appointment. Which sounded fishy to me. Especially since she seemed perfectly fine when she was helping other customers.

No matter what, unless I got the name of Helen's dentist and followed her there—even I drew the line at that—my so-called sleuthing trip to Fancy Francie's was a fizzle.

Tomorrow, I reminded myself, was another day. And I now had two more people coming for dinner, thanks to a combination of perfect hostess skills and a big mouth.

I drummed my fingers on the steering wheel. Who else could I talk to about Will Finnegan this afternoon? Or maybe I should just find a safe place to hide out for a while and sneak a peek at Will's cell phone, which now rested quietly in my car's glove compartment.

My stomach began to growl, a reminder that I never did have lunch after all.

And then, I came up with the perfect solution to satisfy my growling stomach and insatiable curiosity. I pointed the car in the direction of Maria's Trattoria.

One thing I'll say about Maria's. The heavenly aromas that engulf me the instant I walk in the door are guaranteed to pack on a pound or two. But who cares? Not me.

It was too early for dinner, but a perfect time to have a quick bite of whatever the lunch special had been. Assuming there was any left.

I caught sight of Maria in her favorite spot—the open kitchen, where she can not only cook up a storm but keep an eye on how the restaurant patrons are being taken care of.

Maria saw me and held up a plate and fork. I nodded. Boy, she sure knows me well.

In no time flat, she had filled the plate with a sampling of Italian delicacies—I won't tell you which ones because I don't want you to get jealous—and directed me to the booth nearest the kitchen.

"I'd say 'mangia' to you, Carol, but I know I don't have to," Maria said, laughing. "That's one thing I can always count on with you."

Maria took a seat opposite me, then said, "Thank goodness you came in when you did. I needed to sit down for a minute. I'm really going to have to break down and replace the floor in the kitchen. That tile is murder on the feet."

She leaned a little closer. "There's something I wanted to talk to you about. I was hesitant before, but your coming here alone this afternoon has made up my mind."

I looked at her and raised my eyebrows. It was the best I could do—my mouth was full of yummy food.

"It's about Will Finnegan," Maria said. "You mentioned him when you were in here for dinner the other night. I know you saw me react when you said his name. In fact, I'm surprised it took you so long to come back and talk to me."

I could have taken offense at the implied criticism, but Maria has been an occasional part of my sleuthing team for a while. And, as I said before, she knows me very well.

"You know I'm not one to spread gossip, Carol," Maria continued in a low voice.

I nodded. Maria repeated information on a need-to-know basis. Which, as I've explained to Jim, time and again, is not the same thing as gossiping. He still doesn't get the difference. But then, he is a man.

"I know it's not right to speak ill of the dead. But Will Finnegan was a real slick operator. He came in here at least once a week and usually met a different woman. They were very cozy, if you know what I mean. And always left together, sometimes in a real hurry." Maria waggled her eyebrows in case I didn't get her meaning.

"He always ordered the same meal. Veal Marsala. And at least one bottle of Pinot Grigio.

"I'm no prude, and the whole thing fascinated me." Maria laughed self-consciously. "Maybe I read too many romance novels.

"Anyway, I confess that I asked the servers to report back on whatever snippets of the conversation they could hear, without being too obvious that they were eavesdropping. It was the same thing every time. Will told the woman that she was his soul mate, and he'd been waiting for her all his life. And he wanted to show her how much he loved her. What bunk. But it always worked."

I was so fascinated by what Maria was saying that I actually put my fork down and gave her my undivided attention. Something I never do.

"I began to notice that there was a regular rotation of women," Maria continued. "The same ones began to reappear. And on the same day of the week that they had been in the previous time. I couldn't figure it out. But maybe you can. If you're interested, that is."

Boy, was I!

"As a matter of fact," I said, "a dear friend has asked me to look into Will Finnegan's sudden death. I assume you heard what happened the night of his wake?"

Maria nodded. She looked thoughtful, then added, "After being in a classroom for years, and now running a restaurant, I'm pretty good at reading people. That Will Finnegan may have been as phony as a three-dollar bill, but he was charming and very good looking. If he turned all that charisma in my direction, I probably would have fallen for it, too. I bet he had a little black book filled with girlfriends' names."

Or, maybe, a cell phone.

So you can imagine my surprise when I finally smuggled Will's phone into the house, locked myself in the guest bathroom, and checked out his contact list and call log.

The only call that showed up was the one Deanna had made to his wife the night Will died.

And phone's contact list only listed one name: Deanna's.

Chapter 34

Experience is the thing you have left when everything else is gone.

"I may be temporarily sidetracked," I announced to Lucy and Ethel the next morning, "but I'm not finished yet. Something's definitely up with Will Finnegan's death. And I'm going to figure out what it is. Just as soon as I figure out what to cook for dinner tonight. We're having company, in case I didn't tell you that last night."

"You didn't tell me that, either, Carol," said Jim, strolling into the kitchen fresh from his shower. "I finally figured out that the best way I can find out what's happening in the house is to ask Lucy and Ethel. Because you tell them everything."

He wrapped his arms around me and gave me a quick smooch.

"You smell good," I said. "I like that new aftershave you're wearing." I turned around to face my husband. "I haven't had a chance to fill you in yet on what's new with Mary Alice. She has a new male friend, Isaac Weichert. I met him yesterday, and ended up inviting them both to dinner tonight. He seems really nice, but I wanted you to check him out, too. You know we have to protect Mary Alice. I don't want her to be hurt again, after all she's been through. And she admits that she's a novice at the dating game. Your opinion is important."

Jim gave me a cheeky grin. "It's nice to know that my opinion is still important after all these years. So, what are we having for dinner?"

I frowned. "Beats me. Something easy to make, and delicious. I haven't figured that part out yet. But I will."

"Why don't you check out that new cooking show with Chef Paulette for ideas?" Jim suggested. "Everything she makes is with natural ingredients. I heard about it at the Business Association breakfast. I think the show is called *Love On A Plate*. It's on two mornings a week at ten o'clock." He frowned. "But I can't remember which mornings."

Isn't that just like a man? Sharing all the details, except the most crucial one.

"I'll look for it," I promised. After all, Jim did remember the name of the television show. He got definite points for that. And maybe Chef Paulette did catering. Like, for tonight.

No, Carol, tonight is all on you.

Then I had one of my truly terrific ideas. With a slight ulterior motive, which should come as no surprise to any of you.

"How about if we make this dinner a real party?" I said. " Let's invite Jenny and Mark to dinner tonight, too. Hopefully, Mark isn't working. I miss her. I mean, them." I tried not to let my voice tremble when I said the last part.

Which Jim immediately picked up on.

"You can't expect Jenny to call you every day and fill you in on her life, Carol," he said. "She's not a little girl any more. She's all grown up, and her primary priorities in life are her husband and her teaching career."

"Well, I know that," I snapped back. But I was worried that Jenny, and especially Mark, were mad at me for being critical of Paul Wheeler's investigative prowess. Especially in case that would be added to my list of sins and deny me babysitting rights for my hopefully to-be-born grandchildren.

I held out the phone. "Here, you call her."

"You really are the limit, Carol," he said. "I'll do it right now." And he padded into the family room to make the call.

I tried not to overhear. Honestly, I did. But I was delighted when I heard Jim say, "I'm not sure what time, Jenny. Let me ask your mom. Hang on."

In an instant, I was by his side and grabbed the phone.

"Hi, honey. It's just an informal meal so we can get to know the new man Mary Alice is dating. I already met him at lunch yesterday, and he seems very nice. I wanted Dad to meet him, too. And then I remembered how special your relationship with Mary Alice is, and wondered if you and Mark would like to come. I'm planning to serve around six o'clock."

"I'd love to come, Mom," Jenny said. "But I'll have to text Mark and see what his schedule is. He's been up to his eyeballs with all those house break-ins. Have you read about them in the paper? All upscale houses, some north of the Merritt Parkway, and more close to the beach. Mark says there doesn't seem to be any pattern to the break-ins, and because so many of the homes are owned by some of Fairport's movers and shakers, there's a lot of pressure from the first selectman and the police chief to get the case solved."

"I hope you both can come, sweetie," I said. "Don't bother letting me know. Just show up at six. Oh, and Jenny...."

"Yes, Mom?"

"If you want to bring something for dessert, that'd be great."

Jenny laughed. "I'll bring something extra fattening. But I promise I'll take all the calories out before I get there."

"Jenny will be here for dinner," I said to Jim as I handed him back the phone. "But Mark may be working. And she'll bring dessert. But I still have to figure out what to serve for the main course."

"How about if I take care of that, Carol?" my husband asked.

I laughed. "I know you'll take care of the 'eating' part. It's the 'cooking' part I'm talking about."

"That's what I'm talking about, too, smarty," Jim said. "Since you want me to get to know Isaac better, how about if we do something on the new gas grill?"

I was absolutely shocked. But not for long.

"Do you mean you'll take over cooking the whole meal?"

"Not the whole meal," Jim said. "How about if you take care of appetizers and any side dishes, and I take care of the rest. How does a nice London Broil sound?"

"It sounds great, Jim. I could do baked potatoes, and make a big salad. And a cheese and cracker tray. Maybe some shrimp cocktail."

"I'll even go shopping and get the beef," Jim said. He mentioned a local specialty shop whose meat prices were so high that I never dared cross its threshold. Especially after Jim retired.

"You're kidding. It's so expensive. You'd shop there?"

"Of course. The store is part of the Business Association, and give a member discount."

I should have known there'd be a discount involved.

I gave my hero a big smooch. "This dinner will be a piece of cake!"

"Not so fast, Carol," Jim said.

Uh oh. I knew there had to be a catch to this.

"You have to promise me that you will not, under any circumstances, bring up Will Finnegan's death tonight. Remember the trouble you caused the last time Jenny and Mark were here. Maybe that's why we haven't heard from them for a while. Is it a deal?"

Rats. Well, what could I do?

"It's a deal, Jim," I said. *A really, really rotten deal.*

I didn't say that last part. Of course.

Chapter 35

I serve three meals: frozen, microwave and take-out

My day had suddenly opened up, thanks to Jim. I mean, how long does it take to throw a salad together and prep potatoes for baking? Even I can handle those chores in about fifteen minutes. And if I were really clever, I might be able to talk Jim into roasting the potatoes on the grill, along with the meat.

Of course, I did have to give the house a cursory cleaning. A lick and a promise, as my late mother used to say.

I decided that house cleaning should be first on my to-do list. Cleaning is so mindless that, on the rare occasions I do it, I use the time to figure out solutions to any problems I may be wrestling with at that particular moment.

Plus, cleaning is a form of exercise, right? So it burns calories. Gotta love that bonus. Maybe I should attempt it more often.

Nah.

I started by doing my least favorite household chore—cleaning the bathrooms. I had the whole day to sleuth around, and I better not waste it. Especially since my dear husband had laid down the law to me that I was not to bring up the Will Finnegan death at dinner tonight.

The cell phone Deanna had given me turned out to be a dead end, pardon the pun. I could send her a quick text and tell her that, but if she were busy with customers, I figured it was best to leave her alone.

Jim's mention of the Fairport Business Association brought me back to my original plan, interviewing local merchants on my suspect list for a possible newspaper column. I had no desire to go back to Fancy Francie's again this soon, although I still hadn't figured out why Helen K. had made such a speedy exit yesterday.

I was using glass cleaner on the faucets in the guest bathroom—who knew they could be so shiny?—when it suddenly occurred to me where I should start my interviews. The single place in town that every person will have to visit, eventually.

Mallory and Mallory Funeral Home.

"I'm Carol Andrews," I said to the young woman who greeted me. "I guess I should have called ahead for an appointment."

I recognized the woman right away from the night of Will Finnegan's wake. But I decided not to mention that.

"That's perfectly all right, Mrs. Andrews," the woman said, ushering me into what appeared to be her office. "We're used to people arriving in moments of crisis, without phoning ahead first. In fact, we expect it.

"I'm Melinda Mallory. Please accept my sincere sympathy on your loss. We'll try to make this experience as easy as possible for you and your family."

That threw me completely off. In fact, for just a tiny minute, my eyes filled with tears. Because I realized it was only a matter of time before I would be at Mallory and Mallory making final arrangements for, well, you know. Or, he would be, for me.

"I'm not here to make final arrangements for anyone," I said. "I apologize. I should have made that clear."

Melinda nodded. "I understand. I can see that you're a person who plans ahead." She reached in her desk drawer and pulled out some brochures.

"This is basic information on all the services we provide. It's very common for people your age to make arrangements in advance for their last journey. In fact, some people even ask for music and dancing. A farewell party, if you will. It's a little unusual, but we have done it."

Well! I tried not to be offended by Melinda's remark about "people my age." It wasn't easy.

But I certainly was intrigued by the idea of a farewell party instead of a memorial service. Sort of a last sock hop, if you're old enough to get that reference. I filed that idea away, for now, and got down to business.

I whipped out my reporter's notebook (I'm old-fashioned) and said, "That's very interesting, Melinda. I'll add that to my notes. I'm here to interview you for a new column I'm writing for the local newspaper."

Melinda gave me a huge smile, probably at the thought of all that free publicity. "Oh, that's wonderful. Could you wait until I call my father? I know he'd be thrilled to be part of this story, and he is the founder and guiding light behind our business."

I shook my head. "I'm sorry, Melinda, but my editor has given me a tight deadline to hand in this column. I need to wrap this up as soon as possible."

I reached for the brochures and pretended to look at them. "Of course, I'll take these with me. For background information. But I'm very intrigued by what you said about unusual funeral arrangements. You mentioned farewell parties, I believe. How many of those have you done?"

Melinda shifted in her chair. "Only two, in the five years I've been here. I'd appreciate it if you wouldn't include that kind of information in your column. We don't want to get the wrong kind of reputation in town. We are, after all, a traditional funeral home offering traditional services for the deceased. But if a client requests something a little unusual, well, we can do that. I hope you understand what I mean."

"Of course," I said. "But I wonder if you could tell me, just between us, if you've ever had a request for two different services for the same person." I laughed at my own silly question. "I read a lot of romance novels, and I've always wanted to know what would happen if a person dies, and both the widow and the mistress want separate services. Has that ever happened here?"

I raised my pen expectantly and watched Melinda's reaction. Her face was flushed.

"This is strictly off the record, of course," I assured her. "I didn't mean to upset you."

"As a matter of fact," Melinda said slowly, "we did have a request exactly like that recently. For Will Finnegan."

Was it my imagination that Melissa's voice trembled a bit when she said Will's name?

"We had to allow at least thirty minutes between the first wake and the second, so all the guests from the first wake could leave without being seen. The girlfriend didn't want the widow to know what was going on. And since she was paying us, too, we had to do what she asked."

Bingo! Thirty minutes was plenty of time for some unknown person to slip into Slumber Room A and plant the scissors in the guest of honor's chest.

"But please, don't mention that in your column, either."

I made a zipping motion across my lips. "I won't."

After a few more minutes of lame questions, and a tour of the funeral home, including a side trip to the room where all the different styles of caskets were housed, I couldn't wait to get out of there.

But then, I had another brilliant idea. "You've been so helpful, Melinda. I wonder if you'd mind if I took your picture. For the newspaper. I'm not sure if we'll have room for it," (or if the column will ever run at all) "but I'd rather have one. Is that all right?"

Melinda tried not to look pleased. But she fluffed out her hair and said, "Of course."

I hadn't planned to take a picture. But it had suddenly occurred to me that Maria might be able to identify Will's regular dinner dates at the restaurant. And Melinda did fit the general profile—she was an attractive woman. A little young for Will, in my opinion, but if you know me well, you know that I'm never judgmental.

In the push of a button on my phone, I had my picture. And I was outta there. With more information than I ever wanted to know about planning a funeral.

I sat in the funeral home parking lot and made some notes. I tried to write legibly, because sometimes even I can't make out my scribbles.

What were the most important things I learned? The Finnegan family did not know about the first wake. The funeral home cooperated in keeping the two sets of mourners separate. There was a half hour break between the two wakes—plenty of time for someone to slip in and plant the scissors. But where did the scissors come from? Did someone from the first wake hang around? Deanna? Lisa? Unknown person? Or did someone come to the second wake extra early and do the deed?

But Jenny and I were early, and we hadn't seen anyone in Slumber Room A except the guest of honor. Unless the person planted the scissors, and then hid.

AARRGH. I was making myself nuts, and my notepad was now a mass of illegible scrawls.

And what about Melinda Mallory? Did she know Will? Did she have a romantic relationship with him? I put a big red circle around that question.

Lots to ponder. More questions than answers.

I sighed, then put my car in gear and headed for my next stop, the grocery store. I had a dinner party happening tonight, and the guests were arriving in less than four hours.

Carol Andrews, Super Sleuth, would have to go on temporary hiatus, replaced by the rarely seen Carol Andrews, Domestic Diva.

Chapter 36

I don't trust anyone under fifty.

"This is so nice, Carol," Mary Alice said. "The men look like they're getting along very well."

I gazed out my kitchen window at the three chefs. "There's nothing like standing outside around a gas grill watching a piece of meat cook to form lifelong friendships," I said, laughing.

"Especially if they all have their hands in their pockets," my daughter added. "I always wondered why they do that."

"In this case, it's probably to keep their hands warm," I said. "You know how guys are. They never admit that they're cold."

I handed Mary Alice a stack of my second-best china. "Your choice on where to set the table. We can eat supper in the kitchen, or step it up and eat in the dining room."

"I think a barbecue calls for eating in the kitchen," she said. "It's more casual."

Then, to my complete amazement, Mary Alice put down the plates and gave me a big hug. "You can't know how much this means to me, Carol," she said.

I was confused. "It's just an informal supper, Mary Alice. We're glad to have you and Isaac come. Besides, you've had supper here many times over the years. You know you're always welcome, no matter how meager the menu may be."

"You don't understand, Carol. This is the first time since Brian died that I've been here as part of a couple. Just think how long that's been. This night is very important to me. I feel like I'm finally closing the chapter on the sad part of my life, and starting a brand new, happy one."

Impulsively, my daughter threw her arms around Mary Alice and me. "You're like another mom to me, Mary Alice," Jenny said. "I'm honored to be part of this night."

I wiped my eyes with my apron—I do keep one around for appearances only. "I'm such a jerk," I said. "I never realized everything you've been going through all these years."

"How could you, Carol?" Mary Alice replied. "You have all this," and she gestured around my kitchen, including my beautiful daughter. "I've had a good life, all things considered. It's only recently that I realized how much I've missed being part of a couple."

She picked up the plates and headed toward the table.

Jenny and I made eye contact, and I knew she was thinking the same thing I was. Isaac Weichert better not break Mary Alice's heart, or he'd have us to answer to.

A few more minutes and the table was set, the vegetables were ready, the rolls were piping hot, and the salad was tossed. Everything was done, except for the main course.

My cell phone beeped, indicating an incoming text. It was from Jim.

"For God's sake, Carol, open the kitchen door. U locked us out!" Ooops.

"A person can't be too careful these days, Jim," I said as the chefs trooped into the kitchen. "But I guess it's safe to let you three inside. Especially since you have the main course. And we three females are starving."

"Thanks for not asking me for a password," Jim said, heading toward the counter with the platter of meat. "We've been knocking on the door for five minutes. Didn't you hear us?"

"We were talking, Dad," Jenny said. "I hadn't seen Mary Alice for a long time, and we had lots to catch up on."

She gave her husband an affectionate hug. "Were you a big help out there, Mark? Did Dad share all his grilling secrets with you?"

Mark laughed. "I don't think I'm a candidate for any top chef award. Not yet, anyway."

"Practice makes perfect," my daughter said. "And I'll be glad to give you all the practice time in the kitchen you want."

"Isaac was the expert," Jim said, clapping our visitor on the back. "He gave me some new grilling tips. And I thought I knew everything."

You always think you know everything, dear.

I didn't really say that, of course.

Isaac blushed. I always think that's a charming thing for a man to do. It shows he's not ashamed to show his emotions. Or something.

"I had lots of practice back in the day," he said, pulling out a chair for Mary Alice. I noticed that he sat right beside her.

"I'd like to propose a toast," Jim said, placing the platter in front of him so he could serve everyone. "To old friends, new friends, and family, the ones who are here tonight, and the ones who are far away. Cheers."

Jim's toast made me miss our son so much that I felt an ache in my heart. Darn that Mike anyway, moving so far away. I made a mental note to text him later tonight and find out what was going on in his life. And tell him what was going on in ours.

Hmm. Mike was always good with Internet sleuthing. Now, that was a really good idea. I could contact my darling son, check up on him (not that I expected him to tell me much, but I have learned to read between the lines of his brief messages), and give him a new assignment—finding out all he could about Will Finnegan.

I was so lost in thought that I jumped when I heard Jim say, "Earth to Carol. Would you pass me your plate, please? Unless you don't want to eat any of the beef we slaved over for you."

"I was thinking about Mike," I said defensively. "Mike's our son," I explained to Isaac. "He lives in Miami now, and we don't get to see him very often."

I suddenly realized how awkward this dinner could be for Isaac. He barely knew us—well, he knew Mary Alice a little better. I needed to make more of an effort to include him in the dinner table chatter.

I reached across the table and patted Mark's hand. "But Mark's like another son to us, Isaac. He has been since he was a little boy. And now, he's officially part of the family."

"Something Carol had been praying for, for years," Jim added.

I shot him a look which Jim, of course, ignored.

Isaac saw an opening and jumped into the conversation. "So, what do you do, Mark? Do you work here in Fairport? We never got around to talking about that when we were outside."

"He's a detective on the Fairport police force," Jenny said

179

proudly. "And I'm so happy that he's off duty tonight and was able to come to dinner. I haven't seen much of my husband lately." She gave him a loving look. "And I've missed him."

Mark matched his wife's look with one of his own. Ah, young love. There's nothing like it.

"I don't want to bore you talking about my job," Mark said.

Which tipped me off right away that he was working on a very important case. Then I remembered—the burglaries.

Since Mark already knew how nosy I was, I figured it wouldn't hurt if I asked him a little about his current case. Men usually like to talk about their work, right? As long as it isn't confidential information.

That never stops me, of course.

"How are you coming with the break-ins, Mark?" I asked, passing him the salad. "I saw an article on the front page of this week's *Fairport News* asking for the public's help. The photos of the stolen jewelry were incredible. I still can't believe people around here have so much money. And what they choose to spend it on.

"Unless you can't talk about the case." I looked at him questioningly.

Mark ran his hand through his hair in what I recognized as a gesture of frustration. "Normally, I don't talk about what I'm working on. But the chief decided we'd never get anywhere solving these burglaries without the public's help.

"The main problem seems to be that the houses being burglarized are second homes. So the owners aren't there on a regular basis. Sometimes, the thefts aren't discovered until months after they happened. By that time, the pieces have been fenced or pawned. There's a lot of pressure to solve this case."

He looked at Jenny. "Sorry if it's meant that I haven't been home too much these days. I promise, I'll make it up to you when the case is solved. Because it will be. Eventually."

"I often thought about being a policeman," Isaac said. Mary Alice looked surprised. "You never mentioned that."

Then, she looked embarrassed. "Not that you had to, of course."

"I guess the subject hadn't come up yet," Isaac said. "Anyway, I signed up for the Citizens Police Academy to learn a little more about how the department works. At my stage of life, it's too late to make a radical career change. But detective work has always fascinated me."

Me, too.

"Isaac is a paramedic with Fairport Ambulance," I said.

I suddenly realized I was treading on dangerous ground. What if Isaac inadvertently mentioned our vehicle encounter?

So I switched gears. "Tell me a little more about the Citizens Police Academy," I said. "I've seen it advertised in the local paper, but I really don't know much about it."

"It's an opportunity for Fairport citizens to see all the aspects of police work from the inside," Mark explained.

"You're not kidding," Isaac said with a laugh. "We even got to sit in one of the holding cells at the station. Of course, the door wasn't locked. But it was still an experience I'd rather not repeat."

"Students also get to go along with a policeman on his regular shift," Mark continued.

"Or her shift," Jenny put in.

"Correction duly noted," Mark said. "That's called a ride-along."

"I did that, too," Isaac said. "That was some night."

"What do you mean?" Mary Alice asked. "Was it dangerous?"

"Oh, no," Isaac said. "I wouldn't call it dangerous. Just an unusual experience. Even for me. And in my line of work, I thought I'd seen almost everything."

"Don't keep us in suspense," I said. "What happened?"

"Well, I was on the ride-along with Paul Wheeler."

"What a coincidence," Mark said. "He's my partner."

He's my nemesis.

I didn't say that out loud, of course.

"After we cruised around town for a while," Isaac continued, "a call came in from the police dispatcher about something weird that had happened at Mallory and Mallory Funeral Home. Since we were in the area, Paul radioed that he'd check it out.

"I stayed in the patrol car while Paul went inside. He was back in a few minutes and told me what had happened. There was a scissors in the chest of the deceased."

I kept my eyes riveted on my dinner plate. I was afraid to make eye contact with anyone. Even though this conversation was not my doing.

"Then what happened?" Mary Alice asked. "Did you go inside?"

"Not right away," Isaac said. "Paul ordered me to stay put while he conducted a preliminary investigation. I stayed outside for about fifteen minutes, and then I figured it couldn't hurt anyone if I just went inside the front door and listened to what was being said. After all, interrogating possible witnesses is an important part of police work, right?"

He directed the last remark at my son-in-law, who, so far, had said nothing.

"I stayed out of the way. But when I saw the name of the deceased, I couldn't believe it. My partner, Pam Augustine, and I were the paramedics who answered Will Finnegan's nine-one-one call and took him to Fairport Hospital. I really thought he was going to make it."

Isaac shook his head. "Someone must have really hated him, to do something as vicious as that to the poor guy after he was already dead."

I snuck a quick look at Jim, whose face was like a thundercloud.

I shrugged and telegraphed, *Don't blame me. I didn't bring up Will Finnegan.*

Jenny's face mirrored mine—complete surprise. Mine, of course, also had a huge dose of curiosity—all right, nosiness— thrown in.

And Mark, well, Mark had changed his expression from loving husband and son-in-law to that of Detective Mark Anderson of the Fairport Police.

I opened my mouth, but shut it immediately. I had a million questions I wanted to ask Isaac, but I didn't dare. Mark was in charge now.

Mark cleared his throat, then asked, "So, Isaac, what happened then?"

"I went home," Isaac said. "Paul finally noticed me and told me he was going to be interviewing people for quite a while. I asked if I could stay and listen, and he said no, that it wasn't proper police procedure, and he always made sure to do everything by the book. He suggested that I just go home. So, that's what I did."

"And did you tell Paul that you were one of the paramedics who responded to the Finnegan nine-one-one call?"

Isaac seemed surprised at the question. "Why, no, I didn't. It never even occurred to me that I should. Why? Is that important?"

Mark pushed back his chair and got to his feet. "I can't say if it's important or not. But it's information that the police didn't have before, and may help in the investigations. Would you mind coming with me to police headquarters now so you can make an official statement?"

"Why, of course. I'd be glad to." Isaac looked at Mary Alice. "If you don't mind. I don't want you to think that I'm trying to end our date early."

"Don't worry," Mary Alice said with a smile. "That thought never crossed my mind."

I couldn't hold my mouth still any longer. "Mark, one question, please. You said 'investigations.' What did you mean by that? Is there more than one?'

"I should have known you'd pick up on that, Carol," Mark said. "But since you asked, and not to be repeated," he looked at me sternly, "the police are now investigating two different aspects to Will Finnegan's death. The attack in the funeral home. And his sudden death. It's possible that he did not die of natural causes."

Mark shook his finger at me. "But this is none of your business, Carol. I know Paul has already called and told you to stay out of it. See that you do."

I nodded my head. "Of course, Mark." I gave him my most innocent look. "Cross my heart."

For once, I was telling the complete truth.

I had no reason to get involved with any police investigation. I had my own investigation to pursue.

And we'd see who cracked the case first.

Chapter 37

One nice thing about egotists: they don't talk about other people.

"I'll finish cleaning up, Jim," I said. "You must be exhausted after all those hours standing in front of a gas grill."

My hubby gave me a playful swat on my keester with a damp dish towel. "Very funny. I get your message, loud and clear. You womenfolk not only plan the meal, shop for the ingredients, and cook the meal, but then you magically make the kitchen sparkle. All before you go to bed. And without breaking a sweat. Whereas we guys are mere mortals, destined to only do one task, and then collapse."

Close, but not quite what I was getting at.

"You forgot one important thing," I said to Jim. "We accomplish this Herculean task every single day, without any applause from our captive audience. And without complaining."

"I get it. I get it," Jim said, laughing. "You are a domestic goddess beyond compare. And I am very grateful for the manner in which you have kept my castle for the last several decades." He gave me a mock bow. "Tomorrow I'll go out and buy you a crown."

Now it was my turn to swat him.

"Oh, go to bed," I said, laughing. "No crown is necessary. I'd have to go out and buy myself a whole new wardrobe to match it. And you know you wouldn't like that!"

Jim gave me a smooch on the cheek and shuffled off toward

the bedroom, followed closely by Lucy and Ethel. I hoped they didn't sprawl all over the bed like they usually did and leave no room for me.

I took my time drying the wine glasses. They can't be washed in the dishwasher, and whatever possessed me to buy them, I'll never know. I had one ear cocked to the sounds of Jim getting himself to bed. I was waiting for the snoring to start, so I'd know that he was really out cold.

In less than ten minutes, I heard my husband's unmistakable, rhythmic snore. And I headed toward my other favorite late-night date, my computer.

As the machine hummed to life, I pondered my options. So many possibilities for an Internet search. Finnegan's Rakes, and the man himself, were right at the top of my list. Along with Mallory and Mallory Funeral Home and its family of owners, Helen K., and, yes, let's be honest here. Isaac Weichert. I was really curious to check him out, to be sure Mary Alice wasn't getting involved with a creep.

Because, there was no doubt about it. My shy friend was definitely getting involved. I had seen the looks she sent in his direction when she didn't think I was watching.

Was he really as nice as he seemed? And what about his surprising connection to Will Finnegan's death?

I shook my head to clear it.

Isaac's a paramedic, for heaven's sake. It was just a freaky coincidence that he and his partner, the lovely Pam, happened to answer the Finnegan emergency call.

Then, there was Jack Finnegan, and Will's widow, Louisa. I wondered if I could find out anything about them online.

And what about Deanna and her daughter? I'd known Deanna for years, and yet I never knew she had a secret daughter. I wondered what other things she'd been hiding.

Don't go there unless you absolutely have to. Who knows what else you might unearth?

I nodded my head. I do give myself good advice. And sometimes, I even take it.

I checked the time on my computer. Almost midnight. Maybe it was too early to contact Mike and get him on the job. His Miami bar and restaurant, Cosmo's, didn't close until 1:00 in the morning.

I yawned. The only times I ever stayed up that late was when I was cramming for a final exam.

I yawned again. Maybe it was too late to do any sleuthing. I was exhausted.

I put the computer on sleep, and decided that's what I needed to do, too. Tomorrow morning would be here in a flash, and I was usually more brilliant after a quick shot of caffeine.

That's when I noticed my own phone, perched on the side of the desk. Odd. Since I've joined the texting generation, I rarely let it out of my sight. I'm so afraid I'm going to miss something important that requires an immediate response.

Like a fifty percent off sale at the local shoe store.

One text was waiting for me. It had arrived about 10:30, while Jim and I were cleaning up the kitchen.

Got something in mail 2day from Will. Don't know what 2 do. Need ur help!

Louisa Marino (a.k.a. Finnegan)

Rats. I'd never get to sleep now.

Chapter 38

If swimming is good for your figure, how do you explain whales?

"You're up bright and early this morning, Carol," Jim said, heading toward the kitchen island with the morning paper tucked under his arm. "I figured you'd want to sleep in this morning. What time did you finally come to bed?"

I placed a cup of coffee in Jim's general vicinity—not too close to the newspaper, of course. I didn't want to risk upsetting a coffee cup.

Or, come to think of it, upsetting a husband.

"I didn't stay up too late," I responded. "Just long enough to check my e-mails to see if I'd heard from Mike." I managed the crestfallen mommy look with no difficulty whatsoever. "Of course, there were none. I miss him."

Jim grunted from behind the newspaper, which I took as an agreement. "I know. You miss him, too. We really should plan a trip to Florida sometime soon to see him."

Jim's hand snaked out from behind the newspaper, headed toward the coffee. Then disappeared behind the paper again.

"This is pretty good coffee," he said after a minute.

"Almost as good as yours," I said.

"So, what are you up to today, Carol?"

I chose my words carefully. "I got a text last night from a woman I met recently, Louisa Marino. She wants to get together today. You don't know her."

Because, if you did, you'd put me under temporary house arrest.

I didn't really say that last part, of course.

Then, I had a sudden inspiration. "But you'd probably recognize her. Louisa's the choir director at St. Ambrose Church. You know how beautiful the music is there."

"Maybe she'll be a good influence on you," my husband said. "Being associated with a church."

Staying married for a long time often requires selective hearing. So instead of responding to Jim's crack with one of my usual zingers, I ignored it.

"It was too late to answer Louisa last night. I'd better text her back now and tell her I'm available any time today. And we have plenty of leftovers from last night, so you don't have to worry about your supper."

"That was an interesting dinner party last night," Jim said, lowering the newspaper and giving me the full benefit of a husbandly stare. "I was proud of you for letting Mark ask the questions about the Finnegan case, without jumping in with some of your own."

"What a strange coincidence," I said. "I never imagined that Mary Alice's new beau could be involved in Will Finnegan's death. I wonder what happened at the police station last night."

"Knowing you, you'll have all the details before noon," Jim said.

I took that remark as a compliment.

My hand was jammed into my sweat pants pocket, fingering my phone. I was getting antsy. Enough of the small talk. Time to text Louisa Marino back and find out what was up.

"Well, I'm off to take a quick shower," I said, pulling the newspaper down to be sure Jim was paying attention.

"I'll feed the dogs and walk them," Jim said. "Give me a holler when you're through with your shower."

I nodded and practically sprinted toward the master bedroom, closed the door, and pulled out my phone.

Me: *Got ur text. What did you get from Will? I can meet you anytime 2day.*

Carol A.

Ping! An immediate response. Louisa must have been as anxious as I was to make contact.

Louisa: *Come 2 my house. 2 complicated 2 explain by text. Can u b here at 10?*

Me: *Okay.*

I might even be early. I can hardly wait to see what your dead husband mailed to you.

I didn't really text her that last part. Of course.

I got to Louisa's house in record time. Thank goodness Fairport's finest weren't cruising around the beach area on the lookout for speeders to increase their monthly quota of traffic tickets. I wasn't sure my son-in-law would make an effort to minimize my fine.

Especially if he knew where I was headed. And why.

The door swung open as I started to knock, revealing Jack Finnegan on the other side. I jumped back at the sudden sight of him. His close resemblance to his dead brother still gave me the heebie jeebies.

"Come in, Carol," he said, pulling me inside and shutting the door quickly. "They're in the kitchen. Everyone's pretty upset. The kids freaked out when this envelope arrived from Will. It's like a direct communication from the great beyond."

"Or a local session of *Long Island Medium*?" I asked, naming a popular reality television show that I have been known to watch when nobody else is around to criticize my viewing habits.

Jack laughed. "A little bit, I guess." He immediately turned solemn. "But this is no reality TV show. Hell, I'm not even sure it's reality, period."

I followed Jack toward the back of the house, and stopped dead at the doorway to the kitchen. Louisa was at the table, cradling a coffee cup.

And to her right was Deanna.

My facial expression must have mirrored my shock. Jack guided me to a chair and I sank into it. Talk about an unlikely duo—the scorned wife and the long-time girlfriend. Oy vey.

Although I was certain they didn't lack for conversation topics.

Louisa spoke first. "I really appreciate your coming, Carol," she said. "I didn't know who to call when this arrived in yesterday's mail." She pushed a brown envelope across the table toward me. "I understand you've had some experience solving mysteries. This certainly is a mystery."

Not quite as much as you and Deanna sitting here having coffee like BFFs. But close.

You know by now that I didn't really say that, right?

I realized that I had better be darn careful how I handled the envelope and whatever was inside. There could be fingerprints, and I didn't want to compromise them. I *should* bring the envelope directly to the police.

Of course, I had absolutely no intention of doing that. But I wanted to assure you that the thought did cross my mind. Briefly.

All right. Very briefly. And then I dismissed it. After all, Louisa and Jack had handled the envelope already, as well as the mail carrier and heaven knew how many others in the postal service.

Still, I did put my black leather gloves back on before I picked up the envelope. Just to be safe.

The envelope had been mailed ten days ago from Fairport, and had no return address or name. It was addressed to Louisa Finnegan, 240 Fairport Beach Road, Fairport. The post office had crossed out the address and marked it as "Undeliverable. Not at this address."

I looked at Louisa. I was confused. "Why did this take so long to get to you?" I asked. "I don't understand."

"I'm Louisa Marino now," she reminded me. "We had a substitute mail carrier last week, and the name 'Louisa Finnegan' meant nothing to him. He must have returned the envelope to the post office. When our regular mailman came back from vacation, he figured it out and delivered it to me yesterday."

I nodded. That made some sense.

I opened the envelope, very carefully, and a key fell out, along with a scribbled note.

Louisa, I know you think I have treated you and the children badly the last several years, and you're right. I have. I want to make it up to you. Use the enclosed key to find out how. Go to Box 701 at the Fairport Post Office. You'll find two items there. Take the one marked with your name. Please leave the other one for my good friend, Deanna. Say goodbye to the children for me. I'll miss you all.

Your husband, Will

I looked at Louisa, and noted that Jack was standing right behind her. His hands were resting on her shoulders.

Deanna spoke before I had a chance to say anything. Which was a darn good thing, because I didn't know what to say.

"It's my turn now." She looked at Louisa, as if asking permission. Louisa nodded. "Go ahead. You're certainly part of this, too."

Deanna reached into her handbag and pulled out an identical brown envelope. Except that this one had the name "Deanna" written on it.

"I went to Will's condo last night to look for some personal items I had left there." Her face turned red with obvious embarrassment.

"Will and I had been separated for years," Louisa reminded Deanna. "Whatever you say isn't going to hurt me now."

Deanna took a deep breath, then continued with her story. "I wanted to be quick, in case that horrible police detective, Paul Wheeler, happened to stop in. I didn't want to be accused of breaking and entering. Although there was no police tape across the doorway. And I do have a key."

"And then?" I asked, shifting in my chair. "What about the envelope? Where did you find it?"

"I'm getting to that, Carol," Deanna snapped back. "It was very emotional for me to be there, in case you haven't figured that out."

I sat back, properly reprimanded.

"Anyway, I pulled a few clothes from the closet," Deanna said, "and then I decided to check the top dresser drawer." She colored again. "That was my designated drawer. Will didn't want my things mixed up with his.

"I opened the drawer, and the envelope was right on top of my...things." She pushed the envelope toward me. "Open it, and read the letter."

Once again, my conscience pricked at me. And once again, I ignored it.

I shook the envelope, and another key, identical to the one in Louisa's envelope, dropped onto the table. Along with a note. This one was typed, however.

My darling Deanna: By the time you read this, I'll be gone. Life in Fairport has become much too complicated, and although I will miss you terribly, I believe that you will realize that my leaving is for the best. Especially for you. You are a wonderful woman and I do not deserve your love. I want to leave you something to remember me by. Take the enclosed key to Box 701 at the Fairport Post Office. You may find two items there. Please take the one with your name on it, and leave the other one inside, to be picked up by my wife. I'll always love you, even if I didn't show it enough.

Will

Silence can be deafening. It certainly was in Louisa's kitchen at that moment. Jack, Louisa, Deanna, and I were as still as four statues, staring at the two identical post office box keys.

Finally, Deanna spoke again. "I grabbed the envelope and my clothes and got out of Will's condo as fast as I could. I was so upset. I didn't think Will could hurt me any more than he already had. But he was planning to leave me! To leave me, after all these years. I couldn't believe it." She shook her head. "The louse."

Louise covered Deanna's hands with her own. "I know how you feel."

Then she turned to me. "Deanna called me when she got back to Crimpers last night and told me what she had found. We decided it was time to get you involved, Carol. You're the only one we trust to figure this whole mess out. You'll help us, won't you? Please?"

Oh, what the hell. Ignoring all those little warning bells ringing in my head, I stood up.

"Who wants to drive?" I asked.

"Where are we going?" Deanna asked.

"To the Fairport Post Office, of course. You've got mail."

Chapter 39

I'm having an out-of-money experience.

"I forgot there were so many school buses in Fairport," I groused as we were stopped behind still another set of flashing red lights. "How come the students got out so early?"

"It's a half day, because the teachers have some sort of in-service program this afternoon," Deanna said.

I looked at her, surprised that she knew that since she had no children in the Fairport school system. At least, none that I knew of.

"I had three mothers call me in a panic late yesterday," Deanna explained. "They needed to reschedule their hair appointments because their children would be home early. But in the long run, it worked out well for me, because I was able to close the salon for a few hours."

She frowned. "I seem to be doing a lot of that lately. I hope I don't lose any customers because of my erratic schedule. Heaven knows, I could never afford that."

"I think I see a parking spot across the street from the post office," Louisa said to Jack, who had insisted on doing the driving for our little adventure.

I sure hoped so. We four were packed in like sardines in the Finnegan's Rakes truck, and it was incredibly uncomfortable. Especially for me. Because I had the shortest legs, I was smushed in the center of the front seat, and every time Jack had to shift, well, I'm sure you get the picture. And if you don't, I'm not going to draw it for you.

Remember, I went to Catholic school.

We piled out of the truck like the Keystone cops, and as soon as there was a break in the traffic on Fairport Turnpike, ran across the busy road, holding hands like kindergarteners.

The post office boxes were massed along the back wall, and we headed in that direction. Not that we were racing to see who got there first, mind you.

Box 701 was in the top row, which meant that some of us had to stand on tippy-toes to get to it. Both Louisa and Deanna, keys in hand, reached for the lock at the same time.

Deanna stepped back. "You do it, Louisa," she said. "After all, you were married to the guy and had his children. You're more entitled than I am."

Louisa hesitated, then plunged her key into the lock and swung the door open. There were two small items inside, just as the letters had promised.

Deanna grabbed hers and started to tear it open, but I had a brief moment of common sense and reached out to stop her.

Despite the fact that the suspense was killing me.

"Not here," I said. I looked around the busy post office. "We don't know who any of these people are. And we have no idea what's in the packages. It'd be better to find a private place to open them."

Jack took charge. "Carol's right. Let's go back to the house."

"I have a better idea," I said. "Let's go to Maria's Trattoria. There's a banquet space upstairs where we won't be disturbed. And it's not that far, so we can walk."

And, by the way, I was also curious to know if Maria could identify Louisa as one of Will Finnegan's regular dining companions.

Hey, ya never know.

Fortunately, I can do more than one thing at a time. Years of motherhood has made me a multi-tasker extraordinaire. So I was able to text Maria and give her a head's up about our immediate visit to the Trattoria. And be sure the upstairs room was available for our private use.

All this, by the way, as I was hoofing it up Fairport Turnpike, trying desperately to keep up with the Louisa, Jack, and Deanna. I tried to ignore the stitch in my side that increased with every step I took. And hoped I wouldn't have a heart attack right there on the pavement.

I was sure that the other three wouldn't even notice I was missing.

Of course, I was the last one to arrive at the restaurant. Maria didn't waste time on preliminaries. "What's going on?" she hissed in my ear. "I couldn't make much sense out of your text. Everyone made a beeline for the upstairs banquet room. Even Deanna. She didn't even say hello to me."

"Did you recognize the other woman?" I asked. "Was she one of Will Finnegan's regular dinner dates?"

Maria shook her head. "I never saw her before. Why?"

"I'll explain later," I said. "I'd better join the others."

Maria thrust a glass of water in my hand. "Better take this with you. You look like you need it."

"Thanks," I said. "This shouldn't take too long." And I headed to the banquet room. And the surprise of my life.

Well, at least one of them.

"Oh, my gosh!" squealed Louisa. "This necklace is absolutely gorgeous."

"I never knew my brother had such good taste," Jack said. "That must be worth a fortune."

"He certainly improved his buying habits since he met you, Deanna," Louisa said. "I guess you were a good influence on him."

Deanna just sat at the table, staring at the contents of a small box. "I can't believe this. I simply can't believe this. Where did he ever find the money to buy these diamond earrings? I asked him for a pair so often that it became a joke between us. He'd always wink at me and say I'd have to be a very good girl before he'd even consider spending that kind of money. And the brooch is stunning. I love the seahorse design."

"Will certainly said goodbye to both of us in style," Louisa said. Then, she noticed me hovering at the door. "Carol, come and look at what Will left Deanna and me." She held up the necklace so the diamonds could catch the light. "I'll probably be afraid to wear this thing in public, though."

I was starting to get a sick feeling in the pit of my stomach. Because I'd recently read about an expensive brooch in the shape of the seahorse. And had seen a photo of it, as well.

But I pasted a bright smile on my face, because, well, maybe I was wrong. You all know how I am—I jump to conclusions a lot. Too much.

I took the necklace from Louisa and gave it a close glance. I was sure those diamonds were set in platinum, and the clasp alone was worth over $5,000.

I handed the necklace back to Louisa and looked at the seahorse brooch. "Do you mind if I take it out of the box?" I asked Deanna. "I'd like to see if there's a jeweler's mark on the back."

I held the brooch closer to the light and turned it over. Yep, there it was. Tiffany & Company. This brooch was one of a kind, and had been commissioned for a special birthday for a very special Tiffany client.

I cleared my throat. This wasn't going to be easy.

"You can't keep these," I croaked.

"Why on earth not, Carol?" asked Deanna. "They were a gift."

"And we earned them, right, Deanna?" Louisa asked. "After all that rat put both of us through over the years."

I started again. "You can't keep them because they weren't Will's to give to you. Well, that's not exactly right. I guess he thought he could give them to you. But he didn't pay for them."

"What in the world are you talking about?" Jack said.

"This jewelry is part of what's been stolen from houses all around town over the past year or so. There was an article about it on the front page of this week's paper. With photos. One of the photos was of this seahorse brooch.

"We have to take the jewelry to the police right away."

Chapter 40

Show me a man with both feet firmly on the ground, and I'll show you a man who can't get his pants off.

We were a pretty quiet quartet during our ride to the Fairport Police Station. I didn't even complain about being squashed in the middle of the front seat, once again straddling the stick shift.

Deanna and Louisa were each holding onto their treasures so tightly that I was afraid they'd never turn them over to the authorities. Not that I could blame them.

For a brief time, they each thought they'd gotten the gift of a lifetime from someone they'd loved. And they'd had their hearts broken by him again.

"I feel like I never knew Will at all," Deanna finally said. "After all those years together, the more I find out about him, the less I understand him."

"I know exactly what you mean," Louisa said. "I don't know how I'm going to tell the kids about this. They'll hate him even more."

"We'll do it together," Jack said, giving Louisa's hand a brief squeeze. "After all, before he was your husband, he was my big brother. I looked up to him so much when we were growing up. But after what he did to you and the kids, I began to realize what a rat he could be.

"We'll face this together, as a family," Jack said. "And hopefully, we'll be able to put this behind us and be a real family at last."

I was sitting there, quiet as a mouse, taking all this in. And I realized what a revealing comment that was. I still hadn't taken Jack and Louisa off my list of suspects.

Although it was wildly improbable that Jack himself was the thief, and had set it up to look like it was Will instead, it was not impossible. Who better to imitate Will's handwriting than his own brother? And, I reminded myself, the note to Deanna was typed.

If the late Will Finnegan were publicly labeled as the person behind all the high profile burglaries, that would put the last nail in his coffin. Metaphorically speaking. And Jack and Louisa could live happily ever after on the remaining proceeds of the burglaries.

It sounded like a wild theory. But then, I have a pretty wild imagination.

"I still can't believe it," Deanna said. "Not only was he planning to leave town without saying a word to any of us, but it turns out he was a thief, too."

As we turned into the police station parking lot, a horrible thought struck me. Since I'd made the connection between Will Finnegan and the home burglaries, I'd assumed that we'd turn the jewelry over to Mark. But Paul Wheeler was the detective assigned to investigate Will Finnegan's death. Did that mean we had to deal with him, instead? After the tongue lashing Paul had given me on the phone about not interfering in police business, I knew he'd be extra hard on me for what he'd interpret as my meddling. Once again.

But the heavens smiled on me. As we were pulling into a Visitors parking space, I caught a glimpse of my nemesis in an unmarked car, heading toward the exit, off to keep the town of Fairport safe.

Phew.

Since I had more of a first-hand acquaintance with the Fairport Police Station than anyone else, I elected myself the leader of our group, and marched everyone into the lobby in the direction of the information desk. I knew that, more likely than not, the booth would be staffed by a helpful volunteer, as financial constraints have put a stranglehold on the police budget.

I turned around to be sure none of my group had made a break for the exit. I could only imagine how tempting it must be to want to hang onto the jewels, no matter what.

"Carol? Why, hello. What can I do for you?"

I was startled to hear a familiar voice from behind the

information desk. Last night's dinner guest, Isaac Weichert.

I switched into hostess-speak. "I'm so glad you were able to come to dinner last night, Isaac. It was a wonderful evening, wasn't it? Did you and Mark enjoy getting to know each other better?"

Translation: Did my son-in-law grill you like the beef we had for last night's dinner?

"We had a nice talk, Carol. I hope I was helpful," he said. Which told me absolutely nothing.

"Are you here for a particular reason, Carol?" Isaac asked. "Or did you just come to say a quick hello to your son-in-law?"

"If he's not too busy," I said, "I have some people with me who'd love to meet him. And, perhaps, see his office."

Isaac, to his credit, didn't probe for any more information. I guess police volunteers are trained to keep their questions to a minimum.

Which is one big reason why I could never be a police volunteer.

In less than five minutes, Mark appeared. He did not seem overjoyed to see me. In fact, he seemed downright angry.

"What's going on, Carol?" he said in a low voice. "You know I'm up to my ears in an important case. I have no time to spend giving your friends a tour of the police station. Or whatever else you've brought them here for."

Mark looked behind me at Louisa, Deanna, and Jack. "No offense, folks, but I'm on a tight schedule today. Maybe another time, when I'm not so busy, I can show you around. Or I can find another staff person to help you."

I leaned over and whispered in my son-in-law's ear. "Just trust me on this. You'll want to take them your office. They have something to show you. I promise, you won't be sorry. This meeting might even get you a raise."

"Five minutes," Mark growled. "That's all I can spare. Come on."

My son-in-law must have found his good manners gene, because by the time we got to his office on the third floor, he was, at least, polite. Correction: He was polite to the other three in the group. He ignored me entirely.

After gesturing everyone to take seats around a small conference table, Mark looked directly at Jack. "You seem familiar to me. Have we met before?"

I piped up. Well, you didn't think I was just going to sit there, quietly, and let everyone else have the limelight, did you?

"Perhaps I'd better make the introductions, Mark," I said. "This is Jack Finnegan. He's Will Finnegan's younger brother. And this is Will's widow, Louisa, and Deanna, Will's, ah, longtime companion."

Mark gave me a stern look. "Somehow, I knew that you'd get involved in the Finnegan case, Carol. Despite an official warning to stay out of it."

He rose to his feet. "But you're talking to the wrong police detective, folks. Paul Wheeler and I are usually partners, but I'm not involved in this case. If you have any information at all about that case, you have to talk to him."

His expression softened. "I'm sorry about your loss. It must be a very difficult time for the family. I don't mean to sound uncaring. But we have strict procedures we have to follow here."

"Before you turn us over to Paul," I said, knowing full well that he wasn't in the building, thank goodness, "Louisa and Deanna have some things to show you. And after you see them, you'll realize why we came to you, instead of Paul. Why don't you sit down and let us explain."

"I don't mean to be rude," Mark said, "but this better be good. I have a meeting with the chief in ten minutes about the Fairport burglaries. He's asking for a progress report."

"Then you'll want to bring these with you," I said, grabbing the box from Louisa and sliding it across Mark's desk.

I turned to Deanna and said, "Show Mark what you have, too."

Mark opened Louisa's box first. His eyes widened when he saw the diamond necklace inside. He swiveled around to face his computer and, in an instant, a list of some of the stolen jewelry appeared. Along with photos that had been provided by the victims.

Mark reached for Deanna's box. I noticed his hands were trembling. He immediately recognized the seahorse brooch, which was not surprising. It was a unique piece of jewelry.

I don't know what I was expecting him to do. Run around his desk and give us all hugs? That would have been nice. Or congratulate us (me) on solving the mystery of the Fairport burglaries? That would have been terrific. Recommend me for a medal from the Fairport Police for being a good citizen? Make me an honorary member of the police force?

All of the above?

Instead, Mark looked at me with fire in his eyes. "How the hell did you get these things?"

Then, he shook his head. "I don't know how you do it, Carol. You stick your nose in police business after you've been specifically told not to interfere. You're...uncontrollable."

That made me mad. How dare my son-in-law ream me out in front of Jack, Louisa, and Deanna like I was a disobedient child? And after I cracked another case for him. Some gratitude.

I jumped up and shook my finger at him, the way I did years ago when I found him helping himself to extra cookies without asking my permission first.

"Now listen, Mark," I said, "at no time did you ever forbid me to nose around and see what I could find out about the Fairport burglaries. Am I right?"

Without waiting for him to respond, because I knew I was right, I continued my rant. "And if you would just listen to what Louisa and Deanna have to say, you'll understand how this happened. I didn't find out about the jewelry until this morning. When I was summoned to the Finnegan house by Louisa herself. And my first instinct, when I recognized the gems, was to take them straight to you."

I glared at Mark, and then sat down again.

Mark's cheeks flushed pink. I guess he didn't like being reamed out in public, either. He reached for his phone and punched a few numbers. Then I heard him say, "Chief, I'm sorry to keep you waiting. But I have some witnesses in my office who are giving me valuable information about the burglaries. I may have an answer for you soon, if you'll give me a little more time."

The answer from the other end of the phone must have been affirmative, because Mark replied, "Yes, sir. As soon as I can." And terminated the call.

He looked at Louisa. "Why don't you start? I'm listening."

Sorry to say, I tuned out at that point. I'd heard the story before—too many stories, in fact. I was having some trouble separating all the facts, and putting them into a logical sequence.

I know. Being "logical" is not my strong suit. But I do try.

I found a crumpled grocery list buried in my purse and started to make a few notes on it. I wasn't sure Mark would see a connection between the burglaries and Will Finnegan's suspicious death, and I knew there had to be one.

It was up to me to "guide" him. In a subtle way, of course.

I started with some names: Will and Louisa (estranged wife), Will and Deanna (longtime, now spurned girlfriend), Will and dinner date number one (according to Maria Lesco), Will and dinner date number two (also according to Maria), Will and ? Were there more girlfriends? According to the pattern that was emerging about Will's love life, he liked variety. The more, the merrier. So to speak.

Which brought up an interesting question: Was Will skipping town on his own, or was he bringing a girlfriend with him? According to his m.o., he didn't like to be lonely. Or maybe he was counting on making new "friends" to go along with his new life.

Hmm. Louisa and Deanna each received goodbye letters from Will, with expensive jewelry as a parting gift. Did any other girlfriends receive a similar letter and lavish farewell gift?

I crossed that idea out. It made no sense for Will to have rented more than one post office box. Although that could easily be checked with the Fairport postmaster. And there were only two items in box 701.

But what if Will sent his other girlfriends an "It's been nice but I'm leaving town" letter with no gift of any kind? How would that make a woman feel? Mad enough to want revenge?

Nah. I crossed that out idea, too. Louisa just received her letter yesterday, and Deanna found hers by accident.

Except that the delivery of Louisa's letter was delayed because there was a substitute mail carrier who didn't recognize the last name. The letter must have been mailed before Will's death.

I interrupted Deanna, who by this time was telling her own sad tale.

"Could I take a quick look at Louisa's letter again?" I asked Mark. I really wanted to grab it off his desk, but I knew that wouldn't win me any points with my son-in-law. He'd probably slap me in a jail cell for an hour or so for tampering with evidence.

Mark sighed, then handed over the envelope. "By this time, there's no hope of tracing any prints. Go ahead."

I think Mark rolled his eyes at that point. But, hey, I could be wrong. Maybe he had something in his eye and was trying to remove it.

Despite his long-suffering manner, I sensed that he realized I could be onto something.

I whipped out my bifocals and looked at the postmark on the envelope. It had been mailed two days before Will's death.

"What if Will sent out more goodbye letters before he died?" I asked the group, although I was staring straight at Mark. "We're pretty sure he had several other girlfriends."

Deanna choked back a little sob, which made me feel bad for her.

"I'm sorry, Deanna, but you know that's true. Maria Lesco told me Will brought women into her restaurant all the time."

I soldiered on, picking my words carefully to be sure I was making myself clear. .

"The letters Will wrote to Louisa and Deanna led them to the jewelry. But what if the letters to his other girlfriends were just kiss-offs? Maybe one of those letters made a spurned girlfriend mad enough to knock Will off. And another girlfriend could have planted the scissors in Will the night of the wake, as a special parting gift of her own."

I sat back in my chair, waiting for my brilliant reasoning to draw the applause it (I) deserved. And got nada. Zip. Nothing. No reaction at all from anyone.

Finally, Mark spoke. "There's a lot of jumping to wild conclusions in your theory, Carol. And no way to prove any of it. As usual."

Well!

Then my no-longer-favorite son-in-law rose to his feet. "I'm taking this jewelry to the chief right away. Thank you all for bringing them. I'll be back in touch when we need you to make an official statement."

I was shocked. Mark was dismissing us (me) without giving us (me) a chance to expand on my theory. And convince him that it wasn't far-fetched at all. In fact, it made a lot of sense. Any woman alive would immediately understand that. Especially if she'd been dumped by a boyfriend sometime in her life.

And therein lay the problem. Mark was a guy. A terrific guy, yes. But a guy, nevertheless. He lacked the innate intuition that females are born with.

Plus, I was betting that Mark was a teeny bit embarrassed at having his mother-in-law one-up him still again. I wondered how he planned to explain to his boss how the stolen jewelry came into his possession.

I was down, but certainly not out. If that's the way he wanted to play it, fine with me. So I bit back my usual smarty pants response and said, "I'm glad we could be helpful."

And I was going to be even more helpful. Once I figured out how to do it.

Chapter 41

Senior Texting Code: BFF—Best Friend Fainted

"So, you see, girls," I said to my usual canine cohorts, cuddled up next to me on the family room couch, "I've already solved the Fairport burglaries case. That wasn't hard at all. And I still have plenty of time to crack the mystery of Will Finnegan's death before I nuke last night's leftovers for supper."

Lucy opened one eye, decided it was too much effort to respond to what she obviously considered another example of my shading the truth, and rolled over on her back.

Ethel didn't respond at all. Except to increase the volume of her snoring.

"If it hadn't been for me," I insisted, "Louisa and Deanna wouldn't have taken the jewelry to the police. They would have kept it for themselves."

At that outrageous comment, Lucy and Ethel both opened their eyes and gave me a hard stare.

I immediately felt guilty, so I rushed to explain. "What I meant was, they might not have made the connection between the gifts from Will and the Fairport burglaries. And kept the gifts for themselves."

I sighed, remembering how gorgeous the gems were. In all my life, I had never seen such beautiful jewelry, except perhaps on the rare occasions I visit Tiffany and stroll around the main floor.

Without breakfast.

I punched a throw pillow couch in frustration. "That Mark is so stubborn. I didn't expect a brass band and confetti for what I did, but a simple, courteous, heartfelt 'thank you, Carol, we couldn't have solved this case without you,' would certainly have been appreciated."

I was so mad that I had a good mind to let the Fairport police— that would be that twerpy Paul Wheeler—try and figure out the riddle of Will Finnegan's death without any help from me.

He couldn't, of course. He just didn't know it. And even if he did subconsciously know it, he'd never admit it.

Just to confuse myself even more, I wondered if I were just trying to show off. I hate to criticize myself, but I had to admit that could be my underlying motive.

Means, motive, and opportunity. Those were the keys to unraveling a crime, according to all the mystery books I've read.

There certainly was no lack of motive in this instance. Will Finnegan was a no-good rat who dumped his wife and kids, then cheated on his long-time girlfriend. At the same time, he also used his easy access to customers' homes to rob them when the houses were empty. And then, he betrayed everybody and tried to sneak out of town. Motives galore for someone to bump Will off.

Means? Well, I wasn't exactly sure about that part, yet. Because I still wasn't clear on how many people were involved in Will's death.

But in a moment of extreme clarity—rare for me—it suddenly dawned on me who had the best opportunity to plant the scissors the night of the wake. In fact, this was the only logical way it could have happened.

I noodled this scenario around for a few minutes, and decided I liked it. So I texted Maria Lesco, who responded immediately, in the affirmative.

Wahoo! I felt a surge of excitement. Maybe I was finally on the right track. But in order to convince the police—especially my cynical son-in-law—I knew I needed more information.

And a tiny, unimportant thing called proof.

"I was wrong," I said aloud. "I can't figure this one out all by myself."

Lucy nuzzled my hand, reminding me that she was always available to be my partner-in-crime-solving.

"Not this time, Lucy," I said, smiling. "But thanks for the offer.

This time I need some human assistance."

I tried to channel one of my all-time favorite mystery writers, Agatha Christie. I was sure that Dame Agatha would have figured out a way to get all the people involved in this maddening puzzle together at one time. She'd have the suspects lined up in one place, and then reveal how the crime was committed. And by whom.

Easy peasy.

I slumped back on the sofa. The only Agatha I'd known personally was a beautiful grey cat that the kids adopted many years ago. And who was now using that great litter box in the sky.

We never figured out what happened to our Agatha. One night, she just didn't come home. We looked for her everywhere, but never found her. We even posted her picture all over town. But she just vanished from our lives.

Jenny and Mike were heartbroken. Jim and I had a difficult time consoling them, especially since they never had the chance to say goodbye to their beloved pet.

Hmm. There was a germ of an idea there. Will Finnegan had touched the lives of many people in Fairport, some of them in the biblical sense. And so far, he hadn't had a proper wake or memorial service, due to what could be politely termed "extenuating circumstances."

Maybe it was time he had that service. It was a perfect way to get everyone together for a grand goodbye.

And I knew who was the perfect person to organize it. Me, of course. I just had to convince Louisa, and make her think the service was all her idea.

I sent up a silent prayer of thanks to Agatha—the mystery writer and the cat.

But I realized that, in order to pull this scheme off, I needed backup. You know what I mean, right? All those crime shows on television usually have a moment when the police detective radios headquarters and says, "Send backup to…" and he rattles off the address where he's staking out a perp.

That's another "official" crime term, by the way.

First, I called Louisa, and she didn't take much convincing to go along with my organizing a second memorial service. Especially since I stressed that, the sooner we found out what really happened to Will, the sooner she, and Deanna, could get on with their lives.

Having accomplished my primary objective, I texted my personal backup team with an offer I knew none of them could refuse.

Emergency meeting. My house. 3:00 today. Chocolate ice cream with hot fudge sauce. Whipped cream optional.

And then I waited for the three instantaneous *pings* I knew were sure to come.

Nancy: *Hope the ice cream is low fat!*

Claire: *Short notice, but I'll be there.*

Mary Alice: *Want me 2 bring anything?*

Notice that no one asked what the emergency was. They didn't need to. Chocolate ice cream with hot fudge sauce was a private code from our high school days. We used it when we wanted to get out of the house for a date on a school night. It translated to, "Cover for me. I told my parents I'm going to study for a math test at your house."

The police may have their codes, but ours is more fun!

Chapter 42

My husband says I shoot from the lip.

"So, what's this all about, Carol?" Claire asked, licking ice cream from her fingers in lieu of using a napkin. "Or did you just use us as an excuse to have ice cream yourself? Not that I'm complaining."

"What a treat," Nancy said, helping herself to the tiniest possible portion of ice cream. "This is all I want. I'm on a diet."

I looked at my very best friend, who is a size six on her fattest days. "You're just ridiculous. You know that, right?"

"You're not in the dating pool these days, Carol," Nancy shot back. "Jim doesn't care how fat you get. He loves you, anyway."

"Now, just a minute!"

"I think Carol looks beautiful exactly the way she is," Mary Alice said diplomatically. "And so do Nancy and Claire. We all approach beauty in a different way. We should be supportive of each other, no matter what.

"And speaking of supportive, thanks again for inviting Isaac and me to dinner last night, Carol. It was a lovely evening."

That, of course, turned the conversation away from my waistline and onto the new man in Mary Alice's life. Which I was sure was exactly what she had intended.

I gave the gang five minutes to interrogate Mary Alice about her current love life, then took my spoon and clinked it against my bowl.

"All right, everybody. It's time we got down to business."

Nancy looked surprised. "I thought we already had. There's more?"

"Of course there's more," I said. "The ice cream was just a clever ploy to get you all over here. Aren't you curious about what's going on with Deanna? And the investigation into Will Finnegan's death? Boy, do I have news for you."

I tried not to look smug. And failed miserably. It's one of my all-time favorite facial expressions.

Instead, I raised my hand to stop the barrage of questions coming at me and said, "It turns out that, not only did Will Finnegan desert his wife, he was cheating on Deanna, too. He had a string of girlfriends in his life. And if that isn't bad enough, he was also responsible for all the burglaries we've had in Fairport over the past year. He was planning on leaving town last week. And instead of manning up and telling all his girlfriends goodbye personally, he sent them each a kiss-off letter. What a rat."

I paused. "Will did leave both Louisa—that's his wife's name— and Deanna expensive pieces of jewelry as parting gifts. That's what tied him to the burglaries. I, of course, figured that part out. And the jewelry was turned over to Mark today."

There came that smug look again. I just can't help myself sometimes.

"I might have known something was going on when I didn't hear anything from you for the past few days," Nancy said, looking a little put-out. "It seems like you've been having all the fun and leaving the rest of us out. I thought we worked as a team."

My smug expression gave way to a guilty one. Something I've had years of experience with after all my Catholic school training.

"You're right," I admitted. "But everything was happening so fast. I should have let you all in on what was going on. Well, Mary Alice does know a little about it, because Isaac is involved, too."

That did it. Major pandemonium. Questions from all sides.

Suddenly, I wished I could whistle through my teeth, the way some people in New York can whistle for a cab. It seems to work every time, but I could never get the hang of it.

So I clapped my hands together, like Sister Rose, our former high school teacher and new pal, used to do in English class to get us girls to stop jabbering. My palms were sore from repeating the exercise, but finally, I got the group's attention.

I cleared my throat. "Okay, everybody. I have a plan. But I need all of you to help pull it off."

"Somehow, I just knew you'd have a plan, Mom," said a familiar voice from the doorway to the kitchen.

"Jenny," I said as my darling daughter made the rounds of her three honorary moms and exchanged hugs with them, "what are you doing here? And what do you mean about expecting me to have a plan?" I narrowed my eyes. "Have you been talking to Mark?"

"Well, he is my husband," Jenny said with a grin. "Of course I talk to him."

"That's not what I meant, and you know it," I said. "Did you talk to him after I was at the police station today?"

Jenny nodded, then handed me a gift bag loaded with Godiva chocolates. "Here's a peace offering from Mark. He said he was pretty hard on you today when you brought in some of the stolen jewelry and solved the burglary case for him. I think he was embarrassed. You figured it out when he was stumped. Chief Flanagan was very impressed."

Jenny dimpled and said, "As a matter of fact, there's some talk about making you an official member of the Fairport Police."

"You're kidding," Nancy said. "You must be."

"I am," Jenny said. "But check out the look on Mom's face. I think she believes me."

Jenny helped herself to some ice cream, then asked, "So, what's the plan, Mom?"

I was torn. This was my first-born child, whom I loved beyond reason. And she also was with me the night of the Finnegan wake debacle, so she was already involved in my sleuthing.

But she was also the wife of a Fairport police detective, and her first loyalty was now to him, not to dear old Mom and Dad. And I just knew that if I shared my brilliant plan while she was still here, she'd tell Mark all about it and he'd put an end to my sleuthing, once and for all.

The group looked at me expectantly. "Well," Nancy said, "we're waiting, Carol. And I have a client coming in approximately half an hour, so quit stalling."

"I think Mom's nervous because she figures I'll tell Mark what she's up to, and he'll order her to leave the detecting to the professionals. I'm right, aren't I, Mom?"

"Well...."

"Would it make it easier it I told you that Louisa already called Mark to tell him about the memorial service for Will? She wanted the police to know in advance, in case anything bizarre happened at this one, too. She said it was your idea, and you were going to organize it."

"Carol, that's a great idea," Mary Alice said. I flashed her a grateful smile.

"It *was* a great idea," I said. "Emphasis on the word 'was.' I bet Mark doesn't want me involved at all."

"That's where you're wrong, Mom," Jenny said. "Don't forget, you're the fair-haired girl around the Fairport police station right now. Chief Flanagan thinks you're brilliant. He's ordered Mark and Paul Wheeler to cooperate with you completely. The chief thinks you can crack this case, too. So, what's our first move?"

"Now I know you're kidding," I said, immediately suspicious. "There's no way the Fairport police chief would allow me—no, make that, 'encourage' me—to, as you so quaintly put it, crack an official investigation. Did April Fools' Day come late this year? My calendar must be wrong."

"Well, there are strings attached," Jenny admitted. "You don't exactly get free rein in all of this."

"Aha!" I said, as it suddenly dawned on me that my darling daughter, whom I'd raised to tell the truth under any circumstances, might not be putting me on after all. "I knew there'd be a catch." I narrowed my eyes. "And why are you here giving me this so-called legitimate assignment? Why not Mark?"

Or, heaven forbid, Paul?

Jenny checked her Cinderella wrist watch, a childhood leftover she refuses to part with. "Mark said he'd be over to talk to you around three o'clock this afternoon. Right now, he and Paul are mapping out specific parameters with Chief Flanagan. I asked if I could give you advance warning. Because if he contacted you first, you probably wouldn't believe him."

"Or you'd faint," said Claire, who can never resist adding her two cents' worth.

"What are the strings you mentioned, Jenny?" Mary Alice asked.

"Yes," I echoed. "What are the strings?'

"That's what the meeting is all about," Jenny said. "But I'd guess that, at the very minimum, you have to let Mark and Paul know exactly what you're doing at all times. No going off on your own with one of your schemes."

"Well, of course I will," I said, crossing my heart and looking as sincere as possible.

"And your assignment is only for organizing the memorial service, nothing else," Jenny said. "Mark was emphatic about that."

"I still don't understand how you got to tell your mother about official police business," Claire said. "I've never heard of anything like that before."

"Claire, you're always such a stickler for proper procedure," Nancy said, putting her arm around me. "Obviously, this is an unusual case. And unusual cases call for unusual procedures. Besides, Mark would never bend the rules without permission. He doesn't want to lose his job."

Claire tsked. I think she was a little jealous, although I knew she'd never admit it.

"Have you fixed a date for the memorial service?" asked Nancy. "I want to mark it in my datebook."

"You didn't even know the guy," Claire said. "Why in heaven's name do you want to go?"

"Because, with Carol in charge, I'm betting it will be the most entertaining memorial service Fairport has ever seen. And I don't want to miss a minute of it!

"And, besides, you'll need our help, right Carol?" Nancy continued. "Remember how organized I was when we were planning our high school reunion a while ago? We've now morphed into the official Finnegan's Wake planning committee."

Oh, boy. I thought I'd never recover from all those endless reunion planning meetings Nancy had insisted upon. And her checklists and timelines.

Although, why couldn't the memorial service be entertaining? I'd bet that would be a surprise to everyone, especially if we served liquor. Not enough to cause a drunken brawl. But just enough to loosen a few tongues. Like a pleasant interlude at a local pub.

The more I thought about it, the more I liked this idea. We'd give Will Finnegan an Irish wake of sorts, and send him off in style. What could be more appropriate? And Louisa had given me free rein to organize anything I wanted. She and Deanna just wanted the whole thing over and done.

Jenny's phone pinged. After she checked it out, she rose to her feet and said, "That text was from Mark. He and Paul are on their way over here now."

She sent back a quick reply, then said, "All right, everybody out. Except Mom, of course. They want to talk to her alone."

My face must have registered my dismay. I would have been a lot more comfortable with this police visit if my cohorts were with me for moral support.

Jenny gave me a quick peck on the cheek. "Don't worry, Mom. You'll be fine on your own. After all, it's your brain they need right now."

Then she threw her arms around me and gave me a fierce hug. And whispered, "Just don't be too bossy, okay? Let them talk, too."

Chapter 43

If there's a Guinness Stout, is there also a Guinness Thin?

"This is the most irregular police investigation I've ever been involved in," fumed Paul, following Mark and me into the dining room. "It's absolutely ridiculous to rely on the assistance of someone from the general public to solve a criminal case. Especially someone who has a track record of sticking her nose into things that are none of her business. I think Chief Flanagan is way off base."

"Be sure you let him know that when it's time for your performance review," said Mark. "Somehow, I don't think it'll get you a promotion. Or a raise in salary."

He pulled out the chair at the head of the table and gestured for me to sit in it. Which immediately calmed my nerves. Although Mark had his professional detective face on, that gesture assured me that, for this meeting, I was in charge.

Or, at the very least, I would be taken seriously.

My mind flashed back to the last time Mark and Paul were in my house together on police business. It seemed like a million years ago, right before Jim's retirement. That visit, because Jim was suspected of his retirement coach's murder, marked the beginning of my sleuthing career. And also led to Mark and Jenny reconnecting after so many years apart, leading to their recent marriage. And the potential births of my possible grandchildren.

I smiled.

"It's not funny," said Paul, misinterpreting my reaction as usual.

I ignored him and turned my attention to my son-in-law. Chocolates or not, he had some explaining to do. And an apology would also be nice.

"This certainly is a surprise," I said. "You couldn't get me out of your office fast enough earlier today. What gives?"

And I gave him my sternest mommy look.

Mark blushed, something he used to do when he was a little boy and was under pressure. "I was out of line, Carol. You really caught me off guard. And when I gave the jewelry…"

"The jewelry that *I* brought to you," I reminded him.

"When I gave the jewelry *you* brought in to Chief Flanagan," Mark continued, "he saw a chance to use your involvement to get some positive publicity. The department just finished an online survey, and we took a lot of heat about not being involved enough with the community. I guess he figured this would be a great way to show how the public can assist the police in solving crimes. Go figure."

"I don't get it, myself," said Paul.

"You don't have to get it," Mark reminded him. "Or like it. We're here under orders from the chief."

He turned his attention to me. "So, what's all this about another memorial service for Will Finnegan at Mallory and Mallory?"

I shifted in my chair. I still wasn't sure how to approach this with Mark and Paul. No matter how impressed the Fairport police chief was with me at the moment, apparently the whole thing was an attempt to get favorable publicity for the police department, not take me seriously as a sleuth.

Especially when I told them I was throwing an Irish wake.

But what the heck. I knew that, more often than not, my instincts about people were right on target. And as far as the other times, well, I'd rather not go into them, if you don't mind.

"In all the mystery stories I've read, especially Agatha Christie's," I began, ignoring a snort of disgust coming from across the table, "the mystery is always solved when the detective gathers all the suspects together in one place and reconstructs the crime. I figured that if a memorial service were finally held for Will Finnegan, people who had a connection to him, especially his girlfriends, would show up."

Another snort of disgust from Paul. Or was this one from Mark?

I ignored it and smiled at both of them. Sweetly. "I'm so glad you're both open to ideas, because I have a few more."

"Sarcasm duly noted, Carol," Mark said, his lips twitching. "Go on. I, at least, am listening."

"As I was saying, Will Finnegan was a real Romeo. And I'm betting that Will sent all his girlfriends a 'goodbye, it's-been-nice-knowing-you' letter before he left town. Which was a fatal mistake."

I took a deep breath and continued with my theory. "I'm sure that one of Will's jilted girlfriends murdered him, and another one planted the scissors. Or maybe it was the same person who did both. But that doesn't make any sense."

"None of this makes any sense," Paul said with a scowl. "In fact, it's the stupidest, thinnest case of circumstantial evidence I've ever heard. Based on sheer speculation and the overactive imagination of an elderly woman with too much time on her hands."

Elderly woman! That did it. I sprang from my seat, ready to smack him one, then realized I could be arrested for assaulting a police officer.

"Take it easy, Carol," Mark said, putting a restraining hand on my arm and pulling me back into my chair. "Ignore him. Talk to me. I'm willing to go along with this scheme because you've been right on target with some ideas in the past."

Mark shifted his gaze to Paul. "Just in case you've forgotten about that. And I don't see you making much progress on the Finnegan case, yourself."

"I'm following up some leads," Paul said, a little too loudly. "These things take time in the real world, unlike what's shown in fictional detective stories." He glared at me, daring me to contradict him.

"Who have you talked to?" Mark asked.

"That hairstylist, Deanna, for one," Paul said. "She's definitely on my suspect list. I already talked to her once, and I was going back this afternoon to talk to her again. I think she knows more than she's saying."

"I'm sure she'll be at the memorial service," I said.

If I haven't solved the case by then, maybe you can talk to her there.

I didn't really say that last part. Of course.

Then I turned my full attention to my son-in-law. "Helen Konisburg from Fancy Francie's should provide the food for the service. I have a hunch that she was another one of Will's girlfriends."

I suppose, at this point, I should have been clearer about exactly what kind of food was going to be served, but I chickened out. I had to get them to buy into the idea of the memorial service first, before I sprang the Irish wake theme on them.

"And Melinda Mallory will be there, since the memorial will be at the funeral home her family owns," I said. "She could be another of the girlfriends."

I was pleased to see that Mark was making a few notes while I was talking. At least he was taking what I said seriously.

Time for me to switch gears and ask Mark to share some information.

"What about Isaac Weichert? I know you talked to him last night. Did he tell you anything important?"

Then, a horrible thought struck me. "You don't think he's involved, do you? I mean, he's not on the suspect list, is he? That would just devastate Mary Alice. It's the first time she's shown a real interest in another man since her husband died."

Mark put on his official cop face. "He told me a few things that may or may not be helpful, Carol. And that's all I'm saying."

I gave up. Gracefully. I knew from previous experience that, when he had that official look on his face, pressing him for more information would only make him defensive. And angry.

Besides, I had other fish to fry.

"Of course, Will's widow, Louisa, will be at the memorial service," I continued, "as well as other family members. Including Will's brother Jack. Who's been in love with Louisa for years."

I waited for a beat to let that information sink in, then added, "That gives both of them a motive for wanting Will out of the way. Permanently. I hope I'm wrong about that, though. They're both really nice people."

Of course, Paul couldn't wait to shoot my theory down. "You're jumping to conclusions again, with no real evidence to back it up," he said. "Typical behavior for someone who bases her knowledge of detective work on reading mysteries." He sat back in his chair, confident that he had poked enough holes in my theory that I shouldn't be taken seriously.

"How in the world do you know about this so-called romance?" Mark asked, his face mirroring skepticism.

"I paid a condolence call on the family, delivered some food, and got to talking with Louisa. I wasn't prying, no matter what you may think. It just came out in the course of our conversation."

I shrugged and tried to look innocent. "People confide in me."

In the interest of family harmony, Mark raised his eyebrows and let that remark pass. But he seemed more and more interested in my so-called wild theories. And he was definitely taking more notes.

"Jack's resemblance to his late brother is amazing," I said. "In fact, he came to my door a few days after Will's death and scared the heck out of me. For a few seconds, I thought it was Will, back from the dead."

Hmm. Now that was an interesting thought.

I wondered if other people—particularly Will's girlfriends— would react the same way I did when they saw Jack at the memorial service. I already knew that he'd arrived late to the first one, so none of the guests, a.k.a. Will's possible girlfriends, had seen him.

"You've got that pensive expression on your face that always scares me, Carol," Mark said. "What are you thinking about now?"

To share, or not to share? That, indeed, was the question.

"It just occurred to me," I said slowly, "that Jack's appearance at the service could be a real shock to some people, because he looks so much like his dead brother. Maybe, enough of a shock to force a confession out of one of the guests."

"Assuming he's not guilty, himself," Mark said.

I flushed bright red. First I'd come up with a reasonable scenario with Jack in the starring role as First Murderer. Then I came up with an equally reasonable scenario with Jack as the bait to identify the murderer.

"I guess I can't have it both ways," I admitted. "But I think that Jack is key to clearing up this whole thing. One way, or the other."

Time to come clean on my Big Idea.

"I'm sure this memorial will be something people will talk about for years. Especially since it will be done as an Irish wake."

Both Mark and Paul looked puzzled. "What's that?" Mark asked. "I've never heard that phrase."

"Oh, you know how the Irish are," I said. "Any excuse for a party. Good food, maybe a little fiddle music. Some Jameson's whiskey. And a wee pint, or two, of Guinness to drink a toast to the deceased. All bound to loosen people's tongues. Don't you think?"

I smiled at them sweetly. "I'm sure Chief Flanagan will love the idea, being such a good Irish lad himself."

Chapter 44

If anyone has the nerve to ask me how old I am, I always add on at least ten years. That way, everybody tells me how fantastic I look for my age.

"Tell me again why we had to be here so early," Claire said. "The newspaper article said the memorial service won't start until eleven o'clock. That means we'll be sitting around, with nothing to do, for at least an hour. You wouldn't even let us stop to get coffee."

"Oh, stop griping," said Nancy. She slammed the car door shut and turned to me. "I'm sure Carol has a good reason. But it really is weird that we're here so far ahead of the family."

I ignored the two of them. Claire always complains about anything she's not in charge of, and Nancy...well, Nancy sometimes joins her. But they both go along with me. Eventually.

I turned to the third member of my group. "Are you absolutely sure that Isaac and his partner are working today, Mary Alice? You checked with him this morning, right? Neither of them called in sick, did they?"

Claire rolled her eyes. Even the usually patient Mary Alice seemed annoyed at my questions.

"Carol, for heaven's sake. You've asked me about Isaac at least ten times since I got in the car. And the answer is always the same. I talked to Isaac at eight o'clock. He seemed surprised to hear from me so early, but he confirmed that he and his regular partner are working the nine-to-four shift today. Please, don't ask me again. You're starting to sound like a broken record."

"A damaged CD," Nancy said. "Nobody plays records anymore."

"And why is that so important to you, Carol?" Claire asked.

"I was wondering the same thing," Mary Alice said. Then, her eyes widened. "Oh, my gosh. Isaac isn't a suspect, is he? He's such a nice guy."

"Don't worry, Mary Alice," I said, sidestepping a direct answer. "Isaac's not high on my list. But by an odd coincidence, he and his partner were the paramedics who answered Will Finnegan's nine-one-one call the night he died."

I didn't want to add that Isaac was also on a ride-along with Paul Wheeler the night of the first memorial service. That would have necessitated a lot of questions about the community police course, and what a ride-along meant, and gotten us way off track.

Something I never do.

And I never would have mentioned how key Isaac could be to clearing up this whole mess. After all, Mark had hinted that Isaac gave him some helpful information, which he refused to share with me.

Well, I had some inside information of my own. Not that this was a competition between me and the police. Of course not.

"Who's Isaac's partner?" Nancy asked. "Is he single?"

That made me laugh. "Nancy, you really are too much sometimes."

"Isaac's partner is a woman, Nancy," Mary Alice said. "Her name is Pam Augustine, and she's absolutely gorgeous. Carol and I met her at Fancy Francie's a few days ago."

Mary Alice shook her head. "I don't understand why Isaac is dating me when he could be dating her."

"Because you're gorgeous, too," I said. "And besides, Pam Augustine is much too young for him. Isaac has the good sense to choose to spend his time with someone who can relate to the same things he can."

"I guess you're right, Carol," Mary Alice said. "Thanks for giving my ego a boost."

"Any time," I said. Time to get back to business.

"When we get inside the funeral home," I said to my team, "I'm going straight to the office to talk to Melinda Mallory. One of the things I want you to do right away is figure out which spots in Slumber Room A are the best for keeping an eye on everyone's comings and goings. That needs to happen before anyone else gets here."

Nancy raised a perfectly shaped eyebrow and said, "Slumber Room A? You've got to be kidding."

"Nope. That's what the rooms are called." I reached into my car and pulled out a cardboard box filled with photos. "Here," I said, handing the box to Claire, "take this inside. Deanna gave me these pictures of Will from vacations they took together. Spread them around the room, so that, everywhere people look, they'll see Will. Let me know if you need more. I have another whole box from Louisa. She was glad to get rid of them."

Should I feel guilty that the box I gave Claire was very heavy? Nah.

As we headed toward the front door of the funeral parlor, I noted with satisfaction that Fancy Francie's van was already here. Two women, one of whom was Helen K., were busily unloading food.

I shooed Mary Alice, Claire, and Nancy into Slumber Room A, then turned to make my way toward Melinda Mallory's office.

I screeched to a halt when I saw the woman in question sprinting toward me, her face like a thundercloud.

"Carol, what the hell do you think you're doing," Melinda hissed, grabbing me by the elbow and pulling me into Slumber Room B which was, mercifully, unoccupied. "This is a respectable funeral home, not an Irish bar. You asked me to reserve Slumber Room A for a memorial service. We do not serve alcohol at a memorial service. It simply isn't done."

"It's done all the time at Irish wakes," I countered. "And the widow requested that Will Finnegan's memorial service be handled like an Irish wake. With all the trimmings."

Only a tiny lie, but I was sure that, if I'd bothered to consult Louisa, she would have agreed. And if she didn't, I was certain I could sway her to my point of view, especially if we shared an Irish coffee or two while we were having a chat.

"And on top of the Irish whiskey you ordered, and more Guinness Stout than Fairport's St. Patrick's Day celebration," Melinda said, ignoring my explanation and continuing her tirade, "there are two strange women in our kitchen—which is reserved for staff only—warming up corned beef and cabbage and heaven knows what else."

Melinda wrinkled her nose. "The smell of the cabbage is overpowering. I'm very sensitive to odors." And she sneezed for extra emphasis.

"We could lose our license for this…this…function," she said. "It's probably illegal, too. What if the police show up? What'll I do? And with my father away at a conference on new embalming techniques, I'm completely on my own."

The police were showing up, of course. That is, assuming Mark and Paul came through. But shutting down the memorial for illegal service of alcohol would not be tops on their agenda.

"Now, Melinda," I said in the voice I use to coax Lucy and Ethel into taking their monthly heartworm pills, "everything will be fine. The memorial service will only last two hours, two and a half, tops. When it's over, I promise to help clean everything up. And Will Finnegan will have the sendoff he rightly deserves, after the unfortunate first attempt to hold a service for him here.

"It's the right thing to do," I finished, yanking my arm free. "You'll see. Everything will work out exactly as it's meant to this time. You have my promise."

"Well, at this point, there really isn't anything I can do to stop the service," Melinda said. "Just be sure that you keep it as proper as possible. I don't want anyone getting drunk here. Or, heaven forbid, sick from too much food and drink. We just had the carpeting cleaned."

She spun around and marched down the hallway to her office.

I waited until I was sure her door was closed, and then raced to Slumber Room A to see how my gang was doing. Louisa and Jack were due to arrive in less than half an hour, and everything had to be completely ready before they got here.

Wow. Nancy, Claire, and Mary Alice had done an amazing job.

Slumber Room A had been completely transformed during the time I'd been having my "discussion" with Melinda. Framed photos of Will Finnegan graced every possible surface in the room, including a large poster of a smiling Will that had been hung dead center—pardon the pun—right where a casket would be if this were a traditional service.

The chairs had been rearranged in clusters around each of the photo displays, and Irish music played in the background. A row of chairs had been placed to the left of the poster, where Louisa, her children (assuming they showed up), Jack and Deanna would sit.

I know you're thinking how weird it was to put Will's girlfriend in the same row with his official widow. But, be assured that I checked the Emily Post etiquette book and found nothing to forbid that seating arrangement.

In fact, I found nothing that covered that situation at all. So I just went ahead and did it.

"The room is fabulous," I said, congratulating my three cohorts. "After a few drams of Irish whiskey, I'm sure people will start to relax. Someone's bound to say something incriminating."

Claire narrowed her eyes and gave me a look. "Are you crazy, Carol? That's it? That's all you're going to do to force a confession, serve Irish whiskey? That's the dumbest idea I ever heard."

"Of course that's not all I'm going to do," I snapped. "I have a brilliant plan, but you don't need to know all the details."

I turned my attention to Nancy and Mary Alice. "Your job is very important. When people start to arrive, act as hostesses and keep the food and drinks coming. Especially, the drinks.

"It would really help move things along if you acted like you were both Will's girlfriends, too. Try to start conversations with women about the special relationship you had with him. If you could cry a little, that'd be a nice touch."

Nancy nodded her head. Like me, she's a fabulous weeper when called upon. Her ability to whip up tears on demand got us out of lots of tight situations when we were in high school.

Mary Alice looked scared. "I can't do that, Carol. Pretend I was one of Will's girlfriends, I mean. What if somebody I know sees me and doesn't know I'm pretending. I'll be so embarrassed."

"Just do the best you can," I said. "And keep your ears open. If you hear anything important, tell me right away."

"What about me?" Claire asked. "Am I supposed to be one of the girlfriends, too?"

"No, I have a much more important job for you," I said. "I want you to keep your eye on Helen K. from Fancy Francie's. She's in the kitchen now, preparing the food to be served. She's near the top of my list of Will's jilted girlfriends. Cozy up to her, ask if she needs any help, that sort of thing. And start a conversation about Will. Say he did your landscaping or something. See if you can get her to talk."

Claire nodded. "Got it."

"Remember, the main purpose today is to find out the truth about Will Finnegan's death," I said.

"I've never done anything like this before," Mary Alice said. "What if we do find out what happened? Do we call the police? You don't expect us to handle this all on our own, do you?"

"Relax," I said. "Mark will be here all during the service. Along with our least favorite police detective, Paul Wheeler. They're counting on us to start the ball rolling. We're their official helpers."

Claire raised a skeptical eyebrow.

"No, this time we really are," I said.

"You've given us our orders," Nancy said. "What are you going to be doing? Leading the memorial service?"

"Don't be silly," I said. Although it wasn't a bad idea. Too bad I didn't think of it earlier.

"I'll be overseeing everything, and everyone. If things work out the way I hope, someone's going to get the surprise of a lifetime."

I spied Deanna, the first to arrive, standing stock still at the doorway, her face white as she stared at the huge poster of the smiling Will. Nudging Mary Alice, I said, "Go help Deanna find her seat. It's time to get this show on the road."

Deanna was followed immediately by Jack, Louisa, and two sullen-faced young people. I hadn't seen that look since Jim and I took away Mike's driver's license for coming home reeking of beer when he was seventeen.

I noted that the boy was wearing wrinkled chinos and flip flops, an odd wardrobe choice since it was a chilly late fall day in our corner of the world. The girl was similarly dressed down in old sweatpants and a matching sweatshirt. And flip flops.

The quartet stood in the doorway and gaped at the poster of Will. "Gross," said the girl. Louisa shushed her, then started in my direction, holding her in the same kind of death grip Melinda had used on me a short time before.

I was pleased to hear a gasp from Nancy. Or maybe it was Mary Alice.

"My gosh, who is that man? He looks exactly like Will Finnegan."

I smiled. Just the reaction I was hoping for. But from someone else.

I made a beeline for the family before they could settle themselves in for the service, fingers crossed mentally that I'd get a positive reception.

"Carol," Louisa said, gesturing around Slumber Room A, "this really is…something. I never expected anything like this. Will would have loved it." And her eyes filled with tears.

"I'm so glad you approve," I said, uncrossing my fingers. "I had so little time to put the service together, and since Finnegan is an Irish name, that became my theme."

"He didn't deserve it," said the young man. "I'm leaving before this stupid thing starts. Otherwise, I may puke. Come on, sis. Let's get out of here."

Louisa shrugged. "What can I say? They were never reconciled with their dad. I can't really blame them for reacting this way. Maybe it is better that they leave." She looked at Jack for help.

"You're right. I'll go out and tell them they don't have to come back inside, Louisa," he said.

Jack's offer was perfect with me. Because my plan called for Jack to vamoose from Slumber Room A asap.

As Louisa nodded, and she and Deanna took their places as Mourners-in-Chief, I grabbed Jack by the hand and propelled him from the room.

"I know you want to be at Louisa's side all though the service," I said. "But since Will was your brother, I figured it would be appropriate for you to lead the memorial service and give a eulogy of sorts."

Jack looked shocked. Then angry.

"For heaven's sake, Carol, why are you telling me this now? I don't have anything prepared. I'm going to look like a jerk up there. You should have warned me."

"Don't worry, Jack," I said, taking a sheaf of papers from my purse. "I have the whole thing outlined for you. All you have to do is study it and you'll be fine."

I looked around for a private place, and came up with the only one where I was sure none of Will's girlfriends would find Jack. I'm sure you figured out where.

"Just take your time, Jack," I said, pushing him in the door of the men's room. "I'll knock on the door when it's time for you to make your entrance."

"But, what about the kids?"

"I'll take care of them," I said. "I have years of practice as a mom."

And, if I knew kids, they were both long gone by now, anyway.

226

"Thanks a lot, Jack. You really are a sweetie." I gave him a modest peck on the cheek. "Now, remember, don't come out until I rap on the door. That's very important. As a matter of fact, it's critical."

Jack realized there was no arguing with me. "I just hope I can read your handwriting," he said to my retreating back.

Although this whole interchange with Jack had taken less than five minutes, I was shocked at the number of mourners who were already streaming into Slumber Room A. Mostly of whom were female.

The line was moving slowly, as all of them stopped to sign the guest book, then gasped at the huge poster of Will, hanging on the wall to greet them.

Just as I had planned.

Several mourners were paying their respects to Louisa. And I was pleased to see that she was introducing everyone to Deanna as a dear friend of Will's. Isn't it odd how life can work out sometimes?

The bar setup in the corner was doing a brisk business, and the buffet table groaned under the weight of the various food platters. I saw Claire at the buffet, helping Helen K. to arrange the plates and cutlery.

Claire gave me a discreet nod, and I nodded back.

Nancy and Mary Alice were circulating among the mourners as instructed. I was pleased to see that Nancy was clutching a white handkerchief, which she frequently used to dab her eyes.

It was a nice touch, even if it hadn't been my idea.

"Nice party, Mom. Even if the guest of honor isn't here to enjoy it."

I whirled around at the sound of Jenny's voice. "Sweetie! I didn't know you'd be here."

"Oh, come on, Mom. You didn't think I'd miss this, did you? Especially since I was here the first time. Mark told me I could come if I was a very good girl."

"Mark's here? Oh, thank goodness. Where is he?"

"He and Paul are already at the buffet table," Jenny said. "I should tell you that neither of them expect anything to happen today. They came because Chief Flanagan ordered them to. That's why I got to come. If this were an official stakeout, I wouldn't be here."

"I'm glad you're here," I said. "I can use all the support I can get. Now, I have to do something about the music."

I dashed to the adjoining room, where I had stashed a collection of Irish music CDs. I selected the one titled, "Coffin Music For Mourners."

That should do it. Nodding with satisfaction, I loaded it into the CD player and waited. In a few moments, an Irish tenor was singing, "I Am Stretched On Your Grave."

I turned the volume up, in case the sound didn't travel enough to be heard next door, then realized with a start that I heard a soprano voice harmonizing with the tenor's. And the voice was coming from Slumber Room A.

It was Louisa, standing straight and tall in front of her dead husband's poster, tears streaming down her face.

Wow. Either she was the greatest actress in the world, or she really still had feelings for guy, despite everything.

Someone had dimmed the lights, and the room was as silent as, well, a tomb. All eyes were on Louisa. It was quite a moment.

And just what I needed to put the final touch on my plan. So I snuck out and cranked the CD player up to its maximum volume. Then I doubled back to the men's room, tapped on the door, and whispered, "Jack, it's time."

I led him into Slumber Room A. My timing was perfect, because Louisa was just finishing her song. Jack raced to her side and embraced her, then turned to face the mourners.

And all hell broke loose.

Chapter 45

A clear conscience is usually the sign of a faulty memory.

I couldn't tell where the first scream came from. But it was immediately followed by several more.

Just like I expected.

I scanned the crowd and saw Mark and Paul at the front of the room. I was pleased to see that they both had their police persona in place. And were ready to act if necessary.

"What is going on in here?" demanded Melinda Molloy, marching into Slumber Room A from a side door I'd never noticed before and heading straight to me. "Turn that music off right now. I warned you, Carol."

Then she turned and saw Jack. Her face drained of color and she began to yell like a banshee.

"How can you be here? You're dead. I know you're dead. I made sure of that with the scissors!"

Jack backed away from Melinda. Well, who could blame him? He had no idea what was going on. Or who this screaming woman was. Poor guy.

In a flash, Mark and Paul were beside Melinda and led her, weeping, out of the room.

I hoped they planned to question Melinda in the funeral home, because I had a hunch there was more drama to come. No way did I want to handle another hysterical woman, who could also be a murderer, on my own.

By this time, Slumber Room A was in chaos. Louisa and Deanna seemed completely dazed. Jack made his way back to Louisa's side and whispered something in her ear.

Deanna looked at me and mouthed, "What the heck is going on?"

I shrugged my shoulders. "Beats me," I mouthed back.

I grabbed Mary Alice and Nancy, who were standing together near the main exit. "Mingle with the guests. Herd them in the direction of the bar. This isn't over yet. Where's Claire?"

Nancy gestured in the direction of the food. "The last time I saw her, she was over there."

As I started through the crowd, I saw Claire beckoning to me frantically from the edge of the room. From the panicky look on her face, something was very wrong. Claire never loses her cool, no matter what.

She grabbed me and pushed me toward the room where the CD player was still churning out Irish music at a deafening pitch.

Jenny was on her knees, giving mouth-to-mouth resuscitation to a prostrate Helen K.

"I think she's had a heart attack," Claire said. "I've called nine-one-one and Fairfield Ambulance is on the way. If she dies, it will be your fault. This time, you've gone too far, Carol. I hope you're satisfied."

"That's a terrible thing to say to me!" I said. "And it's so unfair. I never wanted this to happen. I just wanted to find out what happened to Will Finnegan. And I thought Helen was involved."

A part of me felt guilty that Helen had collapsed when she thought Will had come back from the dead. Especially because I had counted on that happening, since she'd reacted exactly the same way at Fancy Francie's.

I made a mental note to apologize to her, later. Once I was sure she was off the official suspect list.

"She's coming around," Jenny interrupted. "Stop arguing and help me get her up."

"I guess I overreacted," Claire said as she and I struggled to get the still pale Helen onto the nearest chair.

"What happened to me?" Helen asked. "Why did I collapse? Oh, now I remember. It was stupid of me to react the way I did. Will's not worth it. Alive or dead." She leaned back and closed her eyes.

"Just give me a minute or two, and I'll be fine."

"That was scary," Jenny whispered to me. "I really thought she'd had a heart attack."

"I did, too," Claire said. "That's why I called the paramedics." She pulled out her cell phone. "I better cancel them."

"No, Claire," I said. "Let them come, anyway."

"But why?" Jenny asked. "What if there's a real emergency, and they're here instead and can't respond to it?"

"You have to trust me," I said. "I have a very good reason."

Claire looked mutinous and started to punch numbers on her cell. I grabbed the phone away from her.

"I think Isaac Weichert saw something happen here the night of Will Finnegan's first wake," I said. "We need him here to see if we can jar his memory. And besides, there's always more than one emergency team on call. But I'm betting that Isaac and Pam Augustine will respond to this one." I hope.

I peeked around the corner and saw that the Irish wake was now proceeding full speed ahead. People were clustered in groups, talking loudly about how exciting the scene with Melinda and Jack had been. I guess none of them had ever seen a person confess to a crime before.

The women I had identified as Will's possible girlfriends were now clustered in one large group. Too bad I didn't have the time to eavesdrop. The stories they were exchanging must have been something.

And smack in the middle of this group was Deanna. I bet her stories were the most interesting of all.

Jack and Louisa were still at the front of Slumber Room A, now seated under the poster of Will and holding hands. They both looked a little shell shocked, to tell the truth. And who could blame them?

I heard the wail of a siren. Good. Fairport Ambulance was almost here. I just hoped the rest of my plan worked and Isaac came through. Because if he didn't, I was going into permanent retirement and donating all my Agatha Christie books to our local library.

Out of the corner of my eye—my peripheral vision is still quite good, fortunately—I saw Mark and Paul leading a subdued Melinda Mallory toward the main exit.

Rats. I need them here.

I chased after them as fast as I could. Which, as you know, is not very fast. By the time I caught up with them, puffing all the way, both detectives were already in the parking lot with Melinda.

Isaac and Pam hurried past us, loaded with assorted medical equipment and pushing a stretcher.

Phew. At least, that part of my plan was working.

I was relieved when Mark turned and fell in step behind Isaac and Pam, leaving Paul to deal with a struggling Melinda Mallory. True to form, Paul snarled at me, "I'm taking Ms. Mallory into headquarters. I don't need you here."

Fine with me. So back into Mallory and Mallory (I wondered if the name would have to be changed) I went.

My plan was to make a quick stop at the women's room on my way to Slumber Room A. I figured the two paramedics had to examine Helen first, and that would give me some time. All that excitement had, well, you know what I mean.

Unfortunately, my plan was derailed before I could put it into action by the sight of Phyllis Stevens making her way toward me through the crowd, disapproval radiating from every pore in her body. Poor Bill was, of course, several steps behind his wife, and making little effort to catch up with her.

He gave me a quick wave, turned away, and headed straight for the bar.

I cringed. I didn't have time for a confrontation.

So, I took the offensive.

"Phyllis," I said, throwing my arms around her neck and giving her a bear hug, "you look ten years younger. Welcome home. That cruise must have been wonderful. I can tell that you had a great time, and I can hardly wait to hear all about it. You and Bill must come over later this week for drinks. But right now, I'm needed inside. I'll catch up with you later."

I turned to make my getaway, but Phyllis grabbed my arm. "Not so fast, Carol. What in the world is going on here? I thought Will Finnegan's wake happened while we were away. And why did we have to find out about this…whatever it is…on the Fairfield Patch? You didn't even have the common courtesy to leave us an invitation."

I squirmed out of her grasp. "I'm sorry for the oversight, Phyllis. A lot's happened while you were away. I didn't want to upset you on vacation. And I wasn't sure exactly when you and Bill were coming home."

The upshot of my wasting valuable time placating Phyllis was that I completely missed seeing what happened next, and had to rely on Nancy and Mary Alice to give me the details. Which really irritated me.

I heard it, though—another scream, even louder and more primal.

By the time I hustled myself to Slumber Room A, I saw my son-in-law separating Isaac from an out-of-control Pam Augustine, who was pummeling poor Jack Finnegan with her fists and whatever else was handy.

And Pam was screaming curse words like—well, I'm not going to repeat them. Remember, I went to Catholic school.

Then I heard Mark say to Pam, "You have the right to remain silent."

OMG. I never saw that one coming.

But please don't tell anyone I admitted that.

Chapter 46

Nothing tastes as bitter as humble pie.

It took a while for me to recover from the fact that I had been Completely Wrong about who was to blame for Will Finnegan's death. Almost a whole week, in fact.

I moped around the house, sighing a lot. Everyone avoided me, even Lucy and Ethel. Every now and then, I'd check my e-mail, just for something to pass the time. But I avoided reading the local newspaper. I didn't want to know any of the details of how Detectives Mark Anderson and Paul Wheeler had cracked the Finnegan murder case.

My case.

Some mornings, I stayed in bed until noon. Jim tried to cheer me up by bringing hot coffee into me every morning, but even the lure of caffeine failed to excite me. And I had no interest, whatsoever, in attending the Fairport Merchants Association black tie gala.

Which proves how depressed I was. I never turn down a chance to go shopping for a new outfit. Or two.

How had I gotten the whole thing so completely wrong? Pam Augustine was never on my radar as one of Will's girlfriends, much less the one who did the dastardly deed.

I decided I had to find a new post-retirement hobby and give up sleuthing for good. Jim was right. I meddled in things that were none of my business, and it had to stop.

My pity party didn't even stop when I got a letter of thanks from Chief Flanagan for all I had done to help the police in their investigation.

Poor me.

Then, I got mad. Really mad. At myself, for missing any clues. And at Mark, who hadn't played fair with me.

So I took a nice hot shower, washed my hair, and got dressed in my most professional outfit—a navy pantsuit which makes me look thinner.

I left a note for Jim. "Out for a while doing errands. Back soon."

I only had one errand, of course. And it was at the Fairport Police Station. I had to know how Mark figured out the case, and I hadn't.

"This is a nice surprise, Carol," my son-in-law said, giving me a brilliant smile. "I didn't know you were coming by. I hope you don't have another dead body to report."

"That's not funny," I said, glaring at Mark. "And as far as dead bodies go, I am a concerned private citizen trying to do my duty. And help the police, if the occasion should call for it. Which it has. Frequently. In case you've forgotten."

Mark gestured me into a chair. "Of course I haven't forgotten, Carol. I was just kidding you." He took a closer look at my face, then said, "But I can tell you're not in a kidding mood right now. So, why are you here?"

Don't come across like a cry baby, Carol. Be professional. And remember those grandbabies-to-be.

"I wanted to congratulate you on arresting Pam Augustine for Will Finnegan's murder," I lied.

"Yes," Mark said, "that was an interesting twist to a very confusing case. Or, should I say, cases. In fact, if it hadn't been for you, we probably wouldn't have solved them yet."

Say what?

"You know I'm not at liberty to reveal certain aspects of our investigation," Mark said.

I nodded. Good sport that I was.

"But I guess it won't hurt to tell you that it was Isaac Weichert who pointed us in Pam's direction. Although he didn't really mean to. Let's just say that the conversation I had with him after we left your dinner party proved very enlightening. Especially about paramedics' access to…" He stopped himself.

"That's it? That's all you're going to share?

Mark nodded. "That's all I can share."

You don't think I'd let him off the hook that easily, do you? I was starting to get my confidence back, so I plowed ahead.

"How about if I come up with my own scenario and you tell me if I'm right or wrong?" I asked, an outrageous idea forming in my head.

"Mary Alice has mentioned that paramedics sometimes hang around the hospital emergency room after they deliver a patient. Is that what happened? I know there was a confrontation between Deanna and Louisa about Will. Did Pam overhear it? Is that what happened?

"I bet she'd gotten one of Will's kiss-off letters, too," I said, warming to my scenario even more. "And she figured out a way to send Will on a permanent one-way trip with no one being the wiser."

Mark stood up. A sure sign that our little chat was over. And that I was on the right track.

"Why don't you and Jim come for supper on Sunday night?" Mark said. "It's our turn to cook." And ever so gently, he propelled me out the door.

I pondered what Mark had—and hadn't—told me all the way back home. I knew I'd never give up until I figured out the whole story. And if Mark wouldn't tell me, I'd just keep on digging until I figured it out.

But it was a heartbroken Mary Alice who provided the missing information.

"I should have known it wouldn't last," my sweet friend said, tears forming in her eyes.

"Oh, sweetie, I'm so sorry," Nancy said, patting Mary Alice's hand. "Men can be so hurtful. Just look at Bob as an example."

"Let's not look at Bob right now," I said, putting the brakes on Nancy's attempt to mingle her own male troubles with Mary Alice's. And since the tears were being shed around my kitchen table, I had the right to interfere.

"Carol's right," Claire said. "We're not here to talk about you, Nancy," she said, shooting her a look that is frequently reserved just for me. "We got together to cheer up Mary Alice."

"Would ice cream help?" I asked, falling back on our tried and true way to banish the blues.

"Not this time," Mary Alice said. "Amazingly enough. But it would help if I could just tell you what happened. With no interruptions."

I zipped my lips. "Go ahead. We're all ears."

"Well," Mary Alice said, "Isaac and I went out to dinner last night. And right before dessert, he told me he was leaving Fairport. Not just on a trip." Her lower lip quivered. "He was leaving for good."

She stopped for a second, and took a deep breath.

"Isaac told me that he and Pam Augustine had been in a relationship for a long time. And then she left him for someone else. He never knew who it was. But she hurt him terribly. And he told me that when their ambulance arrived at Fairport Hospital with Will Finnegan, Pam insisted on going inside and waiting with the patient. Although that was unusual, Isaac didn't question it."

"Love can be blind," Nancy said. I kicked her under the table.

"Isaac said he never realized what Pam had done until she went ballistic at the second memorial service. And mistook Jack Finnegan for his dead brother."

"Did Isaac share this with the police?" I asked. Not that the police shared it with me, of course. Despite the fact that it was my dinner party that started that conversation going.

Mary Alice nodded. "But now, he feels so guilty. So, he's leaving town. He told me how special I had been to him, and that he'd always remember me." She sighed. "But I'm still glad I met him. I found out that I'm ready for a relationship again. And we did have fun for a little while."

Nancy raised a glass of water and toasted Mary Alice. "Here's looking at you, kid. And, remember, we'll always have Fairport."

"I like *Everybody Loves Will* better," I said. "I think a television show with that title would have a long run with millions of fans. Just think of the plot twists."

That broke the tension and sent us all, even Mary Alice, into uncontrollable giggles.

"You know," Nancy said, "it's suddenly dawned on me that Isaac really was the hero at the second memorial service. You weren't there, Carol...."

"Don't rub it in," I said.

Nancy looked hurt. "I'm not rubbing it in. I'm merely explaining what happened."

Humph.

"Anyway," she went on, directing her comments to Mary Alice, "remember that Isaac was the one who jumped in and saved Jack Finnegan when Pam was attacking him. If it hadn't been for Isaac, she could have really hurt Jack."

"You're right," Mary Alice said. "I never thought of it that way. And who knows, maybe he will come back to Fairport, someday."

I knew Isaac would have to come back and testify at Pam's trial. But I decided not to share that tidbit.

"You should be very proud of yourself, too, Carol," Claire said. At my puzzled look, she explained, with just a slight grin, "Once again, the always curious Carol Andrews has come through, saving the fair town of Fairport from the bad guys. You solved the jewelry burglaries, and figured out who planted the scissors in poor old Will. An impressive record, for sure."

I suddenly realized that Claire was right. Not that I'm one to brag. But two out of three is a pretty darn good record, right?

Of course, right.

Maybe the library won't be getting my mystery books after all. At least, not yet.

I may need them for future reference.

How to Plan a Funeral

Let's face it. Funerals are events that each of us must face, whether we want to or not. For a spouse or life partner, a family member, a close friend, a neighbor. And, of course, the ultimate one—our own.

In *Funerals Can Be Murder*, Carol Andrews assumes the role of "official funeral planner" to unmask a murderer. But you may be surprised to know that there is a real occupation that's similar to what Carol does in this book—funeral concierge.

Annie Gibbons of Dennis, Massachusetts, is one of the first funeral concierges in the northeast. Her company, *with Amazing Grace*, coordinates all the usual details associated with a funeral, plus many extra, meaningful touches.

Gibbons explains that there many different scenarios under which she and her company are hired. "We may be contacted as a result of a terminal diagnosis, by clients who want to pre-plan, or by families who have experienced a sudden death and are overwhelmed with the details that must be attended to."

Here is a partial list of what *with Amazing Grace* can coordinate:
Help with selecting a funeral home
Selecting, developing, formatting, and printing of
a religious service bulletin, prayers, songs, eulogy.
Travel arrangements
Accommodations
Flowers
Food coordination/ meals after wake
Bereavement gathering, food, music & picture
retrospective video production.
House, baby, elderly and pet sitting
Personalizing of memorial service
Emergency house cleaning

Gibbons says that many Baby Boomers want to plan how their life will be celebrated when they've passed on, often choosing personal stories, music, and pictures for their unique service. For example: a young attorney who died suddenly had a collection of neckties that numbered in the hundreds. "At his life celebration, we displayed all of his ties and had a sign that read, "IF YOU WEAR ONE, TAKE ONE, PUT IT ON, THINK OF JOHN."

Another Gibbons' client was a family planning the celebration of life for their 85-year-old mother, who had died a few months earlier. "She loved doing crossword puzzles with her grandchildren," Gibbons said. "To personalize this celebration, we had square sugar cookies made, frosted and decorated with crossword puzzles using words significant to their family. It was very special."

Annie Gibbons can be reached at 508-237-0595, and her website is www.withamg.com.

There are many resources on the Internet that can be helpful when planning a memorial service, as well. One of the best is www.funerals.org.

A truly innovative life celebration was chronicled in a July 20, 2006 *New York Times* article: "It's My Funeral and I'll Serve Ice Cream If I Want To." Check it out yourselves. You may discover that funerals can be, not murder, but fun.

Believe it or not.

Recipes for an Irish Wake
By Chef Paulette DiAngi

Irish Stew

Sauté in bottom of large pot for two minutes:
2 T olive oil
1½ pounds cubed beef, mutton, lamb or some combination
1 c chopped onions
1 small leek, chopped

Add:
4 c water
2 c Guinness Stout
1 t thyme
2 bay leaves
2 T chopped parsley
6 garlic cloves, minced.

Simmer for 1 to 1.5 hour, till meat is tender.
Add:
2 c carrots, cut chunky
5 potatoes, peeled and cubed
Simmer for additional 20-30 minutes until veggies are cooked
Serve in bowl with slices of buttered wheaten bread.

Irish Wheaten Bread

Mix together, dry:
3 c whole wheat flour
1 c white flour
¼ c rolled oats
2 T sugar

1 T baking soda
pinch salt

Add 2 c buttermilk gradually to make a soft, not sticky, dough. (Can also add up to ¼ cup melted butter if wanting a buttery flavor in the bread.)
Add flour, 1-2 T at a time, to reduce stickiness, if needed.
Cover your hands with flour, and knead dough until smooth.
Shape into one round loaf, place on greased baking tray.
Bake in 200 degree oven for 1 hour.

Irish Spiced Beef

Soak overnight in cold water:
4 lbs grey corned beef

Next day, drain and place in large pot on top of:
1 onion, sliced
1 small turnip. peeled and sliced
3 carrots, peeled and sliced
1 bay leaf

Cover with cold water and simmer gently for 3-4 hours.
Leave to cool in liquid.
Drain meat and dry, place on roasting pan.
Insert 12 whole cloves into top of meat.

Mix into paste consistency:
¼ c brown sugar
juice of 1 lemon
½ t ground cinnamon
½ t ground allspice
½ t ground nutmeg
1 t mustard powder
Cover top of meat with paste.

Add 1-2 c of boiling liquid to bottom of roasting pan. Transfer beef and vegetables to pan, and bake in 350 degree oven for 40 minutes.
Let cool completely, slice thin and serve on Wheaten Bread

with mustard.

Slow Cooker Corned Beef and Cabbage

Place the following in slow cooker in this order:

3 carrots, cut into 3 inch pieces
2 celery stalks, into 3 inch pieces
1 onion, cut into 1-inch wedges, leaving root end intact
½ pound small potatoes, quartered
1 -2 T pickling spices

Add 4-6 c water.
Arrange ½ head Savory cabbage on top of veggies and meat.
Cover and cook for 1-2 hours on low heat.
Slice corned beef against the grain and serve with veggies, some cooking liquid and grainy mustard.

Irish Farm House Barley Broth

Place all ingredients in soup pot:
1 lb neck of lamb
¼ c dried split peas, soaked overnight
5 pints water
½ c barley

Bring to boil and simmer for 1 hour.

Add and simmer for ½ hour:
1 onion, peeled and chopped
2 carrots, peeled and sliced
2 stalks celery, chopped

Remove meat and allow to cool.
Remove meat from bone and return to soup.
Serve warm with bread and butter.

Bangers and Potatoes

Shallow fry 4 potatoes, peeled and sliced, in 1 inch oil or melted lard.

When potatoes are half cooked, add 8 banger sausages, cut into 1 inch pieces.

Toss and finish cooking.

Serve warm with heated baked beans.

Irish Apple Pie

Mix:
2 c all purpose flour
pinch salt

Cut into flour:
¼ c cold butter
¼ c cold lard

Add just enough to make firm dough:
1-2 T ice cold water

Roll out ¾ pastry on floured board.
Line 8 inch pie plate. Fill bottom crust with:
2 pounds tart apples, peeled, cored and sliced thin

Sprinkle apples with:
1 t cinnamon
3 T brown sugar
½ t ground cloves

Roll out remaining crust, place on top of pie, close edges.

Cut vent in center, brush top with milk.
Bake at 400-degrees for about 30 minutes.
Top with warm cream or custard.

Chef Paulette DiAngi is an international award winning Vintner, food alchemist and Ayurvedic Lifestyle Consultant. She indulged her passion for cooking at the Connecticut Culinary Institute after receiving her PhD in Nursing from Case Western Reserve

University. Her goal is to create food to 'fall in love with' that engages all the senses. In addition to her regular day job, she has two cable TV shows: *Paulette's Red Kitchen* and *Love On A Plate*). She also teaches classes in cooking and does demonstration parties for small groups, as well as provides private lessons in her kitchen or yours. Email her at: www.paulettesredkitchen.com.

About the Author

An early member of the Baby Boomer generation, Susan Santangelo has been a feature writer, drama critic, and editor for daily and weekly newspapers in the New York metropolitan area, including a stint at *Cosmopolitan* magazine. A seasoned public relations and marketing professional, she has designed and managed not-for-profit events and programs for over 25 years, and was principal of her own public relations firm, Events Unlimited, in Princeton, NJ for ten years. She also served as Director of Special Events and Volunteers for Carnegie Hall during the Hall's 1990-1991 Centennial season.

Susan divides her time between Cape Cod, MA and the Connecticut shoreline. She is a member of Sisters in Crime and the Cape Cod Writers Center, and also reviews mysteries for Suspense Magazine. She shares her life with her husband Joe and one very spoiled English cocker spaniel, Boomer, who also serves as the model for the books' covers.

A portion of the sales from the Baby Boomer Mysteries is donated to the Breast Cancer Survival Center, a non-profit organization based in Connecticut which Susan founded in 1999 after being diagnosed with cancer herself.

You can contact Susan at ssantangelo@aol.com or find her on Facebook and Twitter. She'd love to hear from you.

Made in the USA
Charleston, SC
24 September 2014